The Affairs of Gods and Men

By

Pauline Crame

The story behind this novel.

Although most of the events in the novel either did not occur at all, or else not in the way they are written, this is the real-life story upon which it is based.

In November 2003 I travelled with my husband Bernard to Nepal, fulfilling for him a life-long dream. During the course of that trip we went trekking in the Annapurna district of the country. Our guide was a young man named Dammar Adhikari.

From their first encounter Bernard and Dammar hit it off as if they were old friends. Because of this we maintained email contact upon our return to England, and in the two subsequent journeys to Nepal again engaged Dammar as our guide.

In August 2008 Bernard died from cancer. Prior to his death he requested that at his funeral money be collected for Dammar and his family.

Several days after Bernard's death I went on line to tell Dammar the sad news only to be greeted by an email from the trekking company to inform me that Dammar himself had died. The two men had passed away within days of each other.

Dammar left behind a widow, four children and his parents, all of whom had been financially dependent upon him. Later that same year I travelled to meet the family and present them the money collected on their behalf at Bernard's funeral. It was this experience that inspired the writing of this book. A year later I quit my job and went to live in Nepal for six months to do exactly that.

Since then the Nepalese family have been made homeless by the earthquake and currently live in a tent on the site of their former home.

The proceeds from this novel will be donated to them in the hope it helps with rebuilding their lives.

And this novel is dedicated to the memory of Bernard Crame and Dammar Adhikari.

CHAPTER ONE.

The rain freshened the early evening air and with it came a mist that brought the first shades of darkness and a slight chill. Kabita pulled her shawl around herself. As she squatted now, beside the tap washing away the remains of the evening meal, she was alerted by the sound of raised male voices. Looking up she saw her brother-in-law, returned unexpectedly from Kathmandu.

He approached her, laid a hand upon her shoulder and said solemnly: "Come into the house."

His tone made a fist clench in Kabita's belly. Sandeep summoned the rest of the family. The fist unclenched and fingers pinched her insides as she waited to hear what the trouble was. But when she did it made no sense. Immediately her mother-in-law began to wail and call her son's name out loud. Kabita sat and stared at the bare stone wall, feeling nothing.

"Kabita," Sandeep spoke gently to her, "did you hear me?"

"Yes. Where is he now?"

"His friends from Kathmandu are bringing him on the night bus. The coroner had to see him."

Once he had dealt with the coroner Sandeep volunteered to go ahead to the village and inform the family, leaving his brother, Khrisna, and Ram's friends to bring him home for his funeral. It was with regret that he left, but later he heard how the driver refused entry to the bus. How Ram slid from the stretcher as they hoisted him onto the roof, causing them to bash his already battered face as they pulled him back on. And then he was grateful for his absence.

Kabita took the mobile phone from the table and rang Ram's number. For a long time there was no answer, but then Khrisna's voice said: "Hello, who is this?" And, "Is Sandeep with you yet?" And then she knew something must be wrong, but not the awful thing they'd told her – not that.

Outside Ram's parents sat on the wall embracing each other and their two older grandsons, all of them weeping. They looked up expectantly as Kabita came towards them, but she turned and walked away, feeling the air charged with questions and accusations.

Just outside the village she sat down, experiencing no discomfort from the stony ground beneath her. In the fast descending darkness there were shadows that warned and mocked as they approached and then receded. Kabita gripped her knees and pulled them towards her responding to the tightness in her abdomen and throat, which erupted now into vomiting just as Sandeep arrived beside her.

He waited until she had recovered herself then said: "Come back to the village."

Kabita didn't move: "Someone has made a mistake."

"There was no mistake. I saw him. Come back to the village, the children need you." Sandeep helped her to her feet and ushered her in that direction.

Kabita obeyed, but she felt turned to stone and had no heart for offering comfort. She sat motionless and emotionless; watching as her parents-in-law, Sandeep and her children huddled into a hump and cried. They were a single solid unit, a suffering heaving mass, but she was the outsider, and she alone knew it wasn't true.

She didn't budge from her position even when Ram's father approached: "It's wrong," she said firmly, but quietly, "this news is a lie." Kabita was certain Ram would have come to her and told her if he was dead.

The family was agreed, and it was sanctioned by Sandeep, Kabita would have to see Ram's body with her own eyes.

Gonesh vomited twice during the night. Indira, congested from hours of crying before she slept, snored and slept fitfully. Sunker cried out in his sleep and called his father's name. Only the two year old Bosiram slept soundly.

Kabita sat, stared, paced, sat, stared and paced wandering in and out of the house all night feeling she had misplaced something.

*

One-thirty was fast approaching and Polly was still a good ten minutes from school. She broke into a slow trot, annoyed with herself for having left it late enough to have to hurry. She had lost sense of time thinking about Ned and so looking forward to his return. The lunchtime walk had become an established habit. On warm days she took her sandwiches and a book to the park, but today wasn't one of these.

The class was waiting when she arrived and was unsurprisingly rowdy, although hush descended immediately as she entered the room. While she composed herself Polly asked: "Who can tell me where we got to?" But before she could go any further the Head Teacher was at the door with Polly's colleague and friend, James.

"Sorry to interrupt," Helen addressed the class, "but I need Mrs. Johnson, I'll leave you in the capable hands of Mr. Law."

Helen's unexpected arrival and her formal tone worried Polly: "Is something wrong?"

The lack of an answer was almost confirmation enough. As Polly was ushered into the Heads office and introduced to two police officers, this was redoubled. Their names and ranks were instantly forgotten: "Please sit down," the male officer said more as if it were an order than a request.

Polly was giddy, hot and impatient with the formalities. "What's happened?"

"There's been an accident, I'm afraid."

"Accident? My daughter? My son?"

"Your husband."

"Ned – in Nepal? What kind of accident?"

"A car accident."

"But he's okay? I mean, obviously not or you wouldn't be here, but he's not. . .?"

The pause was no longer than the space between breaths, but it spoke before the words: "I'm afraid so," which were as loud and shocking as a shot to the head.

"I don't understand."

"I'm sorry we don't know too much either – his colleagues are on their way home I believe, they should be able to tell you more."

Polly tried to stay calm. There was a chance it was a mistake and it was someone else, not Ned. "What do you know?"

"Why don't you sit down?"

"I don't want to." The reply was curt.

"Just that someone ran in the road, the taxi swerved to miss her there was a crash that resulted in the fatality of all three passengers. - Is there anyone else you would like us to contact?"

"No – Yes. My daughter and my son."

"We'll drive you home first."

"I'll be fine, thank you."

"I really don't think you should drive yourself."

"I'll be fine, really."

And she was. An almost maniacal energy flowed, which sharpened her senses and fixed her attention just long enough to get her safely within the front door.

But there was a strange atmosphere in the house as if someone had just left. "Ned?" She called out. "Ned is that you?" Polly waited in anticipation for a second or two, as if really expecting an answer, then picked up the post and shuffled through it without noticing anything. She over filled the kettle, as she put it on for tea, tipped too much water out, filled it again. In the living room she picked up the phone, put it down, wandered back into the kitchen, watched as the kettle reached boiling point, did nothing. Back in the lounge she dialed Ned's Nepali number, but it went straight to answer phone. She tried Richard and Malcolm, but the same was true of theirs. Something was wrong then. Now she dialed Mia's number: "Hi, it's me. I've just had some bad news – they say Ned is dead." After returning the phone to the receiver Polly stood and stared out of the window, feeling nothing. She was still there when Mia arrived.

Polly let her take charge. It didn't matter how many times Polly said it herself, or how many times she was witness to the words from someone else, they still sounded as though they belonged in a melodrama. And while everyone else cried copious amounts of tears her own eyes stayed dry, her heart was shocked into silence.

Her own mother, mother-in-law and both her children offered to stay the night, but she was irritated by their company. It felt as though she had something important to do and they were preventing her from doing it. Mia practically insisted and Polly acquiesced. All night sleep teased her like it was pulling her under water and held her there for an instant, as if someone was pushing on her head. She struggled to the surface, only to find a reality that made her desire the drowning.

*

The sights, sounds and smells were those that greeted her every day. The chickens still scratched the ground. The goats shuffled in their pen, impatient to be released. The water buffalo bellowed and the smell of wood smoke rose from the tin roofed houses. The chatter of children, in the near distance, was lent a musical quality as it mingled with the sound of water running over metal plates.

The mountains, gradually emerging from the morning mist, were lush and green after the rain. Kabita couldn't understand how everything could be the same when nothing ever would be again. She wanted to jump between the beats of her heart and demand that they cease and to scream aloud until the mountains echoed with her pain. Instead she stood, still and silent.

When they came for her Khrisna said: "He doesn't look very nice."

Kabita nodded and allowed herself to be led by the men, who were already prepared for the funeral. Gonesh, who as the eldest son, was responsible for leading the ceremony, looked terrified and no more than a baby with his shaven head.

At the sight of the stretcher Kabita felt faint and thought she would float away. She watched as they uncovered Ram's face feeling at first vindicated in her assertion that it wasn't him, but gradually beneath the bruises and swelling a face she recognised emerged. And then, for a moment, it didn't matter because she saw that his chest was rising and falling with shallow breaths and felt the rush of relief that at last allowed tears to flow. But instantly relief was snatched away, in response to the feel of stony flesh beneath her hand as she reached out to touch his face. And she collapsed in response to the reality; knowing now that all appearance of this being someone other than her husband, was entirely because Ram was no longer with his body.

The women picked Kabita up and helped her home.

*

Malcolm came alone. Polly found his reluctance to answer her questions annoyed her, after all what could be worse than the news of Ned's death. Malcolm's hesitation was borne partly of wanting to spare her imagination the horror of it, but also because he could hardly bare the far too vivid memory himself. "A young woman ran into the road, taxi swerved to avoid her – the drop offs are steep there."

"They went over the side of a cliff?"

Malcolm nodded.

They came around the corner only minutes later, almost colliding themselves with the crowd of people who were gathered in the road rushing from all directions. It wasn't a particularly unusual sight in Nepal, there were often overturned vehicles with crowds attempting to right them, but there was no sign of any vehicle here and people were heading towards the side of the cliff. The taxi was tooting and trying to push through, but Richard ordered: 'wait – stop, wait.'

Then said to his fellow passengers: 'Ned and Ram were just in front, I want to make sure they're okay'. Then they saw him go down on his knees, push his hair back from his crown and heard him shout: 'Oh God! My God, it's them.'

"You are sure? It was him? There couldn't have been a mistake?" Polly asked.

"I wish I weren't so sure."

And there were the faces he knew and loved so well, behind his eyes again. Smashed and battered and blue in the hands of the Nepali men who were heaving them up the side of the bank. And Richard was shouting: "Call an ambulance someone," shaking the man next to him and shouting; "Ambulance!" But Malcolm had seen and knew that was unnecessary.

"They were both my friends. Ram too," Malcolm said more to himself, shaking his head. "He was a fine man, so young, forty at the most. He has – had - a wife and four children. They live in the mountains they're poor."

Rage boiled inside Polly at the mention of Ram's family and she hated Malcolm equally for his sympathy and his dispassionate delivery of the facts. "What happens now?" She asked with reasoned composure.

"We had him sent to the Co-op, just the first place we thought of, if it's not okay we can have him moved. You don't need to worry about the cost of repatriation, we'll see to that." And then: "I'm so sorry, Polly. I really am – we all are, so sorry."

Polly woke to the sound of the telephone and the smell of bacon. For a second it seemed like an ordinary weekend, with Ned cooking the breakfast they'd share in bed, but then she remembered. The room was barely light, even though it was nine-thirty, and it was only just warm enough without the central heating on. Heavy rain pounded against the window. There seemed no good reason for getting up. Christine knocked on the door.

"That was the funeral parlor, Dad's arrived. They want us to go and make arrangements."

The evening before there had been a family discussion on how to proceed. A humanist minister would be employed to read personal statements and a couple of pieces of poetry and prose that Ned had liked. They were unanimous on the dress not being too formal and needed little discussion on which music they should play. The only decision still left to make was to which charity money should be donated.

Remembering how distressing it had been seeing her father, Polly decided to go into the room alone. Her own grief was more than she could cope with.'

"He doesn't look the best, I'm afraid," Linda told her. "We did what we could, but there was quite a lot of swelling to the face."

'His face,' Polly thought. 'His face, not, *the* face.'

"When you're ready he's through here." Linda opened the door and indicated the direction Polly should take.

The very sight of the coffin set Polly trembling uncontrollably. Now she wished someone, anyone was here with her. She closed her eyes and felt her way alongside the coffin to the head. Then said to herself, 'one, two, three:' and opened her eyes. Her initial feeling was relief because it wasn't Ned after all. It was a good likeness, but not quite close enough to convince her. Her heart stopped for a second in response to an apparent breath, but she was prepared for that particular illusion. Then common sense took over and she recognised not only him, but the clothes she had chosen. The long repressed tears flowed at last. 'What have they done to his face?' She thought, as her hand hovered over it, afraid to make contact. She used to love to stroke his face and for him to do the same to her, it seemed such an act of intimacy. Desolation rocked her as her hand contacted with the waxy flesh. And now she understood why it appeared to be someone like Ned, but not quite him; it was simply because Ned had gone.

She composed herself and left the room in as dignified a manner as she could manage, but the sight of her parents-in-law, the one looking defeated, the other terrified, sent her into a further volley of tears. They both embraced her and all three cried together, but Polly couldn't stand their sympathy or their pain, which made her own so much worse. For the remainder of the day people were in and out of Polly's home and though she was often glad of their company she was as often desirous of being alone. And she found it incredibly tiring, so much so that she was in the bath preparing for bed by eight -thirty. As she lay there thinking, she began to wonder about the funeral process in Nepal and to imagine the experience for the family of the man Ned knew so well and she, not at all. And suddenly she realised where money donations should go.

CHAPTER TWO.

In the room, which had been stripped bare of all possessions, Kabita lay on her straw mat curled in a foetal posture. That she herself continued to live, was only confirmed by the occasional breeze on her bare arms and shoulders. Beneath the bathing cloak her naked body felt nothing. Neither did her heart. Her ears witnessed the cries of her daughter and Ram's mother, but her own eyes remained dry and staring. Even when the priest came for prayers and to supervise her bathing, Kabita barely woke from her stupor. And when they came in the evening with the rice and ghee, she ate only the few mouthfuls that were forced upon her.

She, indeed none of the women, bore witness to the kriya ceremony. The sights, smells and sounds of the funeral pyre didn't reach their senses. In thirteen days her sons would return, heads shaven, having witnessed firsthand something that she could only imagine. When her mind stirred enough for thought, it was only to wonder what sin she had committed in her past life to deserve such a fate. And to long for the funeral pyre, so that she could mimic the women of earlier times and the practice of sati.

*

Everyone said the funeral had been a success; personal to Ned and a tribute to his life. Afterwards Polly went home alone. Her mother's near insistence on accompanying her was hard to refuse, but she felt Marianne's pity stifling and more about her own grief than Polly's. Her mother would no doubt feel she offered empathy while Polly, even under these circumstances, would be unable to relinquish her lifelong role as protector. And Marianne's empty life, since the death of her own husband offered neither solace nor hope. If she continued to mourn the loss of a man who had so often made her unhappy then how much worse for Polly, when she and Ned were still very much in love. Polly took the memories of the rows between her parent's home with her, resenting them no less now than she had at the time and understanding them to be the reason behind her need for solitude. A needy mother, an angry sister and father, hardened her heart to free expression of emotion, and it was underlined by shock. Polly sat now, stilted and upright in Ned's leather chair, trying to feel what she knew she ought. She replayed the music from the funeral, hoping to rouse the emotions into action, but it failed her now as then.

Being alone was something to which she was used, but never had she felt lonely before. Ned's job as a carer for people with disabilities required him to sleep away from home several times a week, but she'd always known it was temporary and he was only ever a telephone call away. Then, as now the house had still felt full of him. Intellectually she understood that Ned would never be back, but her body and heart were yet to believe it. It would take experience and time to realise that he would not come home this time. As if in emphasis, she was haunted by the image of Ned's dead face. It was rounded by the swelling, and his mouth made stern by more than a suggestion of fear, but worst of all was the colour. Presumably in an attempt to improve it, the funeral parlor had used some kind of make-up, but the effect created was the appearance of wax work dummy. Polly had been grateful for the computer driven photographs of her husband that played in a loop at the funeral, yet the dead image remained the dominant one.

Now she was filled with the desire to live their whole lives together over again. She dragged a pile of photograph albums from the cupboard and began rifling through them. Twenty-seven years of memories lay between the pages, yet it seemed so little. Only days ago Ned was real, a conscious, thinking, breathing individual; that he no longer existed was impossible to comprehend. All that was left in evidence of his life were a few possessions and these snap shots from the past. How could a photograph have more permanence than a person?

Yet, at least in these there were reminders of his character. His tendency towards self-effacement evidenced in the avoidance of an open lipped smile, so as not to show his uneven teeth. And the way he stood, slightly slouched as if trying to hide. But there was also the softness in his eyes, especially if she was taking the photograph. And what power those photographs possessed now - the power to comfort and yet to heighten her sense of grief and disbelief. How could it be true that he was gone forever? The impermanence of life made a mockery of everything. Someone at the funeral had remarked that his physical presence had left the world, but that he lived on in many unseen ways. Polly understood the words were offered as consolation, but there was none to be had. It was his physical self she craved. To be able to talk with him, see him, touch him and experience the feeling of safety from his embrace. She didn't believe in spiritual survival, but even if she had, what use was a ghost? But perhaps she was wrong. Perhaps nature did have its own version of the video recorder and, as the mystics claimed, a lasting impression of Ned remained for those who had the correct receivers.

It was this thought that led her led to the DVD collection. In these at least there were reminders of his voice and actions that lifted him above the one dimensional. She hadn't got very far when she was interrupted by the doorbell ringing. She responded to it with a mixture of relief and annoyance; the former being more the case when she discovered Mia on the doorstep bearing a casserole dish.

"You can tell me to push off if you want, but I know you won't eat if someone doesn't feed you. I've just got to put this in the oven to finish off."

Polly opened the door fully to allow entry and then returned to the living room. She was in the process of closing the albums and returning them to the cupboard when Mia came in to the room. "Oh! Don't put them away I'd love to look through them with you, if it's okay."

"I guess! I might cry, though."

"How long have I known you Pol? I think I can handle a few tears. – Do you have a favourite?"

"There are a few. This one from soon after we met I like. We look so young don't we? Well, we were, especially me. People had a problem with our relationship at first, you know."

"Because he was older?"

"Yes and not academic and he wasn't good looking. And I was practically engaged. It didn't take people long to understand and grow to love him, though." Polly picked another photograph. "I loved his body. He was so solid and strong."

"Like his character."

"Yes, but not enough to defy death. - I know everyone says it about someone who's died, but he was such a good man wasn't he? And he loved me so much. What'll I do without him?" Now Polly did cry a little, but only a little, because even when the company was Mia she held back. Struggling out of Mia's embrace she picked another album at random.

"Nepal. From what he told me about the state of the roads it's hardly surprising this happened. I wish he hadn't gone, he would still be here if not. But he loved it there so much. The rest of them were probably sick of the place, he never chose anywhere else once he'd been there. That was so like him. Once he found something he liked he'd stick with it rather than try something new. Sometimes he'd play the same CD for weeks on end - used to drive me nuts!"

"Weren't you ever tempted to go to any of these places with him?"

"It's a boy's thing for the hiking club. Although I think a couple of the wives have been. But I wasn't that keen - you know how I feel about flying – wish I'd been with him this time, though."

"Then you'd be dead too and where would the kids be?"

"I'm as good as dead anyway."

Mia held Polly tightly and rocked her like a baby. Polly became aware of her friend crying and it provoked the same in her. Then suddenly Mia stopped, pulled away, patted Polly and returned to the photographs. "Is this the guide who died?"

"No," this time Polly suppressed her tears with difficulty, "this is Ram."

"Gosh! How young and small he is – was."

"Yes. When Ned used to talk about him I had the impression of someone about Ned's age and build because he sounded reliable and competent, but he looks like a kid."

"Any idea yet how much money you got?"

"Anthony's taken charge on that, but he said we've done well and there's more to come."

"How're you going to get it there?"

"Malcolm will sort that for me. I didn't give any of his family a second thought at first, how awful is that?"

"Not awful at all. You couldn't deal with their grief as well as your own."

"I wonder what she's like – his wife. I guess she'll be feeling as wretched as I do. I wonder what she's doing right now."

"I don't expect she's looking through photographs. May be she doesn't even have any."

*

Kabita was eating her first dhal baht since the death. She still wasn't interested in food, it had no taste and its life maintaining quality was one to which she didn't currently subscribe. Even so she forced down a few mouthfuls for the sake of doing just that.

Later, lying in bed, listening to the rhythmic breathing of the children and the shuffling of the animals she tried to rid her mind of the image of Ram's corpse. But, sleeping or waking it haunted her and robbed her of a confident memory of his living face.

In the corner of the room was the bag that had come with Khrisna from Ram's Kathmandu apartment. He had put it there and Kabita had left it untouched, but suddenly she felt the need to unpack it. She crept quietly from the wooden bed, careful not to disturb the sleeping children, and groped around in the dark until she found it. Then she descended the ladder, lit the candle, unzipped the bag and began to rummage through the meagre belongings. The contents totalled a few articles of clothing, a toothbrush, towel and soap, a pair of flip flops and a wallet.

She held the flip flops in her hands and conjured up the memory of the feet that used to wear them. In her mind's eye she traveled upwards the length of his short muscular legs to the small firm buttocks; then up his back, which had been a little too long. Her mind's eye traced the square shoulders and then down the sinewy arms. She tried to picture his face; oval in shape like his eyes and a strong straight nose above a small serious mouth, but the image of his dead face kept getting in the way. Picking up a worn shirt she sniffed the sweet smell of him, breathing deep, inhaling him into her lungs. And the aroma was like a resurrection. So real, so of the present that it served to comfort and confuse. How could there be such a strong scent from someone who was never coming back? A man was solid, could be seen, heard, touched. A smell was no more than an impression yet it outlived the man. Surely a spirit had more substance and yet there was no sign of that. She cradled the shirt as if it were a child and rocked backwards and forwards, crying silently.

*

When Mia left Polly went and lay on the bed. The room was utterly still, so silent, but she was going to have to get used to it. There would be no more whispers in the dark. No more the comfort of spine to spine contact, no more waking to see Ned smiling down at her – no one to make love with anymore. She curled into the pillow and fell asleep, but woke with a start, hearing Ned call her name and the panic in his voice induced the same in her. Her heart beat so loudly it sounded as if it were outside her body, and for a second she believed there was another person in the bed. It was several minutes before equilibrium returned. And as it slowed to normal Polly wished her heart would keep slowing down; down and down until it stopped. But she couldn't die, couldn't even stay asleep, and even when she did reality invaded her dreams. So she got up and wandered the house, passing in and out of rooms feeling as though she was looking for something and every now then realising what it was.

Then she remembered that in Christine's old room there was Ned's rucksack from Kathmandu still waiting to be unpacked. She unzipped the zipper tentatively feeling afraid of the contents. The very first thing she encountered was his diary, which she sat on the bed and began to read. And as she read the descriptions of Nepal and Nepali life the images it evoked made him seem a stranger; the life so alien compared with the one they shared at home, that Polly decided that she must know more.

*

When the crying had subsided Kabita turned her attention to the wallet. Inside were four hundred rupees, a card representing Ram's company and a photograph of him and another man. They had their arms around each other's shoulders. In the candle light it was hard to see, but from what Kabita could make out it made Ram seem a stranger. This Ram, in his sunglasses, combat jacket and hat, camera around his neck, looked very much a city boy. And who was this other man? One of the tourists, she presumed, who kept her husband from her with his desire for glimpses of a life she knew he would never swap for his own. It was because of a tourist he was dead now, she thought bitterly. And yet this man's smile was warm and his friendship with Ram appeared genuine. Besides, the only other photograph she possessed was from their wedding day, so Kabita slid it into the rafters. She extinguished the candle and then returned to bed, turning her back on her children and cradling the shirt.

*

The green burial ground was Anthony's idea. His friend's father had chosen it for himself and Anthony thought it was something of which Ned would have approved. Now Polly waited for the rest of the family to arrive. On her lap she held the red cardboard box that contained the remains of Ned.

"You'll be surprised how heavy it is," Linda told her almost cheerily as she handed it over at the funeral parlour. But, quite to the contrary, Polly thought it much too light. She couldn't have carried the thirteen stone, five feet eleven man Ned had been, but she could carry this box very easily, inside a plastic carrier bag.

She sat in silence, crying tears that were noiseless, except for when they hiccupped from her belly. She licked them from her lips whenever the salty taste became too strong. Polly traced the shape of the box over and over again, like someone with obsessive compulsive disorder, but although she kept telling herself she would, she didn't once raise the lid to look inside. When the first of the family arrived she straightened her shoulders and climbed from the car.

The burial ground was surprisingly quiet given its location near to the motorway and there were several fresh mounds since their last visit only a few days ago. It was a place that told tragic stories for other people, but Polly's story still didn't feel as though it belonged with all those others.

Ned's brother Martin dug the hole next to the wooden post that read Johnson and the date. Then finally Polly lifted the lid and stared at the fine, grey ash inside the box, feeling an impulse to adorn herself like a sahdhu. But not even her hands made contact as she tipped a portion of the ashes into the hole and passed the box to Christine. Polly watched as each of Ned's family took turns at depositing his remains into the hole. Finally, the soil was replaced, forming a solid mound over ash so fine, the smallest of breezes could have blown it away. Polly stayed when everyone else had gone. She stared at the mound, the inscription, the memorial trees, and tried to make herself realise that her husband was really dead.

*

Kabita wandered the length of the river looking for some change, some traces of Ram's remains, but all she saw was the same muddy water. Becoming shallow already as the autumn advanced towards winter; flowing as it always did, over the same rocks, making the same noise, running at the same pace. There was nothing. No confirmation to be found here.

*

CHAPTER THREE.

Polly became an avid reader of the diaries. Ned had written one for every trip, brought them home and added the latest to those already in existence.

November 25th 2003
I can hardly believe I am here. All those years of reading about climbers who have come here and fantasizing about one day visiting Nepal myself and here I am. Kathmandu is just as I imagined, the descriptions I've read are very accurate. I'm so excited, just wish Polly was here too. I'd like to write more, but I'm really tired and feel like a kid at Christmas. In the morning I'll meet the Nepali guide who will be leading the trek.

It was the first reference to Ram and Polly wanted to know what Ned's early impressions had been. She had to read on several pages before she did so.

November 30th 2003
All this uphill walking has made my legs ache, I'm ashamed to say. The other guys say they're the same, but I think they're just being kind to an old man. Anyway, Ram gave them a massage last night and this morning I feel raring to go again. When I first saw Ram I thought he was just a kid, he's only young, not much more than thirty, and he's small in stature. But he has a big personality and a generous and responsible nature. He's restless, always fiddling with things, can't sit still for a minute, yet his manner is controlled and he definitely considers himself the boss. Often he keeps control by creating a little mystery, holding back pieces of information until the last minute, for example. And there's a preparedness about him, like an animal on the alert. It's reassuring because it leaves little doubt that he'd be ready for any eventuality, but sometimes he's so conscientious in the way he looks after us that it can seem stifling. He's very friendly, despite his mostly serious expression, which makes him seem permanently contemplative, almost worried, as if he's thinking ahead all the time. Yet when he smiles he appears almost as a different person it lightens him so much. And he and I get on particularly well. Yes, I like and trust

this man very much.

Polly had skimmed the intervening pages, but went back to them now. Reading the description of the bus journey between Kathmandu and Pokhara, she had a real sense of the place, which made her curious. This was all the more true with reference to the descriptions of mountain life. Perhaps if there was any essence of Ned left behind it was to be found in Nepal rather than here. Not only because it was the site of his death, but also because even when he made a physical return it had always taken some time before he was back spiritually.

She certainly felt no sense of him at home. Not in the garden that had been abandoned to nature for the past seven weeks, weeds thriving on water from the constant rain and nourished by the unusually warm autumn sun. And everywhere in the house she was greeted only with reminders of his absence. Like now as she opened the cupboard and was faced with the mug he no longer used and then, minutes later, emptying the washing machine of clothes that belonged only to her. It was the total lack of a sense of him that was the hardest to bear because it was as if he had never existed at all.

*

Dawn was breaking and the crowing cockerel awoke Kabita. As soon as her mind responded, even before she opened her eyes, she remembered her widowhood and wished to return to her former state of consciousness, but the dictates of life demanded otherwise.

Everything had returned to normal now. The neighbours no longer came for daily visits with food and offers of assistance. The children had returned to school, and every day the hair on the male heads grew thicker. But for Kabita there was no normal anymore and the more ordinary everything appeared the more wrong it felt. Every action, no matter how functional for the needs of her family, seemed utterly worthless.

She never spoke about Ram or what had happened. When she spoke at all it was in a tiny voice that was barely audible. She moved like a murmur. So peripheral was her existence it was as if there was only an impression of a person.

In the whispered concerns of her parents-in-law Kabita imagined they called her 'boksi,' 'witch' and cursed her for Ram's death.

And their gentle treatment of her she believed to be from fear, so alongside her grief she felt a deep shame. She crept in and out of their presence, keeping her eyes averted from their gaze, never recognising their acknowledgement of her pain. For they, like all other observers, could see her suffering in every action and lack of action. So that now, as she squatted beside the tap scrubbing the clothes, it was almost possible to hear her heart yearning for some of Ram's washing to be added to the pile. The one article of Ram's clothing that remained Kabita kept secret. It was like an echo from the past. A reminder of an intimacy only she had known and would never know again.

When the washing was complete she climbed to the bedroom and took the shirt from its hiding place, holding it close and sniffing it hard. But every day she had to inhale a little harder because the smell was fading. What would she do when there was no longer this reminder? What else did she have? When the smell of him was gone, it would be as if he had never existed.

*

Soon there would be a proper plaque, a simple wooden one, which was all the burial ground would allow, but at the moment only the post marked the spot. A post bearing Ned's family name and his date of death seemed so clinical. X marks the spot – the end of the person and his story. The impossible truth, there is an end.

And yet Polly did have some sense of Ned here. And because of that she couldn't stay away, despite her earlier conviction that she would have no need of a particular place to mourn. While she was there she spoke to him; telling him about her day as she had always done and asking him for reassurance that he knew she loved him, forgave her misdemeanors. When she got home she'd look for a sign, read a random page in his diary for example, but all she ever found were references to his love for her and there was never any doubt about that.

Her feelings for him were hard to understand at first, having thought herself in love with David. But there was something about Ned. From the first time they met she felt comfortable in his company, as if she had always known him and as if she could stop trying and just be herself. Mia, rather than Polly, was the one who believed in divine destiny, but over the years the conviction grew within Polly that the universe had intended them to be together. Now it all seemed a lie. What was the point in having a soul mate if he were to be taken from you? What purpose had her life without him?

*

Kabita thought she had seen a ghost. The trick of the early fading light was that it made Sandeep appear as Ram. Kabita's response didn't go unnoticed by him; he saw her stop, tense, push her fist into her belly then sigh and drop her shoulders. He dealt quickly with the matter that brought him there, feeling as if he should offer his apologies for so disappointing his sister-in-law.

For Kabita it had been reminiscent of the early days of her marriage. No particular occasion, but the memory of an ordinary day and Kabita looking up shyly at her new husband as he stood in the doorway watching her busy with some chore.

And then she remembered the first meeting. The two of them catching only a glimpse of each other as the two families discussed the terms of the marriage: each of them looking at the other from the corner of downcast eyes, afraid to meet each other's gaze for the sake of the families and themselves. Kabita felt fortunate that she wasn't marrying a total stranger because she did remember Ram a little. As children they had often encountered each other on the way to school and he would tease her, as he did all of the girls. His flirtatious manner charmed everyone. The whole village, not just her home, was so much more alive when Ram was there. A throng of children always appeared and he would chase them, allow them to climb all over him, enchant them with tales from his treks. The children sat with round eyes gazing, and the adults took a break and squat on their haunches to listen to Ram describe how he and his clients rounded the corner and came upon the yeti. Fortunately with its back to them, so they were able to inch away to a hiding place, where they waited for a whole day without food or water until it was gone. Ram was so serious in the telling that even some of the adults were convinced by the tale. Because, despite his ability to tease, Ram was generally of a serious nature and he had a very strong sense of wishing to do the right thing. Yet he also had his own sense of right and wrong. He was never one for blind acceptance of the rules. Whenever there had been an issue between the two of them, he was happy to discuss it and would as often bend to her will as she would to his. There was however, little disharmony between them, they had an understanding that went beyond the everyday. It was because of this that Kabita had always believed it to be of a nature that defied the grave, but she was wrong. He hadn't even come back to tell her he was gone.

*

Polly was standing gazing out of the kitchen window without thought or purpose. Looking up she spotted Ned walking towards her. She felt her stomach lurch with relief and fear and then, with disappointment, as she realised her mistake and answered the door to Martin.

"Hi, I won't come in, just wanted to leave this for you and the kids to look at. If you're all happy with it, we are, so I'll go ahead and finalise the order."

"Thanks. I'll let you know as soon as possible. You okay?"

"Well, you know. How about you?"

"Yeah! The same."

There wasn't much to it. Italic lettering that read '*In memory of Ned, much loved*' and then his dates of birth and death. Polly stared at the dates, a beginning, an end and nothing to tell of what had gone between. A person's coming and going was acknowledgement by certificates, their ending etched in stone, and for most so little evidence that anything had gone before. At least there were Ned's diaries.

She remembered the first time she saw him, standing in the doorway of the care home he worked in, she a student looking for holiday work. Not an obviously attractive man, but instantly she was attracted to him. His soft blue eyes contrasted completely with his solid physique and strong voice, which later she realised, perfectly described the man.

And it seemed such a short time ago, twenty-seven years – she'd hoped for the same again. Polly had always been a person who questioned the meaning of her life and felt there should be something more, but now that Ned was no longer a part of it she regretted ever having done so - he had been meaning enough. What was she to do with the rest of a life that felt so empty? She wished she could fall into the emptiness and disappear.

*

Kabita watched her youngest son tracing in the dusty soil with a stick, his small body casting long shadows in the late autumn sun. His movements were short and sharp, suggestive of boredom. She looked around for her own stick and on finding one went to Bosiram and drew a picture of a face in the ground.

"Daddy!" Bosiram said, shocking his mother greatly. The drawing was childlike and androgynous. There was nothing about it that
should have provoked such a response in Bosiram. Kabita didn't know how to respond; she looked about her as if expecting to find another explanation for her son's words.

"Daddy!" Bosiram repeated.

She drew a male body beneath the head, as much for her own sake as Bosiram's because it authenticated the face as that of a man. Now she picked her son up and looking into his eyes was startled to see them as empty as her own heart. She ran in doors, took the photograph from the rafters and showed it to Bosiram: "Daddy," she pointed emphatically at the photograph. "He didn't want to leave us. Never forget your Daddy," but she knew it wouldn't be long before he had.

"What have you there?" Ram's mother interrupted, coming over standing next to Kabita and looking over her shoulder. Kabita shared the photograph reluctantly and dutifully. Her mother-in-law took it from her, held it to her breast, kissed it, returned it to her breast and then took it away to show to the men.

"But Daddy won't be coming back anymore." Kabita said more to herself than her son and erased the drawing with the same stick that had created it.

How long would it take for Bosiram to forget his father completely? She wondered. Something of him must be in his children, but they were individuals too, they were like him, but they were not him. If his spirit were anywhere surely it would be here, but she had no sense of him and she had no sense of where to find him.

*

CHAPTER FOUR.

"Polly, how are?" Malcolm held her hand a little too long after shaking it.

"Still trying to make sense of it, but mostly okay. What can I get you?"

"I'll get them - wine?"

She chose beer because it was cheaper, although in the current cold weather she would have preferred the wine.

"I want to talk about Nepal."

"I guessed that. The guys and I were discussing it only the other day, wondering which of us should go and when. "

"I'm going to take the money myself. I think it should be me who meets the family, besides I want to. I also want to see where Ned spent his last days. What you can do for me is help me arrange it – you know, advise me on flights, places to stay, someone to act as a guide."

"It's the least I can do. Who will you go with?"

"I'm going on my own."

Malcolm was visibly shocked.

"Plenty of women travel alone."

"I know, but - it seems like quite an undertaking at your - at this time - after what's happened."

"You think I'm too old, is that it?"

Malcolm laughed. "You certainly aren't that, but you haven't ever done this kind of thing, that's all."

"Neither has anyone else until the first time."

"When're you planning on going?"

"I thought towards the end of next year. I need at least a month there, but I'm not ready yet. By then the insurance money will have come through and the mortgage will be paid off. Then I can quit my job without worry."

"Quit?"

"Why not? The summer wouldn't be a good time to go would it? – No, I thought not, but that's the only time I'd have enough holiday. There's always supply teaching or care work. – Don't look so shocked, Ned loved it."

"It just seems a bit – *drastic,* that's all."

"Well, life has dealt me a rather – *drastic* blow."

Now Malcolm looked a little ashamed. "Yes. Will you want to do a trek?"

"I want to do whatever Ned did, go wherever he went."

Everyone had the same reaction to Polly's plans. Several people finding it necessary to remind her of her feelings regarding flying. "I'll get some valium," became her standard reply.

*

Sandeep and Khrisna had called together Kabita and their parents, who now sat around the table on the wooden bench, in a very formal manner. Whatever they had to tell her this time couldn't be worse than the last, Kabita thought and wished they would hurry up so she could hide again in her chores.

It was Sandeep who spoke: "The family finances are suffering without Ram. We need to find a solution."

It was presented as if there would be a discussion, but before anyone had a chance to respond Sandeep continued: "Ram would most definitely have wanted Gonesh to continue with his education."

'And Indira,' Kabita thought. Of the all Ram's children it was Indira to whom learning came most readily, her English was good and Ram had always wanted her to train as a nurse in Europe or the United States.

"We had hoped to be able to pay college fees for Indira, but it just won't be possible. In fact the way it is now it won't be possible for any of them, but we're hoping to find a solution in time for Gonesh. We have to consider our own children first."

Kabita received the news impassively. And though, in her mind's eyes she saw Ram, wearing a disapproving expression, she had neither energy nor right to protest. Without financial independence she had no control over the decision. Besides, Khrisna and Sandeep spoke the truth, it was only right that their own children be considered before those of their deceased brother.

Kabita nodded quietly, keeping her eyes on the floor.

"And when she's ready we have a young man in mind for marriage. He works in the same hotel as me," Khrisna continued. "In the kitchen, but he's studying English so that he can become a waiter. I've already discussed the possibility with the family and they are not opposed."

Kabita raised her head slightly, but held it sideways with her glance: "She's too young."

"Not so young. The boy won't wait forever."

Released Kabita took a knife and time to reflect as she cut cauliflower and sag for the meal, feeling the dry soil gritty between her toes. How, she wondered, would Indira take the news? Before Ram's death it had been taken for granted that college was the next step for her, but in fact Kabita had never really believed it and the idea that her daughter would get to work in a foreign country was too much of a dream for a village girl. Besides, even if it were really possible she was certain Indira would soon be homesick. And if a husband had already been identified, whose family were happy to take Indira now, there was no need for further studies. There was no sense of regret on her own part at the way her life had been– never had she considered anything other than marriage and mountain life. No. The only regret about her own life was her widowhood. She prayed that her karma was not so bad the same would be inflicted on her daughter.

*

Polly did her best to avoid Christmas. Although the glitzy decorations and sentimental music playing in the shops were as superficial as ever they were enough to reduce her to tears. Instead she sat surrounded by photograph albums of bygone years; reliving Christmases past. Christine and Anthony's plump faces stared out from the pages with wonder in their eyes and then later, those same eyes glowered with disdain and boredom. Later still they sparkled under the influence of alcohol. In every album there was Ned. Ned dressed as Santa, Ned holding Anthony upright on his first bicycle, Ned sleeping in his chair, cracker hat upon his head.

At the burial ground she sat on the frosty grass, knees huddled into her chest, with her crying face bowed towards them and hidden under her black woollen hat. Black coat, black hat, black mood, she could have been mistaken for a shadow.

She tried to stay home for Christmas day, but sensitive to everyone's concern, eventually agreed to spend it with her mother and children, vowing to make sure she was in Nepal for the next one.

When dinner was cleared away Christine said: "I've got a couple of DVDs with Dad on, shall we watch them?"

The first was from her graduation ceremony; there was little footage of Ned, but behind all of the scenes was his voice as he narrated and filmed. Embarrassed by the sound of it he spoke in as near to a whisper as nature would allow, but it was a voice too strong for whispering; a voice with enough power to make itself heard from beyond the grave. And hearing it now induced disbelief rather than comfort.

The second film was of a family holiday in Scotland, one part of the celebrations for Polly's fortieth and Ned's fiftieth birthdays. They watched him emerge blurry eyed and bare chested from the tent with his toilet bag and towel, his expression almost disapproving because he hated to be filmed. Eight years ago he had slightly more hair, although it was already balding and what there was had turned grey in keeping with his neatly trimmed beard. The walk was the most familiar, long strides, but a slight limp on the left because of an industrial injury from a time before Polly knew him. An injury which he later claimed as a blessing because it gave him enough money for a deposit on their first home and a career change into a job he loved.

Polly sat through the footage like a child sitting through the Queens speech waiting for the big film to start, and as soon as seemed polite afterwards, said her farewells and left.

Coming home, to the initial opening of the door Polly hated, as the emptiness of the house always hit her in the face as surely as sharp winter breeze. Today, however, it felt different. There was such an expectancy in the air that she knew when she walked into the living room Ned would be sitting in his big leather chair. She slumped down into it herself, allowing her bag of gifts to fall to the floor and her heart with them as disappointment filled the void.

*

The warmth was already leaving the sun and the December day beginning to feel cool by the time Indira reached her home. When she saw her grandparents sitting outside on the wall craning their heads in her direction she felt a grip of panic that stopped her in her tracks and almost made her drop her books in fear of another death. And so it was with initial relief that Indira received the news of her fate and her reaction was as impassive as Kabita's had been. She simply nodded and went back outside, where her grandparents remained sitting on the wall; they looked at her quizzically as she sat down beside them. No one spoke, Indira held her grandmother's hand who eventually said:

"Are you disappointed?"

"I understand about the money, but I don't want to marry yet." She got up and went to the chicken coup, responding to her mother's instructions she rummaged through the hay until she found the eggs, holding them now, two in each hand she imagined herself her grandmother's age; those same hands bearing loose skin and protruding veins, but still holding eggs in the palms. She shooed the chickens into their pen and closed it before sweeping the yard with the straw broom. No college, no job, no Kapil. It was as if every swish of the broom swept a little more of her hope away and when she had finished she turned and looked at the pile of dust, seeing it as indicative of her dreams.

*

Polly's waking thought was that she had had a bad dream in which Ned had died, but in less than a second she remembered it was no dream. And because today she was returning to work she couldn't give in to the instinct to return to sleep. She dreaded this first day; the sympathy from other people that had to be endured.

She sat on the side of the bed for a moment to aid the waking process then turned on the bedside lamp. Just in the instant between darkness and light there appeared to be a solid shape on Ned's side of the bed, but with the light, came the realisation of empty space. Like a vacuum it threatened to suck her in.

Now Polly went downstairs and made herself a cup of tea, leaving it to cool whilst she ran through her morning routine, which she experienced as a betrayal. The small things had always felt the most wrong: single person catering, tidying a half crumbled bed, throwing never to be opened mail into the recycling bin; although all were done from necessity they seemed indicative of acceptance and an abnegation of her love for Ned. As if she were wiping him out a little more with every ordinary action.

But everything was in fact so far from ordinary that Polly sometimes feared for her own sanity. Sometimes she felt insubstantial, as if she were an echo of her real self; yet at others so obsessively self-conscious it was as if her thoughts had rooted her to the spot. Now, as she carefully chose her clothes and styled her hair, Polly felt like an actress preparing for her part in a poorly scripted play and she worried that she would forget her lines, or fail to make an entrance at the appropriate time.

James met her in the car park as he'd promised. He got out of his car as soon as he saw her pull up and strolled towards her, pulling the collar of his full length coat up around his ears and slightly hunching his body against the cold as he did so. It was an action that lent him such a look of vulnerability Polly wondered whether he was really up to the task he had volunteered for, but it was only fleeting. As soon as he reached her side he smiled warmly, put his arm lightly around her shoulder and ushered her gently in the direction of the staff room.

Over the weeks James, along with Mia, had been her main stay of support. She never asked either of them to visit, but both of them did, or telephoned regularly to ensure she was coping.

Mia's support was of a very practical nature. It was she who made sure Polly was taking care of herself and she who made arrangements for lunch time meetings or evenings out.

James's talent on the other hand was for listening without judging, and so it was that Polly had several times unburdened herself with accounts of her harsh words and deeds towards Ned, that she deeply regretted both then and now. James always put it in a new perspective and made it all seem normal and forgivable. And once - she almost cried with him. It had been as much in response to his pain as to her own, when he'd told her that he'd been engaged in his early twenties to a girl who'd died from leukemia. The horror of the three year experience and the broken heart that had never mended were implicit in what he left out of his dispassionate account. Polly had never stopped wondering, despite the reassurances of those at the scene that it was minimal, whether Ned had suffered, if there had been a moment or longer of pain and fear. In James's case he would have witnessed every tiny flicker of both. Perhaps her ignorance was preferable to that.

Now she waited in the staff room. Her first class wasn't until after morning break which allowed her to both refresh herself on the content of the lesson and to get her initial meeting with her colleagues over and done with. These encounters were mostly stilted and commonly once the person had said how sorry they were they went and sat away from her and buried themselves in a book or conversation.

With only a few minutes until the first lesson began Polly,

provoked by the same level of nervousness, remembered her first day. Then, as now, she had known that in a few weeks she would have to announce she would only be with them for two terms. But unlike the day she started when she was asking for maternity leave, this time she would have to tell the Head she wouldn't be back at all.

It had been a different Head in nineteen eighty-eight and his reaction to her news during her very first term had not been favourable; so that she'd felt like an unmarried fifteen-year-old telling her parents and in the same role had wanted to assure him that they hadn't done it on purpose. She had better tell Helen soon, she thought, it being only fair to her and to James who already knew.

By the time break was over, Polly had seen all but two of her colleagues and was only left with the students to face and she very much doubted that they would say anything. But as soon as she arrived in the classroom it became obvious how very wrong she was – on her desk were flowers in a vase and a note which read:

Dear Mrs. Johnson, these are to say welcome back and we're sorry about your husband.

It was signed by each member of the A level class and immediately Polly burst into tears, so that when the first students arrived she had to turn her back on them in order to compose herself. It was with some difficulty, once they were all in the room that she said: "Thank you for the flowers. I hope you all had a good Christmas and I wish you a very Happy New Year - Now, on with the lesson."

*

CHAPTER FIVE.

In her imagination Indira knew the street in New York where she would have her apartment. It would be just like the one she'd seen in the documentary about New York that she had watched on television when visiting her father in Kathmandu. She would share it with a nice American girl, who would teach her how to cook American style and take her to parties where she'd meet a boy and become the wife of a doctor or lawyer. Then they would buy a house big enough for them, their children and her mother, who would care for the children whilst she went to work or returned to her study.

This dream had persisted for several years and had only recently been usurped by one in which she was the wife of Kapil, living instead in the Kathmandu valley, but the rest of the fantasy remained the same. Now it seemed fantasy was all it was destined to be. Indira looked across at Kapil now, but his attention was directed out of the window not at her and they were nearing the end of the journey. She wanted to tell him that she wouldn't be joining him in college after all, but hardly a word had passed between them, only glances and smiles that she might have misconstrued.

They alighted from the bus at the same point and walked the same route for about half-an-hour before their paths separated. Kapil walked with his friend a few paces in front of Indira and her friend Bobita, with whom she strolled hand in hand, silently brooding on the same subject. At the junction where they parted Kapil turned to the girls and smiled, fixing his gaze a little too long on Indira.

"He definitely likes you." Bobita said, teasingly.

Indira slapped her friend's arm by way of response.

"We could get our own apartment – find jobs to help us pay."

"I still wouldn't be able to study."

"Kapil can come and rescue you when he's qualified."

"Stop it!"

They hugged each other as they parted.

Gonesh was already home when Indira arrived, he was on his hands and knees head down buried in his homework. Indira felt a rush of rage and envy because he was performing the task under protest whilst for her it would have been a joy, but there was no point now. As she threw her books down the front cover fell from her English book, she smiled an ironic smile and went to collect wood for the stove, feeling, as she lit it, that she might as well use her school books as fuel. As she helped her mother prepare the meal she watched her intently and saw that she was lost. In her mother's empty eyes Indira saw her own future and felt protest and acceptance in equal measure. The dream of working in Europe was more her father's than her own and was even a little scary, but without her education Kapil would stay a dream too. The unknown and unknowable future was frightening, but how much more so an utterly predictable one. If only it were really possible to support herself financially and continue to study like some of those European girls her father talked about. If only Daddy hadn't died.

*

Polly had always done her housework on Saturdays so that she could spend Sunday with Ned if he was home, or if not she could read, go for a walk or visit a friend. As long as she started straight after breakfast she was done by lunch time so that in the afternoon she could do the weeks shopping.

Today as she dusted, polished and vacuumed she wondered whether she should sell up and move. Would she feel her loss more or less acutely if she did? What would Ned have wanted? What would her children think? The house was much too big for her and echoed with the story of lives past and, although she enjoyed the garden, keeping the weeds away and the grass short was such a chore. She stared out at it now, Ned hadn't particularly enjoyed doing so, but he did maintain it well and everything growing had been planted and nurtured by him. Now, because of her negligence, they were showing signs of neglect, the living reminders of his care were wilting from lack of the same in her, but she had little time and no inclination to cultivate the garden herself.

She wrote her shopping list over lunch, reflecting on how even this had changed, not only was there no more need to buy beer or men's deodorant, but everything lasted so much longer that the weekly shop had lost its necessity and continued only from habit. Meal planning was an automatic response and easier with only her own tastes to consider, although she had yet to enjoy a meal alone.

In the supermarket she met James, he, like her, pushing a family sized trolley that was only a quarter full: "Let's have tea when you're done," he invited.

She told him her thoughts concerning the house.

"Wait and see how you feel after Nepal, I think that's a bit of a milestone for you."

"Yes, it is. I think Ned would have wanted me to go, don't you?"

"I think he would have approved of what you're doing, as for what he would have wanted – that would be the same now as then, for you to be happy."

"He used to joke about dying sometimes, he'd say 'don't waste time mourning me, find yourself another man. And make sure he's handsome and clever this time.'" Polly laughed slightly at the memory.

"I can just hear him say that. He was always so derogatory about himself and yet he always saw the good in others."

"D'you think? Mostly I guess, but he was a better judge of character than me, if he didn't like someone I would take notice because he was usually right."

"He certainly saw it and said it as it was."

"Didn't he just. Do you remember that letter to his boss when she was threatening wage cuts?"

"I do. How brave was that? He had the courage of his convictions that's for sure."

"Sometimes it was embarrassing mind you, his inclination to say so if something wasn't up to scratch. The kids used to hate it. And sometimes his sense of humour was so cutting people misunderstood and thought him rude."

"Only those who took themselves too seriously, as I recall he laid into me pretty heavily the first time we met, but he didn't offend me."

"Didn't he? I thought he had, we fell out about it actually."

"That's a shame - I found it funny. Why don't you pay someone to do your garden?"

"I guess that's a sensible solution. Thanks James."

"What for?"

"Helping me enjoy some memories. I think this is the first time I've had recollections about Ned that haven't been painful."

*

Kabita left the smallest portion of noodle soup for herself and, feeling like a fussy child, only ate the egg because she was aware of her mother-in-law watching. After the meal she and Indira collected the water in the two large urns, the weight of it bore down on her like the weight of her karmic debt. Karma, like water, fluid and insubstantial; yet heavy enough to be a burden. Now she swept the stone floor, brushing the dust into a corner of the yard; then fed the scraps of the meal to the goats, and hay and green leaves to the water buffalo, leaving the corn for the chickens until last as Bosiram liked to help. He always dropped more than he threw from his plump, toddler hands.

As Kabita shook the straw mats from the wooden balcony and hung the duvets to air she wondered if she and Bosiram should return to her mother's home. Her parents-in-law did not deserve the constant reminder of how they had been cursed; but she couldn't take all three boys and Sunker at least was too young to leave.

Checking the crops for weeds and the need to prune was a welcome distraction. Amongst the crops she could hide from the glances of her mother-in-law, but from shame there was no escape, even in sleep it taunted her, whispering through her dreams. And it was there the second consciousness returned, holding hands with grief. Even before Ram's death Kabita had never felt truly at home in this house, despite realising that Ram's parents did their best to make her welcome; unless he was there she felt like a visitor. Now she had to continue to behave with dignity in the midst of her shame and grief, in the knowledge that she would never experience that contentment again.

*

The telephone continued to ring. Christine was in the garden discussing with Dan what needed to be done. She knew her mother didn't answer it because she saw her standing, arms crossed, hard faced, looking out of the French windows. Polly didn't answer her mobile when it rang only seconds later, either.

"She doesn't seem too good today, does she?" Christine said to Dan.

"It's early days yet."

"She's very stoical, but more transparent than she realises. I'll go and have a word with her, if she'll allow me."

Polly had moved away from the window when she realised by their body language that Christine and Dan were discussing her, she looked around now for something to busy herself with, but hadn't found anything by the time her daughter came in to the room.

"Why didn't you answer the phone?" Christine asked.

"It was my mother."

"Poor Nan, she'll worry now."

"I'll call her back when I'm feeling more like talking." Polly's snappy tone surprised her.

"What is it with Nan?" Christine snapped back. "Why are you so cold with her? She only wants to offer you support."

"She can't support me, she's so needy."

"We could the same of you. Then where would you be?'

"On my own - which would suit me just fine."

"The hell it would. You hate being on your own you just can't admit it. Perhaps Nan does actually need you, she loved him too."

"I just can't deal with that at the moment, I. . . .I'm . . .I can't stand anyone feeling sorry for me."

"Why? Isn't it something to be sorry about? We *are* sorry for you and for ourselves"

Christine burst into deep sobbing. Polly wrapped her arms around her daughter and responded in the same way: "I'm so scared without him," she choked out between the tears. "I just don't know what to do with the rest of my life."

"Of course not, but you will." Christine held her mother by the shoulders and looked directly into her eyes. "Dad would want you to get on with your life."

"I know, but I don't know how."

They were cycling on a tandem, Polly on the front, Ned behind. The country road was full of twists and turns, but empty of traffic. Suddenly Polly felt the lack of Ned's weight and looking back for him wobbled and almost fell.

"What are you doing? Ned asked from an unseen place behind her. "Stop a minute."

Polly did as she was instructed. "Why do you keep looking back for me?" Ned asked: "Its making you wobble, you're going to fall and hurt yourself." Polly was aware of him again without seeing him. "There, I've fixed the bike, now you can cycle by yourself."

Polly's tears woke her up: "I don't want to," she cried to the empty room, "and I don't know how."

And yet it was a beautiful dream with a message it was impossible to misinterpret and so typical of Ned that she could almost convince herself it had come directly from him.

It was too late to return to sleep, but too early to get up. Polly looked out of the window to see rain so hard it bounced from the street and the few cars that were about already drove through it at a crawl, with wipers on full blast. She remembered the year of the floods and how Ned had stayed at work for three days because the roads were impassable and his colleagues couldn't get in. The rain pounded the windows so hard she thought the glass would shatter and the sound on the roof was solid, like hands drumming heavily on wood, now she wondered how much worse than this the monsoon rains could be. Her musings brought her to an appropriate time for rising, she would need to leave a little early for work to ensure road safety in these weather conditions.

*

The mountain was high and steep, Kabita was climbing it because she needed to find something, but she wasn't yet sure what that something was.

She scrambled across rocks, pushed aside scrubs, dug into the soil with her bare hands, but she still couldn't find what she was looking for. And then she was alerted by the sound of childish laughter and looking up saw a boy child standing there in front of her. He smiled and held out his hand, but as she approached he turned and skipped playfully down the mountain towards their village, Kabita ran after him her own laughter joining with his.

She woke slowly from the dream at first mistaking the patter of rain on the tin roof for the continuation of laughter. As she came fully to consciousness Kabita recalled the detail of the dream and she knew she had been sent a message. Ram was coming back, she didn't yet know where or to whom, but there would be another sign. All she needed to do was to wait

*

Grief belongs to winter. To wake in darkness and return from work in darkness felt entirely right to Polly, for those were the times when Ned was most upon her mind, and in the hours between she was too busy with the mundane tasks of life to listen to her heart. She resisted the spring with its expanding light and promise of new things. For her spring was too full of optimism. She was fast approaching fifty with all of her plans for the future thwarted and the very real prospect of living thirty or more years on her own. To be with anyone else would be tantamount to forgetting Ned. No, to validate his existence she must grieve forever. And yet, how she missed loving and being loved.

There would be other things she could do of course. She might even sign up for some charity work in Nepal. She could return to study, take up the piano, meditate, write a book; the possibilities were endless. But still she sensed none of these would ever be truly satisfactory.

*

The cockerel's crow was like a knife. Every morning it sliced into Kabita's sleep and forced her into the dawning of another day. Sometimes, when Ram was alive, the lack of variety in her life, the absolute certainty that tomorrow would be like today, had bored her, but now she was grateful for it because in predictability there was no need for thought.

*

CHAPTER SIX.

As Polly walked through the school gates for the final time she felt flat. Sad, excited, apprehensive or even relieved, none of these would have surprised her, but this lack of feeling did. The end of a teaching career that had been as long as her marriage signaled another big change, but she greeted it without interest. Even Helen's farewell speech and the gifts and well wishes from her colleagues failed to make an impact.

Now she opened the front door of her home, walked into the silent living room and, sitting down in Ned's leather chair, reviewed the farewell presents. A passport cover, a Nepali phrase book, a pair of gas powered hair straighteners, all indicated some consideration as to why she was leaving. And then there were the predictable flowers and toiletries.

Normally Polly enjoyed the end of term and celebrated the beginning of a long holiday in whatever way seemed appropriate. Last year had been special. Ned was already home from work when she returned and they had gone for a walk and a picnic and then spent the early evening in bed, before going to the pub. But today, not in the mood to celebrate, she put a baked potato in the oven and was part way through preparing salad when the telephone rang.

"Hi, it's James. Just wondered if you fancied a drink?"

"That would be nice – say eight. Okay I'll see you there."

Getting ready Polly considered wearing her long blue dress, it was Ned's favourite and she'd yet to wear it since his death. She took it from the wardrobe and was deciding what to wear underneath in order to be warm enough, when she changed her mind and opted for the safer option of light trousers and a top. As a compromise she donned matching necklace, earrings and bracelet.

Polly was explaining her feelings regarding retirement from the job and James was commenting on the fact that he thought more fuss could have been made when Malcolm arrived at their table. "Polly, how are you doing?" He asked, taking a sideways glance at James.

"Not bad, I finished work today. This is my colleague James."

"Hello James." They shook hands.

"I'm glad I've bumped into you actually Malcolm, I could do with discussing some details of the trip. I've been wondering about how we let Ram's wife know I'm coming and what we say. Do we tell her about the money for example? What's her name, by-the-way?"

"I wouldn't worry about any of that you can sort it out with Arjun when you arrive. That's the guide's name. I don't know hers I'm afraid. Ram always referred to her as 'my wife.'"

"Did Arjun," she said his name a little doubtfully, "know Ned?"

"He did! And he was very good friend of Ram's and he speaks excellent English."

"Nothing to worry about, then."

"No, just get your pretty little self there, you'll be met at the airport and looked after from there in. Ned was very popular with these guys they are going to want to look after you. - You're looking better by-the-way"

Polly didn't answer.

"Perhaps I could come and see you before you go, give you a bit of a briefing."

"If you like. Better ring first though, I'm a free agent now." As soon as Polly had spoken the words she regretted them, knowing their meaning could be misconstrued and Malcolm was more likely than anyone to do so. And when she looked back at James she thought she detected disapproval in his eyes.

*

The rainy season was a busy one. The rice needed planting and all of the crops required daily attention to ensure they remained free of pests. Kabita walked backwards planting her small crop a few inches apart, the rain beating on the plastic sheeting she wore for protection, running off and soaking the bottom of her sari. Her feet stuck in the mud and squelched with each footstep, the leeches stung as they made contact with her flesh, and she scrapped them off with her machete. She continued to work through the rain and had just about finished when the hail began so she ran for the cover of the house. Before going inside she checked that the goat and chicken pens were properly secure and poured water over her feet to clean off the mud.

Inside Indira was washing lentils in preparation for the meal while her brothers played cards, getting increasingly frustrated with Bosiram who, even though he was sitting on his grandmother's knee and she was supervising the play, kept picking up the cards and refusing to give them back. Ram's father slept, a bundle of covers was all he appeared to be.

Kabita went to the bedroom to change, leaving her sodden clothes in a heap on the floor until there was a lull in the rain that would allow her to wash and dry them. She had tried to avoid wearing either of the only two saris that remained dry as they were both rather bold in colour and not in keeping with her widowhood, but now her only other choice was the white one, which she needed clean for the anniversary. The rain pelting on the tin roof was deafeningly loud, but at least there were no leaks. The bedding smelt damp as it always did by the middle of the rainy season, as soon as there was a break in the rain Kabita decided, she would go and hang it over the balcony to freshen it up. As she descended the ladder into the kitchen she felt conscious that both her daughter and her mother-in-law would think badly of her for her choice of clothes.

Indira had lit candles in response to the darkening sky. With the rain and the hail pounding on the roof it felt as if the house was under attack. The water buffalo bellowed her objection to the weather conditions and the goats could be heard scrambling over each other. At least the scene inside the house was more peaceful now as Bosiram lay on his belly on the floor colouring and the other two boys played happily at their game.

After an hour or two the rain subsided enough to allow the outside work to continue, during this time Kabita took the clothes to the tap and scrubbed them clean with soap and a scrubbing brush, then when it stopped all together she laid them on the wall to dry. Indira swept the hail from the yard and released the animals from their pens, to allow them freedom before the deluge started again. Bosiram followed, barefoot, having lost patience with shoes that stuck in the mud and hampered his movements.

Kabita reminisced as she worked, remembering the previous year and the security and intimacy of having Ram's help and then spending the long evenings in his company. Although this was one of her busiest times of year it had always been one of the happiest too. Now there was nothing to look forward to at the end of a busy day.

*

Mia was at the door. "Hi, I thought you'd be interested in this," she handed a page from the previous days Independent to Polly.

"It's about Nepali men being offered a financial incentive to marry widows. They get a pretty rough deal by the sound of it they're widely considered as bad luck, as being responsible for their husband's deaths because of 'bad karma.' It's worse in rural areas according to this article, so I wonder how your widow's getting on. They've gone on the march in Kathmandu which is quite something I should think. Anyway, you can read it for yourself.

"Thanks, I will." When she did Polly was not only shocked, but also more than a little ashamed at her own feelings, because, when compared with this, bearing her own burden of grief seemed trivial.

Even though there would be no return to work after them Polly experienced the summer holidays as a watershed. Not least because their conclusion marked the end of the first year of widowhood, but also because it was the first one in her entire career spent alone. She filled the days tending the house and garden, which many evenings she sat in drinking tea or wine and reminiscing, often with the aid of music and always with a sense of disbelief. She felt herself to be waiting, without any idea of what for. Projecting into the future Polly tried to imagine herself in ten or twenty years, but it was utterly impossible. And one thing at least was certain, future would all too soon become present however she decided to live, and despite her desire to change the outcome of the recent past.

It was several weeks since Polly had been to the burial ground, she left home early hoping to be the first there, but Ned's parents had beaten her to it. They had flowers, which weren't strictly allowed; Polly wondered if they would think badly of her for arriving without.

When everyone was there the atmosphere was heavy with expectation, but of what no one was clear and no one seemed to have any idea on how to proceed; so they stood by the in their personal meditations, or made the inevitable comments about how it was still hard to believe despite the fact that a year had passed. Sometimes they even spoke on common place subjects, the way people do when standing at the bedside of a dying person, unable to concentrate on the fact of death for too long. After the shared picnic all but Polly left. "I still miss you," she said to the space around the grave. "I'm doing what you would want and getting on with my life, but it doesn't mean anything anymore." Now she cried, deep wrenching sobs from her solar plexus.

'I hope you know I loved you, I keep looking for confirmation, but all I find is how much you loved me.' She thought the words, unable to speak through her tears, but finding her inner voice unsatisfactory, she continued out loud: "I won't come now until after Nepal, we have one and a half thousand pounds for Ram's family, isn't that fantastic? I'll come and tell you all about it when I return."

Polly turned to walk away then, turning back said: "I did love you so much. I hope you knew that."

The scenes of year ago ran through her mind as if she had videoed them, but the feelings weren't the same; without the shock factor she felt the grief even more sharply. There had been no tears on the day, but today they wouldn't stop, they tore at her body and bellowed into the room and Polly was so far inside the experience she was lost.

When she was a little calmer she looked again through the photographs, feeling resentful of the empty spaces left by those she had selected for Ram's widow. Suddenly she felt angry and shouted out loud: "How dare you leave me. How can I, why should I carry on when life has no meaning anymore?" She tugged Ned's work bag from beside his chair and threw it at the wall; his mobile phone fell from it and to the ground in two pieces. "Shit!" Now Polly felt stupid and remorseful as she picked it up and put it back together, then turned it on to make sure it still worked. She flicked through the messages in the in box, there were several from her – all practical in content, but signed: 'love you x'. Then she went to the sent box, wondering why she'd never done so before and there she found the message which read: 'My Dearest Polly, how can I ever thank you for the love you have shown me? I don't know how I would have got this far without you. XN'

The sight of it brought forth a fresh bout of tears through which she checked her own phone for the message, having no memory of this one. It wasn't there; she must have erased it, what a stupid thing to do. Polly read and re read the message, then she curled into a foetal posture on the floor and cried with grief and with relief.

*

There was prayer and feasting. The men and the boys shaved their heads in commemoration of their loss. Kabita dressed in her white sari and fasted for the day while her friends and relatives enjoyed the food she'd prepared. One year on and the only thing that had changed for her was that, alongside all of the other feelings, she felt guilty at her infrequent moments of forgetting or remembering with fondness rather than pain. But today the memory was like a replay of the actual events and she felt her loss as a threat to her own existence.

Suddenly Kabita's desolation turned to rage and she hated everyone for being there in a festive mood. She ran from the village and climbed the hill quickly and clumsily, so that she scratched and bashed and bruised herself, but she enjoyed the pain feeling it a vindication for her heart. Out of breath she sat down and looked towards her home, envisioning herself as she did so, as a bodiless soul; but, far from inducing a sense of freedom the imaginings created an unbearable desire for belonging so that now Kabita worried that Ram's spirit was as lost without her, as she was without him. "How can I help you get back?" She asked into the space around her. "Send me another sign." And she opened her ears, her heart and her mind in seeking, but from the village there was the distant sound of life carrying on. Close to there was only silence.

*

CHAPTER SEVEN.

It was difficult now for Polly to focus on anything but her pending trip, with only just over two weeks to go and the preparations complete she felt bored and restless.

"I think you're going to have a different perspective on life when you come back," James was visiting and was marking homework books as they chatted.

"I think I'll feel even more lost without an aim. D'you want me to mark some of those?"

"If you like," he handed her a small pile. "D'you have any plans for when you're home."

"I'll have to find another job first of all. I thought I might go back to studying too, a language perhaps or learn a musical instrument. I used to complain about not having time for those."

"D'you see yourself in another relationship?" There was a slight catch in James's voice.

"I wouldn't say never, but it wouldn't feel right just yet."

"Of course not. You were with Ned more than half your life."

"I keep thinking I'll wake up one day and know what to do with the rest of my life, but really I guess it's the same as it's always been except for that one thing. So maybe I'll go back to teaching and back to my *normal* life. I don't really see why another man would make all that much difference."

"Well, it's just better with someone to share things with, isn't it?"

"I have people to share things with, I have you and Mia and my kids."

"Yes but. . . don't you miss that special relationship?"

"Sex you mean?"

"Not just that. The whole relationship thing."

"Of course I do, but you can't make that happen with someone."

"Pr'aps not," now he sounded disappointed.

Polly handed James back the pile of books. "Paige Stone, is she still acting up?"

"As ever. You remember her then?" He cast his eyes downwards.

It was only then that it occurred to Polly he might be trying to tell her something. "She'll take a while to forget."

The hug he gave her as he left was more cautious and formal than usual confirming Polly's feeling and now she worried that she had hurt him. For a moment she considered calling him back, but what could she unsay when she had spoken the truth on her feelings?

She lay in bed awake a long time reflecting on her conversation with James. He was such a good friend she'd never thought about him any other way, but now that the seed was planted she considered him. His self-effacing nature and the way he seemed to fold in on himself reminded her very much of Ned, and there was no doubt that his genuine interest in her was attractive: as were his strikingly blue eyes which were full of pathos. When he hugged her he always held her head against his chest, which felt safe, and there was warmth in it that was beyond the merely physical. The problem though was his profound sadness, because although it was indicative of depth of feeling it was also suggestive of neediness.

There was no doubt that sometimes Polly's sexual desire was immense to the point of being disruptive and she felt sure that James would take care of her needs in a gentlemanly way, but she was less sure that it was what she wanted right now. Commitment to him, to anyone but Ned still didn't feel right. And James' apparent neediness scared her more than a little. She was afraid of it because it threatened annihilation of self and promised loss of independence. But, although she didn't fully realise it, she feared it most because she abhorred the recognition of it in herself.

It was only two days later that Malcolm arrived on the doorstep. "Hi, I know you said ring, but I thought I'd take a chance. I thought we could share this," he waved the bottle of red wine at her.

Against her better judgment Polly let him in, knowing what he had come for and, almost certain that he knew she knew, was going to make it difficult to refuse him.

"It's a bit early for me I was just about to make tea," she lied, "would you like one?"

"Might as well, we can save this for later."

Polly's mind wasn't on the small talk they made over the tea, she was distracted by self-contempt at having let him in and by worrying about how she was going to react when he made a pass.

"Shall I crack this bottle open?" He eventually asked.

"I think it'd be better if you didn't, I have a lot to do tomorrow, don't want to get drunk."

"On half a bottle?"

"I've got a low tolerance."

"Just have one glass, then. I've got a high tolerance," he laughed. "You don't need to be worried I've just come to wish you bon voyage. D'you think I'm going to try to seduce you or something?"

Now Polly felt ashamed and that she had misjudged him: "No. I told you I have a busy day tomorrow."

"Just drink that then," Malcolm ordered as he passed her a very full glass. "So how're you feeling, really?"

Polly took a sip of wine. "Oh, you know."

"No, I don't Polly, Ned is the closet person I've lost so far. Of course I miss him, but it must be so much worse for you."

She took another sip. "Well, it's not that I mind being on my own, in fact it's easier in many respects, but I miss Ned enormously." Taking another sip she carried on because Malcolm seemed to be waiting for more and it felt like a relief. "At first you just can't believe it. You want so much for it not to be true that you're sure a mistake has been made, which is terrible because then it would be someone else's husband and it's like you're wishing it on someone else. Then as the days go by and the person's still missing you feel - it's like - have you ever been homesick? – Well, it's a bit like that. Everything familiar and safe has gone, you feel totally lost and without hope. Only it's a thousand times worse because it's always possible to go home, but death is so permanent. It's so permanent that really it's too much to comprehend."

Polly wondered why she was telling this man who really she hardly knew and wasn't even sure she liked all that much, things she didn't seem able to tell her best friends, but Malcolm looked at her with a concern so genuine it was uncomfortable. "I'm sorry. I mean I'm really sorry."

The words sounded sincere and Polly felt herself fall into them. She tried to hold his gaze, but looking him in the eyes was too awkward, so she took a gulp of wine. "People keep telling me I'll feel differently after Nepal."

"Perhaps you will. Are you looking forward to it?"

"Not sure if that's the right word, but it'll be interesting and probably cathartic."

"Ned certainly loved it. Not that the rest of us didn't; there's something about the   place despite the chaos, cold showers and power cuts, which I hope you're prepared for, by-the-way."

"He worried that the rest of you would get bored with it. He was inclined to stick with what he knew; probably why he stuck with me so long."

"He stuck with you from love. No doubt on that one."

"I know. He was a creature of habit though: 'a boring bastard' was how he described himself."

"Sounds about typical. No, we weren't bored with Nepal it's a fascinating place,.." as Malcolm talked about Nepal he pulled Polly's feet into his lap and started to massage them. Instead of pulling away as she knew she should, she poured herself a second glass of wine.

"Are you enjoying this?"

"Of course, but I think you'd better stop."

"Why?"

"May be I'm enjoying it a bit too much."

"Where's the harm?"

"Your wife?"

"Is away in Newcastle with a friend, she'll never know." He lent forward and kissed her and her body responded shamefully.

"I thought you weren't trying to seduce me."

"I lied. Let's go to bed."

"The Government in Nepal is currently bribing men to marry widows, did you know that? For as little as three hundred pounds."

"So you'd prefer I view you as damaged goods rather than want to make love to you? – I didn't think so, come on you know you want to." It was true, she did. Malcolm was very handsome and exuded sexual confidence. Her body was crying out for attention and she wanted to know she was still capable of enjoying sex.

"We can't."

"Why?"

"I told you, your wife."

"And I told you she'll never know."

"It's not right, though."

"I know, but it's me who's doing wrong. Now stop stalling and come to bed."

Without waiting for a reply Malcolm headed for the stairs: "which is your room?"

"First left."

"Just gotta pay a visit."

While Malcolm was in the bathroom Polly quickly undressed to her underwear and leapt into bed. The first pang of guilt came as he climbed in bedside her, but it was for Ned, not Malcolm's wife. He pulled her close, kissed her again, touched her breasts, responded to her nervousness sensitively and coaxed her gently towards acquiescence.

As his demeanour suggested Malcolm was an accomplished lover, but the only part she really enjoyed was the kissing, which was full of promise. A promise Polly had no doubt he was able to live up to if only she could respond appropriately.

Afterwards he said: "I'm glad you didn't insult me by pretending to climax."

"It's not you – it's because – this is the first time, I kind of feel like I've been unfaithful. But I'm glad it was you." What she meant was that she didn't have to try to be in love with him.

'Thanks. That's sweet. May I stay all night?"

"Might as well now."

They were intimate again in the morning. This time Malcolm persisted until she reached a climax; the relief of it brought tears. He was tender and held her she as cried, and then he kissed her on the forehead, showered and left. Polly stayed in bed, thinking. Satisfaction lasted only moments. The click of the front door closing behind Malcolm brought back all the feelings of loss that he had temporarily relieved.

Now she placed the palm of her left hand against her breast and that of her right on her stomach, feeling the synchronised rhythm of her heart beat and breathing, as if it offered confirmation of her identity, because Polly didn't sleep with men who meant so little to her, especially those with wives. And though she recognised her actions were generated by a loneliness she was unwilling to give up, and she knew Malcolm's confidence was as impenetrable as her solitude, nevertheless she felt utter self-contempt. Such was her shame that she vowed to tell no-one, not even Mia, safe in the knowledge that Malcolm would keep it secret too.

*

It was almost a whole day's walk to and from the market; Indira had timed her return to coincide with the college bus drop off, hoping to see Kapil. She wasn't disappointed. "Namaste," she said as he alighted, and in a manner that suggested she hadn't expected to see him.

"Indira. How are you?"

She smiled and nodded: "Thick cha. How are you?"

"I'm good too. – It's good to see you. Shall I carry your dokko, it must be heavy," he was putting his books down even as he spoke and his manner was flirtatious which made Indira flush.

She giggled as she removed the strap from her head and the basket from her back. "Are your studies going well?"

"They are. It's a shame for you."

"Yes."

"Soon I will be moving to college in Kathmandu and then, if things work out as planned to England."

"Oh!" Although it was probably never more than a dream for her, the reality of Kapil's opportunity was painful. They walked along in silence the rest of the way, each looking shyly at the other and smiling from time to time. At the point where their paths separated Kapil suddenly stopped turned to Indira and said: "I'll carry this to the village for you," then very quickly, as if he half hoped her not to hear: "Meet me here tomorrow."

Indira's stomach lurched in response to his request, she smiled and nodded. As they swapped burdens again, he helping to position the dokko correctly, he lightly brushed the back of her neck, which excited her in a way that caused her shame, and they exchanged shy smiles.

Sandeep, home for a few days, had come to visit his parents and saw Kapil's actions; something in the body language disturbed him. Indira's walk towards home was animated, her manner light despite her heavy load.

"Hello," she said cheerily.

"Wasn't that Kapil Adakari?" Sandeep asked.

"Yes."

"He lives near my village, why did he come here?"

"He carried the dokko for me."

"Since when have you needed help from boys?"

"I met him on the road and he offered." Indira felt her face flush with indignation and guilt.

"He's going to study in England. He's too good for you."

"He carried the dokko that's all. We used to go to school together." Indira went into the house with as much dignity as she could manage and handed over the purchases to her mother.

"So much change, you did well."

"I'm tired. I want to rest for a minute." She climbed to the bedroom, feeling tears welling up in her eyes, but Sunker was there with his homework book. She wanted to shout at him just for being there, but instead went back downstairs and out of the house, pushing rudely past her uncle as he came through the doorway. Of course she knew Kapil was too good for her, she thought indignantly, but he needn't have been. Not if she'd been able to go to college like Daddy wanted, his family might have given her a chance then. 'Why did you have to die?' She cried, silently.

Indira walked around for a few minutes until she felt her anger subsiding and then headed back home, ready to apologise to her mother and her uncle, but as she approached the door she overheard the conversation that was taking place.

"His family are willing to take her without a dowry because they know your circumstances and the mother is in poor health, so needs help, but I think they won't wait for long they need someone soon."

"She's still so young."

"Only a year younger than you were."

They looked up together as Indira came into the room. That she had heard was obvious by the way she held herself.

"He's a nice boy, from a decent family, they'll treat you well." Sandeep assured.

She didn't reply.

"This is a highly suitable marriage Indira, but they want it to be soon."

"I thought I might choose my own husband," she said without meaning to.

"Where're you going to meet a suitable husband? The only place you go outside the village is the market." Sandeep's tone was unpleasant, almost sneering. "And we know the kind of boys you meet there."

Indira looked to her mother for a clue as to whether she could expect her support; the answer lay in Kabita's lack of response. Indira bitterly turned her attention towards her chores, making her true feelings known by performing them loudly and exaggeratedly.

"We need to think about it," Kabita said to her brother in-law, but in her mind the urgency of the situation could only mean one thing. This was the sign she'd been waiting for.

CHAPTER EIGHT.

There were tears at the airport as Mia and Christine waved Polly through the barriers, they cried as much from pride, as from the knowledge they would miss her for the next couple of months. Polly cried because she was terrified.

Placing her rucksack on the trolley she joined the queue for Air India, checking her handbag for passport and tickets several times whilst she waited, and talking internal words of reassurance. As they called her through she dropped the documents that she had been clinging to ever since she became third in line, the young man behind her picked them up and offered them with a smile. "Thanks, I'm a bit nervous, not travelled on my own before." Polly found it necessary to justify her clumsiness.

"Now where?" She asked as the rucksack was sent along the conveyer belt and her documents handed back.

"Just follow the signs for departures." There was no suggestion in the words, but Polly felt herself stupid.

Although there was plenty of time she decided to go through the check-in immediately to ensure she was at the right gate and, once she'd done so, as long as she didn't think too much about the flight, she did feel more relaxed. She tried to fill the time with reading, but there were so many distractions: the announcements, the continual movement of people, the fear of the flight; and, most disturbing of all, Malcolm. Who crept into the back of her mind with alarming regularity.

Boarding the plane brought back fear, but she was keeping the valium until later to help her sleep and make the eight hour journey seem shorter. She shuffled into the window seat, finding irony in the fact that she was probably the passenger least likely to make full use of it.

Ned used to say the take-off was exciting, that he loved the way the acceleration pushed him back in his seat and sent a little thrill from his stomach all the way up his spine. Polly wished she could adopt the same attitude. Once the aeroplane levelled out however, and her ears stopped popping she didn't feel so bad so took out her book to read. Concentration was impossible, she stared at the pages making a pretence that was aimed entirely at herself, and when the the food arrived was glad of the distraction.

Turbulence drove her to the valium. It took only twenty minutes for it to transform her attitude, so that now she was able to experience it not as bumping, but as rocking and she was almost comforted by the motion. Then she risked lifting the shutter and when she did, saw how the clouds, wispy and insubstantial as they drifted past, appeared like spirits; a ghostly trail floating its way across the sky. She noticed too that the way their shadows hung over the landscape it was as if the clouds were shadows and the shadows the clouds. Like them she drifted whispery, half-conscious for the rest of the trip. The next time she looked out of the window it was near morning and journey's end. This time a single dark cumulonimbus cloud surrounded in sunrise, gave the impression of an African plain.

They landed on time at Delhi airport and Polly felt reassured by being met from the plane and ushered to the transfer desk. However, when two hours later and with the leader board instructing her to go to check-in, she still had no boarding pass, Polly's confidence began to fail. Eventually, as she was deciding to go and ask for the third time, it did arrive and she hurried through check-in to the boarding gate where she sat for another two hours, waiting for the fog to clear from Kathmandu airport. Finally on board the plane fear crept ever closer towards terror. The aeroplane was small, bumpy and noisy; the only consolation was that the journey was short.

In his diary Ned had written of his first glimpse of the Himalayas:

'It was a peak moment (no pun intended) in my life. This was the one place in the world to which I had always really wanted to come; all others were only of minor interest to me in comparison. I had read about and seen pictures of Nepal as a child and been fascinated with it. And then later about the climbers and awed by how anyone could conquer a mountain five miles high. And now here I was. This ranked alongside meeting Polly and having my kids.'

To Polly they looked like any other mountains as viewed from the air, like contours on a map, but as they neared their destination and the mountains remained full screen, her emotions were much the same as Ned had described. As they came into land the view of the mountains gave way to the view of the city. It offered only a glimpse, flat-roofed buildings, barren landscape and an airport of military appearance. The road leading to the terminal building was dry, dusty and full of holes. The red-bricked building with its asphalt roof had a shed-like appearance; or a bus station at best. As she walked down the corridor following signs in English and Nepali for baggage reclaim Polly noted the rows of black plastic chairs in which a mass of people gazed at the large television screen. Nineteen-sixties style telephones stood on wooden platforms, water filtered from large, grubby plastic containers. Polly was glad she didn't currently have the need to discover the quality of the toilets, which were behind screens like those used by hospitals from the same era.

The chaos in immigration was such that it took a while for it to register the necessity to fill out a form before joining the queue. At first it appeared there were none in English, but then someone handed her one from the pile that had been discarded on the floor. Joining the exit queue Polly was grateful that she had ignored Malcolm's advice and purchased her visa before leaving, as the line for those without was twice as long as hers.

By the time she reached baggage reclaim, having first been confronted with another X-ray machine for hand luggage, Polly's patience was running out, but here was the worst chaos so far. People too impatient to wait for the conveyer belt as it chugged around, clambered amongst the bags, took them off, put them back on, shouted instructions and pushed their way in and out of the hordes. Polly, very English and very tired, stood back and waited. A man dressed in Western clothes, but wearing a typical Nepali hat approached with a trolley and asked: "your bag?" Waving his hand in the general direction of the conveyer, Polly nodded, worrying a little about how she would pay him with only English currency. He then proceeded to throw any bag which vaguely fitted the description she had given in her direction, until she agreed that one was hers. He put it on the trolley, pushed it through the exit doors and seemed happy with the two pound coin with which she presented him.

Sun, dust, tiredness and a valium hangover made concentration impossible, as she scanned the rows of people bearing cardboard plaques with names on and tried to drown out the onslaught of touts advertising their hotel, offering free taxis to theirs. She searched for her own name. Then realised a young man was coming towards her with exactly what she was looking for: "This is you, yes?" He asked, smiling and offering his hand.

"Yes, that was a good guess."

"No guess. I have seen your picture many times."

In her current state this almost provoked tears: "Are you Arjun?" She asked quickly.

"Yes." He shook her hand vigorously.

Now Polly recognised him from the photographs Ned had taken. "I've seen your photo too."

"Yeah?" His smile was a bit crooked and shone out through his eyes, he put his hand gently on Polly's shoulder and ushered her towards the taxi. She wanted to ask him so many things, but time enough for that.

The taxi was a tiny red Toyota with a boot only just big enough for her luggage. It took several attempts to close the door and even then Polly wasn't quite satisfied it would remain that way. It also took several attempts to start it, culminating in the driver lifting the bonnet to adjust something.

Dusty roads with gaping holes in the tarmac made the journey to the hotel bumpy, but at least they were on solid ground this time. Although push bikes, motor bikes and pedestrians continually getting between the car and their own safety meant that was all she could be grateful for. Their driver tooted, as did every other. The smell was of diesel and sewage. On the roads, which were littered with non-biodegradable rubbish, people walked, sometimes in flip flops, sometimes even bare foot. Most of the buildings looked only half-constructed, some bore bamboo scaffold in evidence of that. The sun baked down on this half-baked world, emphasising the dust, but also the colourful clothes and shop fronts. Polly's first impression was one of colour and chaos, in about equal measure.

*

A lie was necessary; Indira told her mother she was meeting Bobita to help her with a mathematics problem. Even as she went to the rendezvous place Indira was sure Kapil would not turn up and she worried about what he would think of her if he discovered that she had. But Kapil was already there when she arrived, sitting reading one of his books, he stood up as she approached: "You came?"

"You asked me to."

"Walk with me. D'you have plenty of time?"

"Yes."

Kapil walked a couple of paces ahead and didn't speak. He looked about him from time to time as if checking no one was following them. The only person they passed was an elderly woman carrying a dokko full of spinach. Indira knew she should ask where they were going and why, but her fear of the answer was matched by a shyness towards Kapil and an excitement that made her reckless.

Finally Kapil stopped: "Here," he held out his hand to Indira. "This is where I come for thinking; no one will disturb us here." The touch of Kapil's hand sent a thrill of guilt and anticipation running through Indira. He helped her crawl into the hidey hole, which was in the side of the rock and only just big enough for the two of them. They had to squeeze in the entrance one at a time. Now she was afraid and her heart was beating so hard she was sure it would attract the attention of any passers-by and alert them to their whereabouts. She knew she shouldn't be there and struggled for something to say, but found no words.

Kapil saved her the trouble: "Why did you come here, Indira?"

"You asked me."

"Didn't you wonder why?"

She giggled, a nervous giggle: "Of course I did."

"But you still came."

"Should I go then?" Now Indira worried for her reputation, especially that he should think badly of her.

"No."

"Why *did* you ask me?" Indira said, indignantly.

Kapil put his arm around her letting his hand lightly brush against her breast, turned her face towards his and kissed her.

She pushed him away: "Stop it!"

"Sorry." He moved away slightly.

"I'm a good girl."

"I know."

Indira was confused by the conflicting messages of her culture and biology, but most of all she wanted Kapil's approval. "Then why?"

"I like you."

"If you like me you won't ask me to do anything shameful."

"It's because I like you that I ask. My family plan for me to go away and study."

"I know. My family want me to get married."

"Then what will we do?"

Indira shrugged: "Don't you want to go to England?" Her tone was hopeful.

"Yes, but when I come back everything will have changed, especially if you get married. That's why I wanted to kiss you."

"You wanted to kiss me? – Promise, that's all. – Okay, go on then."

The kiss was clumsy, but it excited her. Kapil's breathing was hard and Indira could feel that his heart beat like hers. He kissed her again and lay down pulling Indira with him, but, terrified of the consequences she pushed him away and sat up.

"What's the matter?"

"You said just a kiss. I'm going now," she squeezed towards the entrance.

"No wait! I don't want you to think badly of me."

Indira squatted with her arms hugged around her knees. "You will think badly of me if I don't go."

"I won't"

"Is that why you brought me here, you think I'm easy?"

"No. No."

"There will be plenty of girls in England who are only too willing from what I've heard." Indira moved towards the entrance again, but Kapil grabbed her leg and pulled her back.

"You don't understand. I want to be with you."

"You can't. They have a husband planned for me."

"I wish that was me, then."

Kapil's words sent a shiver of excitement right through Indira. "That's impossible, your parents wouldn't agree."

"They couldn't refuse if we really decided. Would you wait?"

"I'm not sure I can, even my mother seems keen on this marriage."

Kapil risked a gentle kiss, when there was no resistance he increased the intensity and laid them both back down. He pushed his groin towards her and she could feel the thing she was afraid of growing in response.

"No. Stop!"

"I want to make you mine."

"We have to wait."

"For years until we're married?"

"We'll never be married."

"If you wait I'll come back for you."

The words were sweet, just what she wanted to hear if only that were really possible. Sensing her warming to him Kapil pulled her close again.

"What if I get pregnant?"

"It's not possible the first time."

"No? – You're sure?"

Then suddenly he sat up and for a moment Indira felt relief and regret in the belief that he'd changed his mind. But all he did was to remove his jacket and lie it down underneath her, then he removed his trousers and underclothes, pushed Indira on to her back and himself inside her before she had a chance to fully realise what was happening. It hurt so much she cried out and he pulled away. "I'm sorry, you weren't ready."

"I won't be. I don't want to," but as Kapil touched and coaxed and said her name over and over with desire in his voice, she began to change her mind, feeling her need for him as a warm glow that spread upwards from where he touched her to her heart. Then he pushed back inside her moving slowly at first, but then speeding up. Indira began to experience the feeling another way, to enjoy his weight on top of her and the feel of him inside her, but just as she started to move in unison with him and want it to carry on he cried out, relaxed his full weight on her and then immediately pulled away.

"Are you okay?"

She nodded.

"I didn't hurt you, did I?"

"No."

"Come here."

This time she voluntarily cuddled into him and they kissed each other. "Will you forgive me?"

"For what?"

He smiled and made a noise somewhere between a sigh and a laugh. "Will you come here with me tomorrow?"

"Yes."

They crawled out of the nest together, Kapil made sure no people were around before he helped her up over the rocks. They parted company without a word to each other, but Indira didn't mind. Her heart was soaring with the eagles. She couldn't marry anyone else now, she would have to wait until Kapil finished studying and she didn't care how long that was.

*

The hotel room was surprisingly modern with plenty of sun and hot water.

"So, what are your plans?" Arjun asked.

"Nothing definite yet. I need to shower and sleep a little before I do anything. Then eat, do they have food here? Would you like to join me for a meal?"

"Okay. We eat and we make a plan. See you later."

He was on his way out of the door. "What time later?"

"I don't mind. Seven?"

As Polly showered and unpacked a few things she felt shocked. It was as if the whole experience was happening inside a diving bell; so unreal it seemed. Then she sent an email to say she'd arrived and lay down to sleep. Now she felt deep regret at never having been here with Ned, satisfaction that she was now here on his behalf, disappointment that the events of her life had made it necessary for her to be here at all.

*

Indira hardly slept. At first feeling too excited by what she and Kapil had done and by the prospect of being his wife, but then, as the sounds of sleep began to penetrate the darkness, she began to feel differently. By their very nature secrets could never be celebrations. Festivities need revelers. A wedding was required to celebrate the loss of virginity; the transformation from child to adult and the life-long union of two people. Not minutes of snatched pleasure in a hole in the rocks. Lying on her back next to Sunker Indira noticed the smell of his body and became worried that hers smelt of what she had done.

Creeping from the bed and then the house, taking the necessary items with her she made her way to the village tap. Even though it was pitch black and there was no one around Indira washed with the sheet around her. Then she curled into a foetus on the ground and cried silently for fear of waking anyone. A rage boiled inside her, sitting up she slapped herself around the head and pulled her hair. How could she be so stupid? Kapil wouldn't marry her; he'd have no respect for her now. She cried and cried and rocked until exhausted she returned home and to bed.

In the morning anger turned to fear. What if he was wrong and it was possible to get pregnant the first time? Suppose she was pregnant now? Wasn't there enough shame on the family with her father's death? Feeling herself a wicked girl and a dishonourable daughter she was unable to look anyone in the eye. Although she knew she didn't deserve it for herself, she also knew there was one way left to save her family more shame, she owed it to them now to do her duty.

Kapil waited almost an hour. He waited the same length of time for the next three days. Then the news of Indira's impending wedding reached his village and he waited no more.

*

CHAPTER NINE.

Over dinner they discussed the letter. "Is easy," Arjun assured her. "My friend's family live near there he can take. You tell me what you want say, I write, I give to him."

Back at the hotel Polly dictated the letter, hoping he put emphasis on the right parts. On his instruction she made no mention of the money, referring to it only as a gift.

"What's her name?" Polly asked. "Ram's widow, what's her name?"

"Kabita."

"Lovely name." And now that she knew it, it felt to Polly as if there was more of a connection between the two of them. She felt a responsibility towards her, as if she had to atone in some way for Ram's death.

"So, tomorrow – what are your requirements?"

"I want to go trekking and to see Ram's family, other than that I have no *requirements.*"

"Okay, I come here nine o'clock; we go to my office, make arrangements, then if you like I take you show you Kathmandu."

"Thank you. I would like that."

"Okay, I go now," he held her hand rather than shook it, placing the other one on her elbow. His touch was very reassuring.

He was waiting in the lobby when she arrived the next morning, slouched on the sofa reading the paper, white baseball cap in his hand. When he saw Polly he stood up, put the cap on, smiled and touched her lightly on the shoulder as he said hello.

It was only a short walk to his office. On the way were shops selling trinkets and clothes: prayer wheels, singing bowls, candle holders, stone and brass Buddhas were amongst the wares. The shops themselves, where people both lived and worked, had a garage-like appearance; two storey bare-bricked buildings with corrugated iron shutters that closed down at night and balconies on the top floor from which hung grubby looking clothes. Street venders approached Polly with wooden flutes, beaded bracelets, hand carved elephants, dropping their prices with every refusal on her part to buy. Around each corner it seemed there was a beggar; amongst them a leper and a one armed child. Polly gave them both one hundred rupees, having no idea whether this was generous or the opposite. Arjun gave to the child too, but Polly didn't see how much. He also shook hands and had a brief conversation with three or four people en route and she knew by the way they looked at her that he had told them who she was, but only one said anything:

"So, you are Ned's wife? He was a very fine man."

"Thank you. He was."

The trekking company office was above a shop selling carpets. They climbed concrete stairs and went through a metal gate that opened sideways. The entrance was spacious, linoleum floored and home to a row of trainers and flip flops of varying sizes. Since Arjun removed his shoes, Polly did too.

In the office she met several men whose names she instantly forgot, but all of whom knew Ned. They made her tea, with milk and sugar, which she didn't want, and talked about Ned; which was exactly what she wanted.

She left the office feeling overwhelmed, but satisfied with the arrangements. She'd leave for Pokhara in the morning; spend a couple of days there before going on the trek and a couple more before visiting Ram's family.

"So, now we go look at Kathmandu. You want to take a taxi or walk?"

"How far is it?

"Not far. We walk."

She was pleased with that decision, finding it fascinating to view the streets of Kathmandu. Streets which were littered with rubbish that fawn coloured scrawny dogs sniffed at; and occupied by nineteen sixties style cars, rickshaws, chickens and even a cow. People walked in every direction, somehow avoiding the traffic and muddy, foul smelling holes in the road. In the doorways of shops more people squatted, some chatting others just squatting. Men played cards, women breast fed babies, flies buzzed around uncovered meat and greasy looking doughnuts and, amongst all the chaos, the very ordered look of children wearing blue or burgundy school uniforms and carrying exercise books.

In Durbar Square they saw the Temple of the Living Goddess. It took Polly a while to realise that this should be taken literally and that the Goddess was actually alive. The pre-pubescent girl in her current incarnation peered out shyly from behind the shuttered windows of her home. It was a beautiful building, eighteenth century oriental style, the wooden balconies and slatted windows were painted black. The Goddess herself, Arjun explained was selected as such after several vigorous tests of her authenticity. These included displaying perfect physical charactcristics and a lack of fear in frightening situations. From her western perspective Polly wondered how one decided what perfect was, and if they had ever heard of shock, but she didn't mention these.

On the outside of one temple were erotic scenes. These, Arjun explained were carved by an earlier king who wanted to encourage the people of Nepal to breed because its population was so low. "He was very successful," he said with a wry smile. "We are now twenty-eight million."

Whilst sight- seeing and planning Polly felt fine, but back in the hotel and alone, her mood dipped rapidly down. With the evening advancing and the sun loosing warmth if not yet light, it seemed a little chilly in the room, so she climbed into bed, pulling the covers over her head. She felt so utterly alone, as if she were the only soul in the universe and as if the very core of her being was empty. Then into the emptiness fell a host of negative thoughts. She was weak. So weak she feared being alone; too weak to admit that to anyone, herself included. It was this that had allowed her to be seduced by a man for whom she felt little and, now that she had, she was afraid she would do it again. He was safe. He didn't care if she loved him, neither would he want to be with her so there was no risk of losing him. It was hard to admit, but she wanted affection and sex, but not commitment because that still felt like infidelity, but she hated herself for that need. Full of self-loathing she tried to sleep, wishing to escape the one person from whom it was impossible to flee, but sleep was fitful and sporadic and in any case made no difference to the way she felt on waking.

There was another need growing in her now too, the need to eat, but Polly didn't want to, because every time she ate she detested herself for doing so. People lost all of their desires with the death of a loved one, but she'd lost none and even when they went unsatisfied she felt their very existence to be an abnegation of her love for Ned and proof of her unworthiness. She should have loved him more.

She ordered from the hotel menu, an omelette to be brought to her room. Then she went back to bed.

*

The horoscopes were a good match. The families' credentials without fault and even Indira seemed quite keen on the idea now, but Kabita felt guilty, feeling she had let her daughter down. Perhaps the dream meant something else altogether, perhaps it meant nothing at all. And if she continued to work the land it was perfectly possible for Indira to stay at home another year or two. Kabita found her daughter outside, staring into space, which she seemed to be doing a lot the past few days.

"If you don't like the boy, you can say no."

"I know."

"If I make sure he sits to the left of the stove, where Daddy used to sit, you can look at him before we call you."

"Yes."

"Indira," Kabita's tone was somewhere between impatient and pleading. "You don't have to do this just for us."

'But I do,' Indira thought. And she wondered if Kapil would have told anyone who might be laughing at her and calling her names. "I do want to."

Despite the other feelings Kabita was relieved.

And actually Hari looked nice. From her vantage point at the top of the steps Indira peered down, she must have made a small movement because he looked up slightly and saw. She moved away quickly, but not too quick to notice how he responded with an inner smile that registered so little on his face the adults, engaged in eating and arranging, failed to notice. But she liked that about him and she liked the way he looked, curly hair, full mouth, straight nose were all confirmed as she raised her eyes momentarily whilst serving drinks.

"Wait a moment," his mother ordered as she was leaving the room, Indira's heart raced in fear that something was wrong. Perhaps her lost virginity showed somehow. "Turn around so we can see you properly. Open your mouth let's have a look at your teeth." Indira did as she was bidden and was then dismissed, her part now over it was impossible not to hear their verdict. "Nice straight, white teeth, I like that, it's a sign of good health and that she takes care of herself. She looks strong too."

Much discussion followed on when the wedding should take place, they would decide on a definite date after checking with the priest for a prestigious date. "The young people have to agree to it first," Sandeep reminded Hari's mother.

"Of course, but he liked her, didn't you Hari?"

The family left noisily, talking in excited tones. Indira sat on the bed, let her hair down and as she brushed it she pulled it across her face and peered out through it, it gave her a different view of her world, like looking through a beaded curtain, everything remained visible, but the details were unclear.

*

Polly's bag was thrown up to the top of the bus and tied there with rope, her small rucksack remaining with her. She was ushered to the window seat and there Arjun left her while he wandered up and down the pavement, shaking hands with people, patting their backs, scrounging cigarettes. Vendors mounted the bus selling newspapers in English and bottles of mineral water, one of which she purchased. When the engine started there was no sign of Arjun and Polly felt a rush of panic, but just as it began to move he appeared by the door and then climbed on and sat beside her.

The journey out of the city was slow, like that in any city at peak times of day. And the further they moved towards the city limits the more squalid the scene from the window became. The piles of rubbish increased in dimension, the homes reduced in size and quality to one room clay shacks with tin roofs and no closing door. The children became dirtier, often naked from the waist down; and the dogs grew thinner. People worked and lived beside the pot-holed roads; a constant film of dust covering their lives.

Polly's view of this world made her feel humble. And, with her mood much the same as the day before, more than a little ashamed that she should live so well whilst others lived so poorly. Although it was very much as she expected, it was also true that it hardly seemed possible that in the twenty-first century people lived such medieval lives.

The seats on the bus were rickety, making it necessary to sit straight and still, almost like riding pillion on a motorbike, so that she and Arjun sat with their legs actually touching and sometimes, as they rounded a corner, he pushed towards her. It felt slightly uncomfortable to Polly, a discomfort that was borne of the belief that in Nepalese culture men and women kept physical distance from each other and also of the fact that Arjun was a very attractive man. As they rounded another corner Polly tried, unsuccessfully, to squeeze her body closer to the window. She felt Arjun's body tense in response and worried that she caused offence, so turned to offer him a reassuring look, but he lowered his eyes from her. And then she thought of Malcolm and how ever since she'd slept with him she had felt an unwanted connection, as if something beyond the physical had passed between them. She thought of him with a level of fondness that matched the level of contempt she felt for herself; remembering what a good friend he'd been to Ned and what a committed father to his children and how pleasant he'd always been to Polly herself. She'd enjoyed the mutual flirtation that has always existed between them, but now they'd crossed the line, she wondered if it would be harder to observe the boundary again. Perhaps there was something to be said for the keeping apart of men and women.

As they left the city the scenery became more green and fertile, and the beautiful foothills of the Himalayas, which weren't visible themselves yet, were worked as farmland, mainly by women it appeared, who squatted in fields with baskets on their backs and hand held tools. Then they walked along the road side carrying baskets of the same kind filled with oranges, spinach and one with stones. Outside every home there were goats or water buffalo in shelters made of hay and wood; and as in the city, children on their way to school, some of them tiny enough to fill Polly with fear for their safety.

Arjun spent most of the journey chatting and laughing with the other guides and porters, sometimes leaving the seat to do so and whenever he returned, touching Polly lightly on the shoulder or arm as if to reassure her. His voice had a musical quality, his face a look of slight amusement.

They stopped for breakfast and later lunch; in both cases in stone and shed shacks. Polly ate porridge for breakfast and cheese on toast for lunch and drank black tea. Here she encountered her first squat toilet, where a water jug replaced the toilet roll.

She felt there were so many things she wanted to ask Arjun, but she couldn't think of one. He sat with the guides, she with some Dutch tourists, four young men, two of them brothers, who were doing the same trek as her. They asked if she was travelling alone, but though one of them at least had noticed her wedding ring, no one asked about her marital status.

Back on the bus Polly asked Arjun: "What was it like in the Maoist uprising? The first time Ned was here it was still going on?"

"Was no problem for the tourists, but not many people came and even now there aren't so many as before."

That wasn't really what she meant, but she didn't explain. "And now they form part of the Government?"

"Yes, now we have coalition Government and they will make constitution."

"And that's good? Things are better now?"

"They will be, but we have to wait – give them a chance. You know? You understand?"

"Yes. I understand. Ned loved the story of how the Maoists came for their tax money, he was always telling people. Two lads hardly more than sixteen with a statement on their cause, rather than the riffles they feared, who had then issued a receipt in proof of payment. Everyone back home loved that." Arjun's expression was no more amused than usual, perhaps she'd said too much. From nervousness she carried on: "He said lots of people made a fuss, but they all paid up."

"They were afraid not to. But Ned he knew, King takes tax keeps for himself, Maoists say they are in charge in mountain and take tax for there."

"Was it anywhere near here that the accident happened?" At last a question she really wanted to ask.

"No, was the other side of Pokhara."

"Could we go there?"

"You want to go?"

"Yes. Yes, I do."

Arjun shrugged and pursed his lips. "Okay, I can show you."

As they neared the city the scenery became once more like that in Kathmandu, but not as squalid and the whole place seemed quieter and less chaotic. From here there was an excellent view of the mountains, vast, barren white with snow, they stood out from behind the green tree covered foothills like a gigantic stage set. Arjun showed Polly to her room. Although more basic than the one in Kathmandu it was clean, light and had an en suite bathroom with a shower and flush toilet. It looked out on several other hotels, all three of four stories high and with a Mediterranean look about them. From the small balcony there was a perfect view of the mountains. And because it was away from the main street there was little noise.

This was the very hotel Ned stayed in, for all she knew this very room. Here as well as Kathmandu she had a strong sense of him, his presence echoed everywhere, it was as if she'd only missed him by minutes; so strong was this sense that she could have believed herself to be the ghost.

CHAPTER TEN.

As he approached Kabita's house Bishnu adjusted his smile, making it welcoming without too much enthusiasm, wishing to obscure his true feelings as much for his own sake as anyone else's.

In the fading light Kabita wasn't immediately sure that the man was who she thought he was, but even so she felt the flutter of nervousness and, as his identity was confirmed she stopped for a moment to compose herself, then approached him slowly, hands clasped in front of her, head slightly bowed.

To Bishnu she looked younger and more vulnerable than the last time they had met, some two years ago now, at the wedding of his youngest sister; her vulnerability at least was hardly surprising. Kabita was remembering that occasion herself and how ill received Ram's absence had been by his elderly relatives.

"Namaste."

Kabita's reply was almost a whisper. "Namaste."

"I have a letter for you," Bishnu held it out to her.

Without looking at either him or the letter Kabita took it. "I'll make tea, come in." She stood back from the doorway to allow him to enter first. As he did so he paused momentarily stepping over the step with unnecessary caution and Kabita felt the warmth from his body brush her aura.

"You're to have a visit from the English widow."

Kabita's back was turned towards him as she put the tea on the stove; nevertheless Bishnu noticed the tiniest of flinches and when she turned towards him he saw too that she was annoyed, but as she handed him the tea Kabita smiled softly and Bishnu decided it wasn't with him.

"I hear there's to be a wedding."

"Yes. So much work."

So that was it. "How soon is the wedding?"

"Six weeks."

"Indira is a lovely girl. I hope they will look after her. Where is she now?"

"She has taken Bosiram to buy shoes."

"You'll miss her, I think." Bishnu knew only too well the pain of separation, having lost his wife to childbirth and his son to the relatives who cared for him.

"It must be hard financially," he risked "without a man to earn for you."

"At least we can provide for ourselves with the crops." Kabita tilted her head and offered a side-ways glance, Bishnu responded with a gentle smile.

"Indeed, but things like shoes and school equipment . . ."

"We manage." Kabita poured more tea for both of them.

"Everyone from the company was so sorry about Ram." It was Bishnu's very private opinion that a representative should have called on Kabita and that some financial help would have been appropriate. "Did you hear that there was a march by widows in Kathmandu?"

Kabita said that she had.

"Our society is so old fashioned. It's about time we caught up with the rest of the world and realised that widowhood is tragic, but not a stigma. It's no one's fault. "

Kabita made no reply, but she did look directly at Bishnu for a second, a pensive look that was generated by many questions; a look that was received as full of anxiety, so much so that he worried he'd spoken out of turn and after a few minutes said: "I'd better go."

"Would you like dhal baht?"

"Do you have enough?"

"You came especially to bring me a message it's the least I can do." Her mouth hardly responded to the quiet smile her eyes offered, as she held his in a slightly protracted gaze. Then, remembering herself and fearing he'd think her forward she looked again to the floor before standing in readiness to make the meal. Bishnu got up too and stood beside her. "Kabita," he said.

"Yes?"

"I. . ."

Kabita's heart beat so fast she was afraid she'd faint and she trembled a little.

"I . . ." the air between them stopped moving. "I expect you'd like some help preparing the food."

"No, you're a guest," the air circulated again, "anyway here's Indira."

Indira shot them a quizzical glance as she said hello. Kabita quickly explained the purpose of Bishnu's visit and just as quickly stooped to admire Bosiram's shoes.

Throughout the meal Kabita's shame grew, so that by the time Bishnu had left she felt sufficient self-contempt to find a quiet place and pray; not only for forgiveness, but also that Ram's soul suffer no ill effects as a result of her behaviour.

*

The taxi wound its way up the hill and around bends sufficiently sharp and steep as to leave Polly in no doubt about how a fatal accident could have occurred. Then the taxi slowed down and quite suddenly came to a stop, Arjun turned to face her in the back of the cab: "Was somewhere here," he held the door open for Polly to climb out. He stood on her right, with his left hand on her left shoulder he ushered her gently forwards. Then he let go and walked slightly ahead, clearly looking for something.

"I not sure exactly where, sorry."

"It's okay. At least I have an idea."

"Was one of these bends, the woman was crossing road and they fell, this side," he indicated, "they were coming down. We go and come same way to trek."

A shiver went through Polly as she stood as close to the edge as she dared and didn't try to stop her imagination plummeting with the taxi down the hundred feet or more drop, her stomach churning at the fear they must have felt. She was a little dismayed at the matter-of-fact manner in which Arjun discussed the deaths. What she didn't know and never would, was what Arjun kept from her; that ambulances were rare in Pokhara and most bystanders were unable or unwilling to pay for a taxi to the hospital. Ned's English friends were just behind in this case though, but with the depth of the fall Arjun presumed that neither taxi, nor ambulance would have saved the lives of his friends.

Polly tried to find a quiet spot free from people, dogs and goats, wishing to be alone with her thoughts for just a few minutes.

"I go sit in car and wait," Arjun said, as if he'd read her thoughts.

Polly wandered up and down the road as if looking for some evidence, but without really knowing what form that would take. On the road from Kathmandu they had seen one over turned bus and two trucks, but she supposed that after a year, even in a place like this where things happened slowly, all clues were likely to have been cleared away. And just to be here, to have Arjun say it was on one of these bends, did make it more real somehow.

*

It was two days before Kabita read the letter. The very fact of the English woman's visit was unwelcome to her. She didn't want to see manifest in a stranger the emotions she herself found it so hard to face and nothing, not the most extravagant gift, could make up for the fact that without her husband's wishes being indulged, Kabita's own husband might still be alive.

*

In Lake Side, Pokhara, Polly began to understand why Ned had liked Nepal so much. Along the main street the shops were similar in style to those in Kathmandu and sold much the same wares, but these were of cleaner and more modern appearance and the traders were less insistent on selling. They often invited her into the shop, but no more than that, they didn't push their wares on her. They always said: 'Namaste' and typically asked more: Which country? How many times in Nepal? Did she have children? In the local shops, in the same street as the hotel, there was no need for such questions, however, because everyone knew who she was. Between the shops there were restaurants offering food from every continent, from nightclubs and bars very western music played and every other premises it seemed advertised yoga of ayurvedic massage. Perhaps she'd treat herself to one of those, Polly thought, or maybe a yoga session.

On a lamppost she noticed a sign which read: 'yoga point 20 mins walk, pay as you like' – Polly made a decision to visit there on her return from the trek. She continued to walk in the same direction as the sign until it pointed up the side of a hill and the street turned into more of a suburb, at which point Polly decided she had better head back. She did so walking along the lake instead of the road. The path, which was undefined and unpaved, was muddy in places with patches of course grass growing here and there and many restaurants backing onto it. On the lake, which was still and clear, were small oriental style, fishing boats manned by a crew of one. Overhead, paragliders enjoyed the best views of the mountains and the foothills which lined the lake. Women refugees from Tibet invited Polly to 'just looking' at their handmade crafts.

Ned had described this walk in his diary and she reflected on the fact that she followed in his footsteps as she watched her own feet tread the path. As she got closer to the end of town where her hotel was located it gradually became busier and at the point where she had to head back to the road there were boats for hire to the Peace Stupa on the other side of the lake and at the top of a hill of about one thousand feet. Polly decided to make the trip, knowing that Ned had done so on his first visit. For five hundred rupees someone would row her across and await her return.

During the crossing Polly sat quietly absorbing the tranquillity, feeling the experience healing. The climb to the top was quite steep and in places slippery from streams or discarded water from the villages. Because it was unplanned Polly was wearing sandals rather than her walking boots so she slipped several times, grazing and cutting her bare lower legs. Her body felt uncharacteristically delicate, so that she felt the sharpness of her injuries intensely and it brought tears to the back of her eyes and throat. In the open air she was hot and removed her thin jacket, under cover of the trees she was chilly and put it back on.

When she reached the top and encountered the Stupa Polly was a bit disappointed, mostly on account of its modernity, but also because it was so commercial with its camera flashing tourists, donations box, professional beggars and even a small café. In which she drank black tea, ate a pastry and gave money to the beggar before beginning the descent, which was arduous due to her fear of falling.

Back at the hotel Polly lay on her bed and tried to read, but her thoughts kept drifting back to Ned. She was half afraid to think of him because it hurt so much, but half afraid not to from fear that if she forgot him, even if only for a second, it would erase him totally from her life.

Later, eating alone in a restaurant it had taken her half-an-hour to choose, Polly felt conspicuous in her aloneness, but also that it was a necessary part of the process of coming to terms with Ned's death. She had chosen it so decidedly that she resisted inviting Arjun to dine with her, even though she thought perhaps it was expected on the night before the trek, and now she avoided eye contact with the lone woman who had sat down opposite her because conversation was the last thing she wanted. When she got back to the hotel it was still early, only eight-thirty and there was no sign of Arjun or any of his friends, for which Polly was very grateful. She went straight to bed, where, feeling cold inside and out, she curled into a foetus. She hadn't been asleep long when there was a gentle knock on the door, followed very quickly by a second one: "Polly. Is Arjun, are you there?"

"Yes. I'm in bed," but she climbed out and opened the door just a crack.

"Sorry! Is there anything you require?"

"No thank you, just to sleep."

"Okay, I sorry for disturb you. We leave at nine tomorrow, you want me to call you?"

"No. I have an alarm."

"Okay. Good night."

*

The college bus had been just ahead of theirs as Indira and Bosiram returned from buying shoes. In order to get home without encountering Kapil they had got off a stop early, but as the bus turned the last corner and climbed the hill Indira caught sight of him and, she was sure he saw her too. Her stomach flipped and she responded irritably to Bosiram's babbling.

Later that same day, with the first niggling pain that indicated her bleeding would start soon, Indira felt deep regret at the loss of Kapil and at her impending marriage and, for the first time, considered the possibility that Kapil had been sincere. Now she wondered how he felt, she hoped he wouldn't think their liaison had meant nothing and that he would realise the circumstances surrounding the marriage. But then, hadn't he spoken of marriage himself and asked for her to wait? So long as there was no pregnancy and it seemed there wasn't, no one would ever have known what they had done. Perhaps Indira should try to meet him and explain, but then, if he had only wanted sex he'd laugh at her and might even now be calling her names to his friends. Names which no one had better hear before her marriage or there would be no wedding. No, she had been right and things were far better left as they were.   *

CHAPTER ELEVEN.

"Taxi goes same way to trek as Ned." Polly needed no reminder, as she was hardly likely to ever forget this patch of road. As they rounded every bend to be confronted by sharp drop offs on either side, Polly's nervousness increased, but with much effort she managed to keep it under control enough, she hoped, to conceal it from her companions. The taxi again was small and into it were crammed Arjun, Jivan the porter, and Polly, plus the driver of course. Polly thought she had kept her bag light, bringing what she considered the essentials, but now that she compared it with the bag Arjun carried, packed with not only his things but Jivan's too, she realised that her idea of essential was probably extravagant.

The point at which the trek started was quite commercial, a fact which for some reason surprised her. The items on sale included bottles of water, snacks, some of which were very western chocolate bars, glasses and cream to protect from the sun and walking sticks made of bamboo. Arjun stopped by one stall and carefully selected a stick which, when he presented it to her, made Polly feel like an old lady, of course when compared to him she was. "You saying I'm old?"

Arjun laughed slightly: "Is steep and slippery sometimes. May be you don't need," he shrugged and pursed his lips, "but if you do we can't buy in mountain. So, you don't want?"

"Yes, thank you. I do want," now she felt a little foolish.

The first part of the walk was relatively flat but very stony and took them through a fast moving stream on the edge of some woodland. Both stones and water made Polly cautious and so she walked slowly, already glad of her stick and often needing a hand from Arjun as well. The feel of his strong grip and large hand made her feel safe, but it also acted as a reminder of something she had lost.

The view of the mountains was completely lost, but Arjun assured her it wasn't for long and that once they reached their final destination in three days she would have a very good view.

"And now," he said at the foot of stone steps similar to those she'd climbed to the Stupa, "we go up."

Polly surprised herself as much as her companions with the speed at which she made her ascent. The biggest problem going up was that, in temperatures of twenty-five degrees Polly got very hot. She stripped down to her vest top from necessity, wondering at the appropriateness of bear arms. They were still climbing through the edge of the woods so there was little to see. Every few minutes someone passed them, some speeding by on the up, others descending in the same manner or as slowly as Polly had traversed the stones. And Arjun was right; already Polly had seen people half her age with two sticks, some of whom looked as if they couldn't wait for the trek to be over, which wasn't altogether encouraging. As they left the wooded area they came upon a small village, houses built of stone and painted blue wood stood either side of the cobbled street. Here they stopped for lunch. As Arjun handed Polly the menu she remembered Ned telling her that the guides were given a certain budget to cover their wages, the hotel fees and the food for themselves their clients and the porter so, the more she ate the less money Arjun made. It was a fact she currently wished she wasn't armed with as she was starving hungry, but now she was afraid to eat for fear of depriving Arjun of moeny. She chose noodle soup, which was delicious, cheap and, as it turned out, filling too.

The afternoon's walk was much more interesting and more as Polly had expected. They passed through several villages, all of which were housed with the same simple properties. They were passed on the way by trekkers wearing boots and hats and carrying walking sticks and by local people wearing flip flops and carrying baskets on their backs. Commonly, whether going up or down the mountain and regardless of the contents of the baskets, the locals pace was at a trot or a run. One man who passed had a cage full of chickens; it took up the whole width of the path so Polly, Arjun and Jivan had to step off to let him pass. Most amazing of all was the man with the double bed.

"I'm glad I haven't got to carry that up here," Polly said.

"If you want something up here, only two ways to get, you make or you carry."

"Yes."

The suspension bridges were a challenge; strung between ravines that promised certain death from a fall. Polly kept her eyes to the front and almost ran to cross them. At one they had to wait for a troupe of ponies that were crossing. They wore headdresses of a ceremonial kind and bells around their necks, which could be heard for some distance after they had passed. Overhead birds of prey hovered on the thermals. Several groups of blue uniformed children passed by always smiling and saying: "Namaste."

"How far do they have to walk?" She asked Arjun.

He shrugged: "May be two hour."

Well, she could just imagine how an English child would feel about that. Her class would be empty.

They reached the village a little after four. Polly was delighted to see the Dutch lads, but realised now how long it must have taken her to walk because they hadn't encountered each other at all until now.

Arjun showed her to her room. Two wooden beds were the only furnishings, the pillow and mattress felt a little hard, but the white sheets were pristine. Jivan had already put her bag on one of them. From the shuttered, glassless window Polly looked out on terraces. The silence was such that she could hear the words of encouragement called to the oxen that ploughed some distance down the hill and the air was clean enough to taste. Polly stood for a moment, picturing Ned in this very place, perhaps he looked out of this same window and onto this same scene. She decided she'd read the diary again later, but right now she needed a shower.

The shower room was concrete with a metal shower head protruding from the wall and two water pipes beside it, one cold, one hot. There was nowhere to put her clothes except the damp window ledge. It put Polly in mind of how it used to be in her school days, clothes left in the changing rooms from a lack of anywhere in the communal shower, so they ran to and from it with towels wrapped around to hide their bodies from each other's critical looks. This shower ran cold, she adjusted the hot tap, waited, still cold, she adjusted the hot tap and waited a second time, this time it ran luke warm. It was just warm enough to stop her from asking for a bucket of warm water.

Afterwards she wandered the length of the village, about ten houses. Every house it seemed had a buffalo and a goat or two, housed inside shelters built of sticks and corrugated iron. There were several children, one a boy of about six, lay on his belly writing in an exercise book. Another, a girl of about eight carried a toddler on her back: "My niece,' she told Polly in excellent

English. There was a small shop in which Polly bought sweets for the children, tucking some into her pocket for the next day for the children en route, again a tip she picked up from the diaries.

Without the aid of mechanical dryers and styling brush her hair dried in a frizz, she tried not to mind, it had occurred to her to bring the gas powered straighteners, but it seemed inappropriate to the occasion. For dinner she ate chow mien, and afterwards watched the two Dutch brothers play chess. As it began to grow dark she checked her watch, it was six-thirty. A fire was lit in a stove made from tin and everyone was invited to sit around it. Arjun picked up the boy Polly had seen earlier and bounced him on his knee.

"D'you have any children, Arjun?" She asked.

"Yes. Three. Two girls, one eight, one ten and my son is one years."

"Oh! I bet you miss them."

"Yes, yes I do." He took on a far- away look for a while, then said: "And your childrens are Christine and Anthony, right?"

"Yes." Polly replied in a tone of surprise.

"Now I think Christine is - um, twenty four or five and Anthony about twenty."

"You have a very good memory."

"No need good memory Ned talk about his family many time. He was very, very proud of his family."

"Thank you."

The woman proprietor of the tea house spoke to Arjun and then said to Polly: "Ned very funny man."

"She tell me how first time Ned came he keep saying he need helicopter off mountain," Arjun informed Polly. Arjun translated as she spoke. "Now she tell me Ned singing songs to the childrens - she say to him very nice voice and he say he think water buffalo sound better. He very, very good friends with Ram, they both funny together, childrens love it when they come. Ned always have sweets and he play trick with childrens, make sweet appear from behind their ear. She say his friends very nice, respectful, but Ned the best and they all very, very sorry for hear of deaths."

"Thank you," Polly said, then to Arjun. "How do I say thank you in Nepali?"

"Dhanyabahd."

"Dhanyabhad," she repeats and then said it to her hostess, who beamed in response and said: "Swahgatam."

"Means you're welcome," Arjun explained.

Although Polly enjoyed hearing about Ned it made her sad too: "I think I'll just go for a little walk."

When she moved away from the fire Polly felt cold enough to require her coat. She had left the padlock off her door; sure that there was no danger of being robbed here. With the electricity currently off the room was pitch black, turning on her torch to find her coat Polly first checked her watch, thinking she might just go to bed instead, but it was still only eight o'clock. Mountain time, she decided, was set at the proper pace, a person's life wouldn't run away so fast in a place like this. She was very conscious of the sound of her footsteps on the wooden landing and descended the ladder as quietly as she was able. All of her companions were still sitting around the fire and didn't seem to notice as she crept out behind them to the edge of the village. Now she looked towards Pokhara, it was a city of tiny lights. Then she looked up for the stars, but few were visible as the sky was cloudy.

Polly wasn't aware of Arjun until he gently touched her and she jumped in response, for which he apologised.

"I came see you're okay. I think maybe you feel sad."

"I am."

"I think we shouldn't talk about Ned."

"No, I want to talk about him, but it does make me sad."

"A year is not long?"

"It doesn't seem like a year. I think because it was sudden it took me most of that year to believe it."

"Why you come here? What you want? I know you bring money for Kabita, but why you want go to trekking?"

It sounded curt, but Polly knew Arjun meant no offence. "Because it happened here and I thought it might make it more real and because it was a part of his life I wasn't involved in. I wanted to know that part of him. D'you understand?"

He shrugged: "I think, but in Nepal is not same like this."

"So, Kabita, didn't she want to see where it happened?"

"I don't think so."

They stood in silence for a few minutes. It was a silence in which Polly was totally comfortable. Then Arjun said: "I think everyone going to bed now."

"Okay, then I'll go too." She wondered how Ned, the night owl adjusted to that.

Polly expected to be awake for some time as well as to wake early in the morning, but she was wrong on both counts. The light had been trickling through the shutters for some time, but was only just bringing her to consciousness when Arjun knocked on her door a little after seven.

*

The bus was full to capacity; there was only room on the roof. Indira said she didn't mind, but Kabita decided they should wait; there would be a truck or two going their way. It wasn't long before one arrived, they hauled themselves up and into the back. The truck bounced over potholes and climbed with great effort around the twisty uphill roads. Since Ram's death Kabita had become quite fearful of travelling, she gripped hold of the overhead rope and concentrated so keenly on holding on that she almost didn't notice when the goat urinated, so only just moved her feet in time. As they passed through a neighbouring village two thin, grubby boys ran up to the truck and, with a little help from the man nearest to the back, climbed into the moving vehicle. His dress and briefcase suggested he was going to town on business. When it was discovered that the boys had no money for their fare he paid the thirty rupees; with a warning that they'd better be telling the truth about being on their way to school.

There was a demonstration as they arrived in to the town. Striking kitchen workers marched with banners declaring their right to more pay and better working conditions. A discussion struck up between the male passengers on how the Maoists were failing in their promises, some were of the opinion they had never been sincere, but others that more time was needed. They hadn't yet had a chance to prove themselves. Kabita would once have agreed with the latter opinion, but now she didn't care enough to have one.

She cared only a little more to be here with Indira choosing material and a tailor for making the wedding sari, thanks to the generosity of Sandeep and Khrisna they were both able to be fitted for new. One of the neighbours had already sent word to her friend's personal tailor, who had recommended a place to buy the best quality material at discount prices because of their acquaintance.

The trip had been postponed for four days by Indira's period, for which she needed to stay close to home to be able to clean herself and her cloth easily. Although Indira often resented having to stay home and out of the kitchen during menstruation she knew too that she was lucky amongst Nepali women, some of whom were sent to sleep in the cowshed for the duration. For this one she was so grateful she would happily have done the same. Indira hoped that her husband would be modern enough to allow any daughters they might have the same treatment she enjoyed. She didn't even get sent away for the first one. Imagining future daughters, future children, was almost impossible and yet inevitable too. Although grateful beyond measure that it hadn't happened, Indira also felt a pang of regret that they wouldn't be fathered by Kapil.

Indira quickly decided upon the material and embroidery design for her sari and was very soon being fitted for the choli. There was portent in the process, a finality to something which had felt almost like a game until now and suddenly she was seized with fear. Now it was certainly too late to change her mind, in only a few weeks she would the property of Hari and his family, her mother as well as her father would be lost to her from then on. She wondered again about Kapil's proposal, if he meant it she could run away – go to Kathmandu and find work and a room while she waited for him, she'd meet him tomorrow from the bus and see what he had to say. But then, how could she run away when it would bring more disgrace to the family? And where could she hide so that her uncles couldn't find her, but Kapil could? It was no use; she had to go through with it now. Hari did look nice; it probably wouldn't be so bad.

During her fitting Kabita saw a full length image of herself in the mirror for the first time since Ram's death. Of course she knew she'd lost weight by the fit of her clothes and she'd noticed the touches of grey in her hair, but the hand held mirror she used for grooming had been kind with the portrait it presented. Ram had sometimes commented ill on her rounded belly and breasts, she wondered how he would have felt about the shapeless body she now possessed.

The visit to the tailors with material and cholis was followed dhal baht in a cafe. Both women were quiet on the journey home. Each haunted by their own desires and fears.

CHAPTER TWELVE.

It was all up hill to Ghorapani. Three thousand steps, Arjun said, as counted by a tourist, a fifteen hundred metre climb, which Polly calculated as about four thousand five hundred feet; about the height of Ben Nevis. But when she and Ned climbed Ben Nevis, some ten years ago, it hadn't taken all day to go up and down. Was she simply less fit? The steps were stone, uneven and in many places so deep Polly had to crouch into the climb. She wished to be able to say that the seven or eight hours seemed less, but if anything it seemed more. Every muscle in her body ached, her breath came in heaving pants, sweat poured from her, so that her hair stuck to her head. They broke for tea in the morning, lunch and tea again in the afternoon, by which time she dared not sit down for fear of seizing up and not being able to carry on. She remembered the diary entry that referred to Ned receiving a massage from Ram. It would hardly be appropriate in her case.

The lunch time stopping place was beautiful. High enough for them to be looking down on the birds of prey they had seen the day before. And with the Himalayas in the background so white and stark in comparison with the busy green foothills, they looked as if they were painted on the sky line. She ate rosti and egg, the rosti, which she interpreted as a misspelling of roasti, was basically bubble and squeak. Earlier in the day they had passed through more forest and seen languor monkeys close to and several water buffalo had wandered across their path.

After the afternoon tea stop Arjun sent Jivan on to Ghorapani and they walked slowly along together. "I'm sorry I'm so slow," she said, assuming impatience on his part.

"Not so slow, most peoples are the same."

"Really?"

"Yes. Even Nepali peoples from city who never walk in mountain before."

"Tell me about the mountains. Which is Machhapurchhre? And why is it considered the holy mountain?"

"That one, the Fishtail," he pointed, but there was no real need because its shape made it obvious. "And is holy because so many peoples died trying to climb. King say God don't want peoples on it, declared it holy and banned any more climbs."

"God knows how anyone could attempt such a climb, I feel like this is going to kill me."

Arjun giggled: "You doing okay, not much further now, maybe twenty minute."

And that was accurate in as much as it brought them to the start of the village, but there was at least that much again to the lodge in which they were to stay. So that by the time their final destination was reached Polly had gone beyond relief and walked on automatic.

Ghorapani was blue, all of its lodges painted a cheap bathroom paint blue, it was also relatively large and from one end to the other there was a considerable incline. There was a smell of wood smoke and diesel, the one from the fires the other from the generators. In the centre of the main room in their lodge was a large wood burning stove with a chimney and even a washing line. There was no problem with hot water in the shower here, it was so hot she almost burnt her hand and the toilet was of the flush variety.

Polly washed not only herself, but her socks, T-shirt and underwear in the washbasin with toilet soap, then hung them to dry around the stove; alongside those of the other guests. Then she sat on one of the benches around the stove and struck up a conversation with a French couple who were in the middle of a tour that seemed to include just about everywhere except Africa. Polly wondered, as they ran off a list of their destinations past and future, how it was possible to fit in so many places in six months. She sat with the same couple during the meal, but immediately afterwards they went to bed, in anticipation of the early start for the sunrise the following day.

Arjun came and sat beside her: "So, I think maybe you need extra fifteen, twenty minute to Poon Hill, is not so far about three hundred metre, but is steep. I think we allow one hour, leave around five-thirty. So, what time you want to get up?"

"I guess five."

"Okay. How you feel now?"

"A bit stiff, but otherwise fine."

"Is all downhill after this."

"I don't like going down, I warn you now, I'm afraid of slipping."

He shrugged and pursed his lips. "Is okay. We no need to hurry, we go 'bistahrai, bistahrai,' slowly, slowly."

During the conversation the tea house manager had come over and stood inches away from Polly looking intently at her. This had happened on several occasions now and Polly began to take it as normal, rather than feel intimidated by it. Arjun turned to the woman and said something, to which she reacted with obvious amazement and, as far as Polly could tell, asked him the same question three times. "I tell her who you are," Arjun explained. "Ned and his friends came here three times, on every trek they stop here."

Then the woman said to Polly: "Your husband. - Oh! Good man, very good man. I sorry."

Polly burst into tears. They came with so little warning she was trapped and her exit to her room, amidst garbled apologies, was clumsy. Once there she made no further attempt to control them and they ripped painfully and noisily from her.

She could hear cautious footsteps outside the door, they receded and returned uncertainly several times and then there was a gentle knock on the door and Arjun called her name. Now, worried that her behaviour might be considered rude, Polly wiped her face with her hand and opened the door. Arjun and the tea house manager were both there. "Do you require anything?" Arjun asked, as if he were not at all sure he was doing the right thing. The woman spoke to him crossly in Nepali then pushed past him into the room, sat on the bed with Polly and waved him away. Arjun closed the door as he left. The woman pulled Polly to her, rocked her, stroked her hair and spoke softly in Nepali as Polly cried and cried.

When the alarm rang at five Polly switched it off. When Arjun knocked on the door at five-thirty she ignored it. He knocked a second time and quietly called her name. She could hear him waiting and imagined his ear to the door. It was several minutes before his footsteps could be heard descending the stairs and then his voice in the dining area.

Polly hadn't slept much. In her half-conscious state she had played games with the truth, reinventing her story, and though the details changed the final conclusion was always the same; Ned hadn't died after all. Now she lay there reflecting on the fact that this was the one outcome over which she had no control. If he'd been injured so badly he needed care for the rest of his life there were several options she could have considered and reconsidered. If he'd left her at least she could still talk to him, try to get him to change his mind, alter her behaviour so that he'd want to come back. In any case, he would never have left her – everyone, even here where she'd never before set foot, kept telling her how much he loved her. It was preposterous; he would not have left her. But he did, he left her completely and she was incomplete without him. Now she felt a rage boiling up inside her and it demanded an outlet. Kneeling on her bunk she punched herself in the head, pulled her hair and bit her hand, opening her mouth she mimicked a scream which only remained silent from courtesy: how dare he – how dare he leave her- how dare life treat her so badly –how dare he die.

Exhausted Polly lay back down, feeling disbelieving, frightened, angry, resentful, desolate with equal intensity and regularity. She simply didn't know how she was ever to come to terms with being without Ned, or how she would ever relearn her life. And as the light began to filter through the shutters Polly remembered that Christmas was only five weeks away. Her second without Ned; last Christmas she had thought about what he'd been doing the one before, but this would be the first occasion on which she could say 'last year he wasn't here'. It would only be the first of many, for her birthday and his and the children's birthdays and their wedding anniversary, this year her comparison would be with his absence the year before.

From downstairs the voices of the tourists returning from Poon Hill could be heard. Polly knew she should get up as they were supposed to be leaving after breakfast, but she couldn't face seeing all of those people. Just as she was deciding what to do there was a knock on the door and the tea house lady came in with a tray of muesli, toast and black tea. She patted Polly's hand as she laid it down and stroked her hair before leaving the room. Polly felt so grateful. Gratitude towards the woman whose name she didn't even know for her loving ministrations.

Arjun came to collect the tray, calling out first so that Polly knew who to expect. She quickly pulled clothes over her pyjamas and brushed her hair, aware that it was sticking up on one side and wishing it were long enough to tie back, and then she let him in. He left the door open and remained standing then, offering a cautious smile, as if he was a little afraid of her, asked:

"How you feel now?

"Better, thank you. I'm sorry if I embarrassed you."

"Embarrassed?" His tone was incredulous.

Polly wasn't sure if it was because the idea was ridiculous or because he didn't understand the word. "Did I make things awkward for you?"

"How so? Anita helped you. No trouble for me. She know better what you want."

Polly still wasn't sure that he understood, but didn't pursue it further. "Do I need to hurry up and get ready? Only I'm very tired."

"You want stay another day? We can go to Poon Hill tomorrow, but only if you like."

"Yes, thank you. I would like.

"Okay," now his smile was more like the usual one.

"I'm sorry I look such a mess. I'll have a shower when some of those people go."

"Why you keep saying sorry when is not your fault?"

"It's very English," her smile almost became a laugh as she said: "in fact I almost said it again then."

After he'd left Polly wondered about her behaviour. Had she been a little too familiar? Why should she care how she looked to him?

Later, as she sat outside trying to read she was distracted by the sight of Arjun scrubbing his jeans clean with a scrubbing brush and a bar of soap under the outside water tap. The veins on his arms stood up with the effort, she noticed the shape of his forearms, they were not as good as Ned's had been, whose arms, even as he grew older remained sinewy and contoured, but the protruding veins created the impression of strength and his skin looked smooth and taut. Arjun must have become aware of her eyes on him because he stopped what he was doing for a moment and looked enquiringly at her and smiled; it was accompanied by a small sound that resembled a sigh.

"Could we go to Poon Hill now?" Polly suddenly asked, the thought having only just occurred as if in defence of her looking at Arjun.

"Right now? Not tomorrow, for sunrise?"

"May be tomorrow too, but they'll be lots of other people there tomorrow I won't be able to experience it properly." When he didn't respond for a second: "I'll pay you extra for your trouble."

"Is not about money," now he sounded a little annoyed and Polly was worried she'd offended him. "Is just . . . ., doesn't matter, we go."

*

Indira made the journey to fetch the wedding saris alone, she enjoyed the trip, finding it a welcome break from home which was often boring now that school had finished for her, but she missed the company of her mother. She had little doubt that marriage, especially if she had children, would bring an end to boredom, but worried that she would be lonely instead. Now, with the garments on her lap and the pending wedding only too real, it was too late for doubts, she realised. Being a wife was a role for which she had been well prepared, practically, if not emotionally, not just by her upbringing, but also by years of tradition. On that first trip for the saris, her mother had talked about her own feelings from the time of her own marriage and assured Indira that she had shared the same concerns, but that everything would be fine. After all hadn't she grown to love Ram so much that she felt incomplete without him now? Indira had no reason to doubt how Kabita felt now, indeed it was part of the problem. She worried that not only she, but her mother too, would be more lonely once she'd left and she knew that the amount of contact they had from then on would be entirely dependent on her in-laws.

Kabita was harvesting the rice, she bent, cut, picked, bent, cut, picked and then laid it on the plastic tarpaulin before beating it with a rock and shaking off the loose rice, which she bagged ready to use as animal feed. Then she loaded the rice into her dokko, carried it up to the house, bundled it up and hung it to dry. She barely filled the dokko, the yield was down on the year before, but at least it would supplement the purchase from the market. In a few days she would need to beat the husks off and package it into sacks. The rice harvest had prevented her from going with Indira to collect the saris, but Kabita didn't mind too much, the truth was that she had enjoyed the first trip so much, had felt such pleasure and comfort in her daughter's company that it had made her frightened of the loss she must face in so short a time. She feared it would be like bereavement and who would console her over this loss? Certainly not her sons, they were too young, and in any case would probably miss Indira themselves, especially Bosiram; and certainly not her parents-in-law, in whose company she felt awkward and who were still grieving the loss of their son. She was going to be so lonely without her daughter .

*

It was steep and Polly had forgotten her stick. It was a little after mid-day and so the full heat of the sun was on them, Polly blamed this and the fact she had not been doing her morning stretches for the difficult and slow climb. Just before the summit there was a sign welcoming them to Poon Hill, but, like the walk through Ghorapani, the climb wasn't over yet and Polly sighed heavily at the realisation.

"I told you was steep."

"Yes, you did."

"Here. Come." Arjun walked two steps up and then took hold of Polly's hand, almost dragging her the last couple of paces. She wondered about the appropriateness of their holding hands, but because Arjun held on so did she. At the top Polly was greeted by a view that more than made the climb worthwhile. They walked on to a kind of plateau with the foothills dropping off behind them and the Himalayas forming a semi-circle, the lack of cloud provided perfect clarity. It was absolutely silent. "Oh!" Was all she was able to say because she had started to cry again, overcome by the beauty and stillness of the place as much as by her usual sadness.

Arjun stood next to her and gently rested his arm around her shoulders. They stood in silence for some time. Polly was afraid to breathe for fear of disturbing the peace; she closed her eyes and listened for her heart. Ned's face appeared behind her eyes wearing such an expression of contentment she wanted to leave him there.

"Hindu's believe in reincarnation, don't they?"

"Yes."

"Is that personal, so that an individual first floats around in the ether somewhere and then finds a body to enter, or is it less conscious than that, more like the energy changing form?"

"Some believe is conscious."

"And what about you Arjun, what do you believe?"

"Reincarnation make sense, everything in universe is recycled, peoples are mostly water and all water that here now was always here, but I don't know how conscious. I mean I look for my father in my son and I think I see him, but of course because his genes are same. If he say to me one day, 'hi son is me, don't you recognise your own father?' Then maybe I believe it," he laughed. "I don't know, is possible individual become individual, but all the same in the end, he won't remember, you won't recognise, because they not same person anyway. The person you knew and love still be gone."

"Yes." Polly swallowed back her tears.

"I think may be this not want you want hear."

"What I want is impossible."

"You want for Ned not be dead."

"Yes."

"But this thing can't be changed. If thing can't be changed maybe a person have to change attitude."

"Yes" Polly said through tears and she reached for Arjun's hand.

He held hers, then he pulled her close and embraced her as she cried, rubbing her back. Polly laid her head in his chest and sobbed. Arjun held her, except for his breathing he was perfectly still and didn't say a word. When her tears subsided Polly pulled away: "Thank you, Arjun."

"Welcome."

"I want to walk around a little now."

He nodded his assent, walked over to the wooden bench and sat down. Polly climbed the viewing tower, thinking as she did so how it spoiled the overall effect of the place, it was an eye sore, she decided, descending again as the view was as good from the bottom.

As she walked around Polly absorbed her surroundings and tried to savour the moment as she knew Ned had done from his diary account, in which he'd written: *my one regret, the one thing that stopped it being perfect was that Polly wasn't there.* Yes, that was her regret now too.

"I'm ready to leave," she told Arjun after about fifteen minutes. "Thank you for bringing me, I couldn't have done this with a group of tourists, but I'll come in the morning too, if that's okay, I would like to see the sunrise."

Arjun nodded. On the way down, as Polly struggled both physically and emotionally, he offered his hand again, this time, as Polly took hold of it, she felt comfortable.

CHAPTER THIRTEEN.

Nature's paint palette changed the mountains from grey to pink as the orange sun reflected on the silver snow and then, as it rose higher in the sky, they became again the white background to the awakening foothills. Polly stood watching with a group of twenty or more, she took few photographs as there were already several at home and she wanted more than anything to be in and of the moment. Immortality was in the moment, she decided, if only she could remain there, no planning, no remembering, only being; perhaps that was what it was like to be dead, if was like anything at all. Being here, looking at the ever present mountains was a reminder of the insignificance of an individual life as measured in natural terms, and yet how highly significant to those who live it. 'No wonder people want to believe in God', she thought, as she took one last look and then turned to leave.

Arjun waited. He stood with his right foot wrapped around his left heel leaning slightly to the left, arms clasped behind his back. He was wearing the blue-green jeans he'd washed the day before, a thick jacket and woollen hat. Polly was dressed in similar manner, the down jacket she wore had been hired for the occasion, but on the way down the temperature began to rise and gradually she removed the layers until she wore only a T-shirt. Arjun remained dressed as when he'd set out.

"How you feel today, Polly?"

"I have a bit of a headache actually – it wouldn't be altitude would it?"

"I don't think, not after two days here and is not common at this height, we only just over three thousand metre – did you have yesterday? – No. I don't think then."

As they were preparing to leave and Polly was making her last minute visit to the toilet she discovered her period had started, well that explained the headache and the out of control tears. She was annoyed at having to unpack her bag enough to find sanitary protection and clean underwear, but also relieved that she hadn't left the required items in her rucksack in Pokhara. Why it couldn't have happened when at the hotel she didn't know. She was of an age where predicting the timing and planning around it was becoming increasingly difficult, but she had to admit that it would have been more inconvenient whilst visiting Kabita. Now, apart from all the other toileting issues, she had to worry about how to dispose of used sanitary towels and tampons, she could hardly ask Arjun about that, but she couldn't remember seeing any bins anywhere. In her trousers were two large side pockets, in one she kept the clean, in the other, wrapped and inside a plastic bag, the used. If there was a fire in the lodge that evening she'd sneakily dispose of them there, she decided, but meantime she'd keep a look out for bins. Now Polly found herself wondering how local women coped.

She tied the wet underwear to the outside of her day sack in such a way as to obscure the nature of the garment; she could hang them to dry properly once they reached their destination.

The downward walk was more arduous than the upward climb. Walking down large steps hurt Polly's knees and she had to concentrate so hard on where she was going she saw little of the scenery. Arjun jumped down ahead of her and held her hand whenever the steps were particularly deep or damp. Jivan skipped on ahead of them and was always waiting at the appointed stopping place when they arrived. With the combination of challenges Polly was having to face that day she felt quite grumpy and was more than a little relieved when they arrived at their destination, although it was the most basic so far. And now she feared spiders would be lurking in the wooden frames and damp in the white washed walls.

Again the shower was housed in a concrete outhouse and was only just luke warm. When she left the shower Polly went into the communal room and sat down at the table, which was covered by blankets. As soon as she did so she felt warmth, but didn't immediately realise that a log fire burned beneath the table, she peered underneath to make sure, then slipped into her room took the used sanitary towels from the plastic bag and put them in her pocket. Back in the lodge she took them one at a time and surreptitiously threw them into the fire, hoping no one came along with logs until they'd burned out; not only because it would cause her some embarrassment, but also because she had read somewhere that Nepali people don't like things being thrown in the fire. This fact made her feel a little guilty, but equally she felt there was no other option.

After the meal she was invited to join two Taiwanese women and their guide around their homemade fire in the porch adjoining the house. Their guide was drinking and offered some to Polly. "What is it?" She asked, looking suspiciously at the clear liquid.

"Petrol." He laughed heartily at his own joke. "No, is Raksi, but taste like petrol." He held the bottle out to her again: "Is local, made from millet."

Because it was local Polly felt she ought to give it a try. All three of her companions laughed as she screwed up her face in response to the taste. "You're right, it does taste like petrol."

"How you know," the guide teased, "when you drink petrol."

"When did you?" Polly teased back and received a slap on the shoulder as he threw his head back in peels of laughter.

"I think Raksi must be very strong and get you drunk fast."

That made him laugh all the more. They were joined by Arjun, who squatted beside them and, as the two men chatted in Nepali, the tone became more and more sober. "We talk about politics," Arjun eventually explained, and as he talked he shelled and ate peanuts throwing the discarded shells into the fire. "He think if constitution not written there will be return of revolution and he think constitution won't be drafted because no one in government can agree on anything. Now he say peoples fed up with strikes and many peoples want King back." Arjun said something to his companion. Then to Polly he said: "I tell him there will be constitution and anyway revolution sometimes necessary for create change."

They continued debating, often excitedly, but it never appeared to be hostile. "Now he say in revolution many peoples dies, and I say many peoples dies anyway from being poor. And many revolutionary changes required in Nepal."

Polly was pleased that Arjun took the trouble to translate. "I tell him Maoists need more time, peoples judge them too quickly, but he think they don't mean what they say, they just want power."

"Well, power does tend to corrupt, but perhaps it's not so easy to keep promises even if they are sincere. Sometimes deals have to made with people even if you don't want to because they have the things you need and it would be impossible to succeed without them."

"You think too straight," the guide told her light heartedly, "you need more raksi."

"No thank you. – Do you think there would be a return to revolution if the constitution isn't drawn up on time?"

"Is possibility, but no one want, so I think constitution will come on time."

"Let's hope so," now Polly became acutely aware of her Taiwanese companions who were talking to each other in their own language. She was waiting for the chance to include them in the conversation, when they were all alerted by the sound of drumming and singing from inside.

"Oh, we go and see," one of them said and Polly went with them. Two young men were playing hand drums and their singing was accompanied by an even younger woman. When Polly and the others came in they became more enthusiastic in their playing and encouraged them to join in the song, repeating the words over and over, but Polly just couldn't retain them. They passed her a drum and tried to teach her the simple rhythm, counting it out for her and slowing down, but as soon as the beat was back up to speed she lost it again. "It's no good I have no sense of rhythm." The drum was passed to one of the Taiwanese women who did a much better job and in the meantime Arjun had written down the words of the song phonetically so that Polly could now sing along. She smiled her thanks to him mid-song, no wanting to stop now that she'd finally got it. Round and round they went with the singing and round and round went the drum.

And then, sounding at first like another percussion instrument, rain drummed down on the tin roof. There was comfort in the sound, it added to the homely atmosphere. Polly went to bed, a little before nine, feeling somewhere near to content.

*

At busy times, such as these; there was so much to do that the days went quickly and the evenings were short; so that by the time the meal was over it was almost time for bed. Kabita thought now about the long summer evenings with neither Ram nor Indira for company and she flew into a rage. She beat the husks off of the rice violently. Her rage was such that she wanted to throw the whole lot on the floor and jump up and down until there was none of it left in a condition that was fit for use. She wanted to destroy her surroundings, to kick down the cowshed, smash holes in the house, rip the chicken coup to pieces with her bare hands. How could she be so stupid as to allow her daughter to leave her? Why did she collude with Sandeep? Had she sacrificed them all for the sake of a stupid dream? How dare she? But how dare he? And how dare Ram die and leave them to their fate unchallenged?

And then, as if in emphasis of her thoughts, Indira approached and as she drew close Kabita was overcome with the sense that, dressed in pink, she looked like a child.

*

They were nearing the end of the trek. As they set out and bid farewell to the Taiwanese women, Polly felt as though she was leaving well established friendships behind and, despite the arduous nature of much of it, wanted to repeat the whole trekking experience. Nepali mountain life was so vastly different from anything she'd previously encountered and, although it was no doubt hard in many ways, especially in the winter and rainy seasons she imagined, there was also an appeal to it. Rhythms set by nature, rather than man, were no doubt healthier and she imagined the same to be true of companionship formed from necessity. But then she could hardly deny the strength of her own companionships with her family and friends. It was just that she had lost the sense of belonging with the loss of Ned and imagined that feeling would be cushioned by being part of a community. Yet for all she knew it may have nothing to do with social support and everything to do with the loss itself. For to have been someone's wife was such an integral part of one's identity that reinvention of self was necessary. And, in that case, with fewer options, it was likely to be worse for Kabita.

"Arjun," he was walking very slightly ahead as he was inclined to do, but stopped now and turned towards Polly. "How much help does Kabita have from her community?"

"Peoples come when first happen, come and stay one, two week then go. I hear she very upset, she don't speak and she collapse."

"But now, who helps her now?"

He looked bemused: "I think no one, may be her childrens when not at school."

"What about money? Do Ram's brothers have to provide for her?"

"Is not requirement. May be they help, but they have own families."

"So how does she survive?"

"She have own land."

"But she must need money for some things. Does she sell what she grows?"

Arjun shrugged. "If she grow enough."

"Will the money I have help much?"

"Yes. I think."

"How much is one and a half thousands pounds worth in Nepali rupees – I don't mean how many rupees I mean how much will it buy."

"How much it buy – aw, I don't know what I compare to."

"Well, how does it compare to Ram's wages."

Arjun thought for a moment, some of it audible as he converted American dollars to pounds. "I think one year or little bit more."

"One year! One's year's wages? Well that should make a big difference surely."

"Yes. Is good."

Polly realised it was comparable with her insurance pay out, but she had savings already, no mortgage and very likely she'd find a job on her return to keep money coming in. If thirty thousand was all she had for her entire life it would be a very different story.

"What about her home, does she have to pay rent on it?"

"No, it belong to Ram's parents, they build when they young."

"Does she have a right to stay there?"

"There is law now to protect widows make sure they have husband's property, but sometimes womens have to fight if brothers try to take, but Ram's family won't do this, Kabita be safe to stay."

Polly nodded thoughtfully and then, because she was concentrating so hard on the things she'd been told she tripped on a raised stone and fell forwards, grazing her hand and her pride. Arjun helped her to her feet and held her up turned palms in his.

"Is sore?" He asked, and gently brushed the grazes with his thumbs. A buzz of tingling energy passed up Polly's arms and into her spine in response, as if he had contacted with an acupuncture point.

"Only a little, I feel more stupid than anything.'

"You thinking too much about Kabita, should be concentrate on where you going. Are you hurt anywhere else?"

"I don't think so," Polly checked her knees as they stung a little, but there was no sign of injury. When she looked at Arjun it was straight into his eyes that were keenly watching her, he smiled and lowered them. "Let's leave talk until lunch time," he said gently putting his arm around her in a comforting manner.

He stayed beside her for the rest of the walk, which took them through a forest that had a jungle-like appearance and was alive with the sounds of running water, crickets and birds. In many places it was damp under foot from the rain the night before and Polly was again grateful for her stick. When they arrived at the stopping place a very bored looking Jivan was waiting for them. He and Arjun had a conversation and then Arjun came and took Polly's order then sat down opposite her. "So, any more questions?" he didn't look at her, but fiddled with the menu and cutlery.

"How well do you know Kabita?"

"Not well. I remember her little bit from school and sometime I see her in Kathmandu or her village when I visit Ram."

"Is your home near to theirs?"

"No, I live near when I was child, but now live in town. My childrens want modern things and television."

"Oh! So your mother doesn't live with you?"
"She does, but is our house, we build."

Polly was nodding thoughtfully again when the food arrived. "You always thinking," Arjun observed.

"I'm just trying to understand Nepal and Nepali life. So much is different and yet so much is the same."

"Of course."

*

The first two months after the winter solstice were quiet times in the tourist industry and Ram had often spent portions of them at home, so that the monotony was relieved by his company. Even when he went to visit friends in neighbouring villages and was gone most of the day the assurance of his company made the days pass quickly, and more happily. Although sometimes he came home full of alcohol and made her angry by staggering around the house and laughing as he crashed into things and she would show her displeasure by chastising him as if he were a child. How she wished she hadn't now. How she wished her memories of him to be untainted. Kabita remembered the Dasain festival two years hence and how they had quarrelled into the night about his drunken behaviour. The she remembered how last year she had wished so much that he were there that she would have made her own raksi and poured it for him from morning until night.

But mostly the memories were good, she remembered how he entertained the children running around with them and exciting them. How the two of them would sit outside on the wall together and talk, he telling her about some of his clients; often the tales were funny and never were they mundane. Kabita had of course heard of the man Ned. In fact Ram had sent a message once to say he was coming for the night, but the visit had been cancelled when Ram was sent on another trek. So, now his widow was coming instead and she would have to be made welcome for Ram's sake. The letter only said that she was coming with a gift; there was no mention of how long she intended to stay or of any other requirements.

Kabita imagined how much easier things were for Ned's widow in a country where, according to things Ram had told her, most women had their own income and where second and even third marriages were considered neither unusual nor shameful.

*

It only took another hour to reach Ghandruk. A village that had grown to town dimensions due to the tourists, Polly was informed. The streets were cobbled, the walls dry stone, but the glaring green and blue of the residences, coupled with garage type doors, lent a tacky appearance. The Peaceful Lodge was very European with its en suite bathroom, garden bench and resident dog. In the bathroom Polly discovered her first plastic bin with a lid; she divested her pocket of unwanted waste before taking a very hot shower, washing her hair and changing her clothes, but, although she enjoyed the luxury, she also felt a little disappointed by the luxury of it, as if she was cheating somehow.

There was no sign of Arjun so Polly decided to go for a walk and when she did so she came across a tiny Buddhist Temple that, much to her disappointment, was locked. She was on her way down the path towards the exit in the dry stone wall when she was alerted by someone calling: "Mam, please Mam," and turned to see a small, Tibetan looking man calling her back. There was no charge for letting her in he assured, but pointed out the donations box on her right as she entered, bare footed.

The temple was simple. Hessian mats lined the floor and the altar, a wooden table covered with cloth, was home to a brass statue of Buddha and a small prayer wheel. Instinctively Polly knelt on one of the cushions that were lined in front of the altar. Ned had always said Buddhist philosophy was the one which came the closet to representing his beliefs. Like Arjun he believed reincarnation made sense, but it didn't really matter to those left behind because the person they had lost was gone forever. It was Ned's opinion that if there were such a thing as karma we should all try to be better people and treat others well, but again, it didn't really matter because we should do that anyway. What he hated about organised religion, indeed what they both disliked, was the hypocrisy and the way it was used to both generate and maintain social injustice. Ned had considered Buddhism to be less guilty of these. Polly however, was not so sure, and she remembered several discussions on the subject because, whilst it was true that as far as she was aware Buddhists never instigated or took part in wars, it was also true that they did little or nothing to combat current injustice. In fact, she had argued with Ned more than once that the preaching of detachment was tantamount to advising acceptance of one's lot. Although Ned had agreed, he also insisted that there were Buddhists who actively sought social change.

The atmosphere in the temple was so peaceful it was difficult to imagine how anything could disturb it. No wonder places of worship were considered sanctuary. In the stillness she considered the concept of conscious reincarnation, there were after all people who claimed to remember past lives, but Polly had always wondered what determined where and when a person was reborn and what laws it was it subject to. Where, for example, would Ned be reborn, here where he'd died, England where he'd lived, or somewhere else entirely? There was without doubt something comforting in the notion and although she completely rejected the Christian idea of individual survival beyond death, since Ned's passing she had wanted to believe it possible. She was very glad for the children they had together because in them she saw traces of their father and the light of immortality shine. She knew really it was as Arjun had said; whatever the truth, the person Ned was gone and she had to come to accept that.

On the way back to the lodge Polly was passed by a group of uniformed children who greeted her with "Namaste," and were rewarded with a sweet. She counted how many were left and calculated there should be enough for the number of children she was likely to encounter in the one and a half days that were left.

There was still no sign of Arjun, or indeed Jivan, when she arrived back at the lodge, so Polly settled down with her book and placed her own order for her meal. It was a little after eight-thirty, as she was preparing herself mentally for bed, that Arjun and Jivan arrived back, walking hand in hand, but side to side as they pulled away from each other, it was immediately obvious that they were very drunk. "Polly," Arjun almost fell on her, 'how are you?"

"Better than you, I think."

"No, I very, very fine," he giggled.

"I hope you'll be very fine tomorrow too," Polly kept her tone light to make it clear she wasn't disapproving.

"You no worry, I take good care of you. You Ned's wife and Ned good man. He Ram's friend, I Ram's friend, that make Ned my friend, you my friend now too," he shook her hand vigorously. "We friends, yes?"

"Yes."

"Okay. Now I go bed. I need sleep."

On his way he tripped up the step, but got up straight away, laughing and waving. Because of his helpless state Polly realised her vulnerability and her total dependence on Arjun.

*

Kabita had boiled the milk she'd freshly taken from the buffalo, collected the eggs and was part way through filling the water urns when Bosiram came running into the yard, his jumper on back to front and his trousers twisted, indicating that he'd dressed himself that morning.

She caught hold of him and put his clothing right, despite his fighting and pulling to get away. He was the child who most reminded her of her father and this was reinforced for her as she observed him take his jumper off and put it on the wrong way around again. It wasn't merely the way he looked, although he was like him with his dark skin and round eyes, but it was more the way he behaved, stubborn, slightly cross much of the time and determined to have his own way. And Kabita had noticed it immediately; as soon as she looked at him she had seen his nature and the recognition of her father in her son had confirmed reincarnation for her. So, she needed no persuading of the fact, only of the details. She didn't, for example, think it safe to assume that Ram would be reborn close to his home or even in Nepal, but then, when she considered the dream she was bound to believe he was coming close to home, otherwise there was no point in him telling her at all. What she did know was that if she ever saw him she would recognise him.

*

The day was hot for walking, twenty degrees or more. Today's trek was mostly downhill and through what Arjun described as 'traditional villages,' by which he meant they hadn't been built for the sake of the tourists, but had been there for years. The inhabitants of these villages were clearly poorer than those in the tourist ones. The clay and wood houses uniformly coloured rust red, with varying amounts of land beside them growing varying quantities and types of vegetables, but there was usually spinach and maize. Here whole families worked together, a boy of no more than twelve or thirteen drove oxen. A mother and daughter beat the husks from millet with poles. A tiny child fed corn to the chickens. Polly handed out her sweets a little more cautiously, aware she wasn't going to be able to buy any more.

They came across a very lowly house where two very thin and grubby children, naked from the waist down, but wearing woollen jumpers and hats, squatted playing listlessly with marbles. Polly stopped to give them sweets and suddenly she was mobbed by a group of about five or six, who came running and screeching, Polly tried to count out two each, but they grabbed at her so that instinctively she held them in the air, where Arjun took them from her and doled them out in pairs and he spoke firmly to them.

As they receded a very thin, dirty, bare footed woman with wispy hair approached held out her hand and smiled a near toothless smile, which never reached her vacant eyes. Polly looked searchingly at Arjun, who shrugged and said: "all gone." Then she rummaged in her pockets as the woman put her hands in prayer, but it only confirmed Arjun's words: "I'm sorry," Polly said, sounding as helpless as she felt. Arjun spoke to the woman, who lowered her hands, head and shoulders in response and started to back away.

"Here, give her this," Polly said handing Arjun a five hundred rupee note. "Will that help?"

"Stop them starving today," he said as he handed it over and the woman bowed and smiled her thanks, her hands in prayer.

Polly was almost in tears as she asked: "should I give her more, then?"

Arjun herded her forward gently as the children followed clearly begging for more. "You don't have enough money to make difference for more than few days."

Just outside the village Polly sat down on a pile of stones, needing to recover from the encounter. She sat with her head in her hands and her eyes closed against the scene, but they were imprinted in her mind, the mother as much as the children had broken her heart.

Arjun came and squatted beside her and put his hand on her shoulder. "You have big heart, Polly. If your pocket as big you could help, but it not."

"Why do you think they are so poor?"

"They are too many. Maybe father don't have job, or run away or kill by war. And they don't have much land for grow own."

"That's the kind of situation that makes me reject reincarnation of the kind that says its karma, because then their plight is their own fault."

"Is nothing to do with karma, is politics."

"Exactly!"

"You upset, you want stop soon? We can walk until afternoon over and be two hour quicker tomorrow, or we can stop after two, three hour."

"Let's keep walking."

"Okay." He sent Jivan ahead again.

Arjun took hold of her hand and didn't let go until they reached the next village, where a much healthier looking baby being nursed by its mother lifted Polly's spirits. Being hand in hand with Arjun only felt uncomfortable to Polly because she was aware of looks from passers-by, but he seemed neither to notice nor to care.

CHAPTER FOURTEEN.

There was less than half a day's walk on the final day of the trek so there was no need to leave until nine or more, but Polly was awake by six-thirty, before it was even properly light. To be sociable the evening before she had drunk mustang coffee, a mixture of coffee, butter and raksi with the group of young Japanese trekkers who shared the accommodation. She didn't enjoy it and it had lain on her stomach all night. So this morning Polly was tired and therefore, glad to be able to take her time getting ready and for the first time since arriving in Nepal did some bending and stretching exercises, hoping to be invigorated by them. Normally she was able to bend forward and touch her hands on the floor and to join her hands behind her back, but today she achieved neither. The backs of her legs were solid and slightly sore, her arms felt bruised her shoulders immoveable.

Looking in the mirror after her shower Polly noticed that there was a small patch of grey in her hair on the right side of her face and that the skin on her neck was beginning to hang loose. The flesh on her hands too was losing its tautness, she thought, as she began to look critically at herself. Soon she would be fifty. The prospect frightened her a little. It felt as though another reinvention of self was required. Alongside the loss of her marital status came the loss of her youth and very soon menstruation would cease for her too. She gathered from what other women had said that with it would come the loss of sexual desire, which would make her life more peaceful she had to admit, especially since without Ned any attempt at release of her desire was accompanied by guilt. Yet the combination of all of these things did make her feel less a woman. Polly didn't know how much she would have questioned her future if Ned hadn't have died. Probably she would have carried on working and living as she always had, but she didn't feel able to anymore. If Ned were still alive he would have reassured her and continued to make her feel special. Of course there were plenty of people who loved her, she never doubted that, but the special love from him was different and she was sure she'd never experience that again. Even if she could overcome her fear of another loss and find the confidence to embark on a relationship it was impossible to believe that she could be loved as Ned had loved her, for a second time. Polly knew she was lucky to have experienced it even once and tried to find consolation in that, but if anything it made her loss the greater.

'If thing can't be changed may be a person have to change attitude.' Arjun's words echoed in her mind, but she wasn't sure how one went about changing their attitude.

"You very quiet today," Arjun observed of Polly as they headed back towards Pokhara.

"Sorry. I don't want the trek to be over. I like it here in the mountains."

"We be in mountain when we go see Ram's family. Maybe you be sick of mountain after that. No tea houses there, no hot water or electricity."

"I know. Were you and Ram friends a long time?"

"Ever since boys in school."

"His death must have been terrible for you, then."

"My heart was broken. And for Ned too, he my friend also."

"And how do you feel now?"

"Sometimes miss him still, but nothing I can do, he is past."

Polly shuddered at the word: "That's exactly what hurts the most, I don't want Ned to be past; I want to keep his memory alive."

"Of course, but happy memory. When person is sad all time is selfish, is all about their loss, does no good for dead person or for living peoples. I tell no one of the pain in my heart."

To Polly Arjun's words sounded very sad but so like her.

Arjun put his arm around her and patted her shoulder: "I think everything be okay for you soon, but first you must want." Again words that struck a chord, Polly was shocked at how well he seemed to read her.

He walked a little ahead once more, ready to offer help down the steps if necessary. His manner of walking was in long slow strides that appeared confident and yet this was contradicted by a slight stoop. He was tall by Nepali standards, maybe five feet ten or more, and slim, but that he was also strong was evident in the fact that his shapely calves were visible through his jeans: "There Pokhara," he said, stopping and pointing out the city.

"Yes. I hear it too," the tooting had annoyed her slightly, but not as much as in Kathmandu, because it wasn't as loud, as there wasn't so much traffic.

As they came off the track there were taxis waiting. Arjun approached one, had a conversation with the driver and then walked away, all in a very low key fashion. When he returned in the same manner beckoning her and Jivan over, she supposed he must have acquired a satisfactory price. Bargaining was not something with which Polly was comfortable, but they all seemed to expect it here.

She failed to recognise the part of the road where the accident had happened, but only realised it as they turned into a busy city street that marked their return to Pokhara.

Back at the hotel they gave her the same room. She went immediately to have a shower and wet her hair so that she could blow dry it, forgetting the situation with the electricity, which was that currently it was off. While she waited for it to dry enough to use the straighteners instead, she unpacked and gathered together her washing, feeling a little anxious that it was getting near lunch time as she needed to eat. Suddenly the light came on indicating that the electricity supply had returned and Polly could now use the blow dryer. She also put on a dress, make-up and jewellery, but none of these things improved her opinion of the way she looked. As she closed the backdoor of her room she looked nostalgically towards the mountains, but they were totally obscured by cloud.

On her way downstairs she decided to offer Arjun lunch. He was reclining on the sofa in the lobby and as she walked up to him he looked up: "Aw!" He said, as if something had really surprised him.

"What?"

"You look beautiful."

"Thank you." Polly said, taken aback and resisted the urge to contradict, feeling genuinely flattered. "I was wondering if you would like to join me for lunch."

"I just had dhal baht, I not hungry."

"Never mind. It was to say thank you. How about dinner tonight."

"Okay."

As Polly walked down the street in search of somewhere to eat it was with a renewed confidence in her appearance.

*

If the milk yield carried on as it was Kabita would soon be able to sell some, she thought as she poured a measure for Uma as usual and sent Sunker over to the house with it. She threw more wood onto the dying embers of the stove to finish cooking the noodle soup. From the room upstairs she heard the coughing of her father-in-law which didn't seem to be improving even though it had been several days now.

The children and Ram's mother ate their soup. Then Kabita sent Indira to her grandfather with his share and a cup of Nepali tea. A few minutes later she returned with the empty cup, but the soup untouched. If this carried on Kabita would have to take him to Kathmandu, she would give it two more days she decided as she poured him some home brewed medicine and sent that to him with Indira.

When Gonesh and Sunker had finished their breakfasts they took their toothbrushes from the rafters and went outside to clean their teeth, closely followed by Bosiram who had climbed up to reach his. Kabita followed and arrived just in time to see him squeeze a considerable amount of toothpaste onto his brush, himself and the ground, but when she took the brush away from him in an attempt to help he shouted and kicked so much she had to allow him to continue unassisted. A few minutes later she sent her daughter to fetch him back from the school he'd followed his brothers to.

As she cleaned her own teeth Kabita looked unfavourably at the gap in between the two front ones, the brown stains that brushing failed to remove and the hollowed cheeks of her face. It hardly mattered what she looked like anymore. With the exception of the wedding there was no one or nothing for whom to make a special effort, but she remembered how she had looked upon her forty year old mother-in-law when they had first met and vowed to never let that happen to her. And now she looked the same, or worse and she hadn't even reached that age.

Indira returned with Bosiram still screaming and trying to pull away from her. Kabita took an old school book of her daughters from the rafters and presented it and two coloured felt pens to him, but he was distracted for only a moment before he stomped off down the hill again with Kabita running after him. When she caught up with him she picked him up and threw him into the air, laughing as his protests turned to giggles. She was out of breath when she got home because he was really too big for throwing around these days, but at least he was happy to stay at home now. She took him to help her pick tomatoes which later they laid out in the sun to dry.

*

At the last minute Polly realised she should invite Jivan too, but he said he was visiting with friends. While they were out Polly consulted Arjun on a suitable tip for Jivan.

"Is up to you, I can't tell you."

"But I have no idea if you don't give me some." Arjun shrugged. "Well can you tell me what would be a small tip and what would be generous?" Polly asked.

"Five hundred would be minimum, five thousand would be good."

"Thank you."

Polly ordered lasagne and Arjun pizza, she drank a glass of red wine and he an Everest beer. As they ate they were accompanied by the music of first Cat Stevens and then Jack Johnson. The restaurant tables were low, the chairs wicker and the menus written in English. All around them, with two exceptions, were white faces from the mouths of which came several languages.

Arjun ate as if it were his first meal for months, using the fork, but no knife. "What yours is like?

"Very nice. What about the pizza."

"Good. I taste this?" His fork was already hovering over Polly's dinner. He took a mouthful and then another. 'So much for Nepalis not liking to share food from the same plate,' Polly thought.

"Perhaps you need to taste it all to make up your mind."

"No, is good." It seemed Arjun had missed the irony.

"So, what do we do about this money?"

"We get in cash and keep in hotel safe."

"I don't suppose she has access to a bank?"

"No. That why we need cash."

"Will it be safe?"

"Of course. What you think someone rob her?"

"No, I. . . " Polly didn't know how to respond to what had probably sounded like an accusation of dishonesty. It was just that she had no idea of what this woman and her circumstances were like. If one believed everything they read then all village women were ignorant, passive and vulnerable, but then so much of what she had read had been contradicted; and Arjun broke just about every rule. "It's just I have no idea what Kabita is like."

Arjun nodded, he picked up his phone and fiddled with it, then did the same with Polly's. He took a toothpick and broke it into little pieces, which he then put back into the saucer they were provided in. "So what you want to do for next two days?"

"Nothing. I'll just wander around here and see what's going on."

Now Arjun started putting the napkin into various shapes, in between he cracked his fingers. Polly wondered what was making him so restless. "Would you like another beer?"

"Okay."

Polly called the waiter over and ordered the beer and another wine: "I should buy a bottle and take to the hotel really, it's so expensive in the restaurants."

"Is more than England?"

"No, not much, but when everything else is so cheap it seems so. I don't eat out very often in England anyway."

"Is expensive in England?"

"Everything is expensive in England."

"I have friends who say in England they could make big income, but is hard to get visa – strong invitation is needed."

"It is true the wages are much higher than here, but so is the cost of living. The only way you might succeed in making money is if you shared accommodation with a lot of other people, or someone put you up very cheaply. Rents on properties are like hotel prices here."

"If I could earn a lot of money I could keep my family really well."

"You could, but earning a lot of money is harder than you think."

Polly felt as if Arjun wasn't really listening. "I suppose it's difficult keeping your family on what you earn especially with it being a seasonal job."

"Yes. But my wife have job too, my mother look after childrens."

"Oh!" Polly was genuinely surprised, although of course she knew there were women who worked. 'What does she do?"

"She teacher."

"Oh! The same as me, then. What does she teach?"

He shrugged and pursed his lips. "She just teach."

"In England we have specialist teachers who teach one or

occasionally two subjects. At least once the children get to secondary school. I teach history. Well, I did, I don't have a job at the moment."

"You're retired?"

"No. I will have to find another job when I get home. I quit so I could do this." "Is easy find job in England?

"For some. What age do the children start and end school in Nepal?"

"In government schools start at five, finish about sixteen" "That's the same as England."

"But government schools here no good, too many student not enough resources."

"That's the same as England too."

"I don't think. In English government school is possible take exam for university yes? This won't happen in Nepal, if you want good education you go private."

Polly didn't say what was on her mind. "Does your wife work in a government school?

"Uh huh!" Arjun was not only absorbed by his beer but by preening himself, he was looking over Polly's shoulder in a manner that suggested a mirror was there. And when she turned around to check she discovered that there was.

"Are you admiring yourself?"

"Yes." He looked at himself sideways as he swept his hair back with the palm of his hand.

Polly giggled. "You're as vain as I am."

"What means this –vain?"

"It means you think you look handsome."

"Don't I, then?"

"Yes, gorgeous, like a famous film star."

Now Arjun giggled: "Yes, I thought."

"I'll get the bill. Are you sure a handsome man like you wants to walk the streets with an old woman like me?"

"I tell them you my mother," he teased.

Polly slapped him playfully on the arm, to which he giggled and snatched it away. "I'm the wrong colour."

"I say I adopted."

As they left Arjun put his arm around her shoulder and pulled her slightly towards him and they walked like that for a few yards.

"I thought Nepali culture didn't like men and women touching in public."

"Is okay if old person need help," Arjun said with a wry smile, but then he dropped his arm and they walked side-by-side without touching.

Polly went straight to her room, all the while she made her preparations for bed, removing make-up, washing her face, brushing her hair and teeth, Polly thought about Arjun. She found the flirtatious nature of his behaviour unsettling, not least because she was very attracted to him, but also because she didn't understand it. She wondered if it was just his way, or if it was because of his relationship with Ned. It was impossible to believe the attraction was mutual she being so much older, but he behaved as though it was. Leaving that aside Polly began to worry about her own motives. Perhaps this was another example of what had driven her into sex with Malcolm. The attentions of a handsome man, coupled with her sexual and emotional needs, was going to her head and making her behave like a fool. True flirting was fun and harmless enough for the most part, but there was danger inherent in it too if Arjun thought, even for a moment, she was in earnest. She mustn't flirt with him again. But he crept between the text of her book as she tried to read, and a self-accusatory voice reminded her that she did very much mean it. She lay down to sleep in an analytic frame of mind, in which she wondered how she would ever resolve the conflicting feelings of wanting love and sex and wanting to only ever be Ned's wife.

When she woke a little before seven to the light and the sound of retching, she was still tired. Someone, she supposed must have eaten the wrong thing, she sincerely hoped it wasn't going to be the case for her, especially not while at Kabita's. Polly had chlorine tablets for the water and avoided eating either meat or anything uncooked and so far had remained well.

She did her stretching and bending exercise and pelvic floor before showering in tepid water. Polly knew if she waited for an hour the solar panels would have heated the water, but by then the electricity would be off and she wouldn't be able to blow dry her hair. It hadn't mattered in the mountains, but with the facilities available she wanted to groom herself properly. It was quite hot already and she felt the short sleeved top might be too warm, but didn't want to cause offence by showing too much of her body. Polly wondered if she had already made that mistake in the mountains, but her hormones made it impossible for her to tolerate any more than a vest top whilst walking.

There was no sign of Arjun when Polly went for breakfast and there was no sign of anyone else either. She went into the dining area, which was light and airy with a pink and grey marble floor and only protected from the elements by a tin roof with wooden ceiling. There were railings painted in the same bathroom blue as the houses in Ghorapani, which opened it on one side, and on the other there were rooms. Polly sat at one of the three small tables whose Formica tops were covered by pink chequered table clothes on top of each was a glass containing rose pink serviettes. In the corner stood a very noisy, nineteen-sixties style fridge, which ceased its hum with a shudder as the electricity supply cut out bang on eight o'clock. Polly sat self-consciously thumbing the pages of the menu while she waited for someone to come.

When, after several minutes, no one did, she wandered down the corridor and into the garden which was already bathed in sunlight. Here there were two round blue tables one of which was covered with flies and the remains of a rice meal, so Polly chose the other which was out of the direct sunlight under cover of a tree. With some amusement she noticed that the trunk had blue rings painted around it. At the bottom of the garden a young man swept up leaves with a broom made from twigs and an even younger girl squatted by a tap washing dishes. Neither of them took any notice of Polly, so she approached the lad and asked: "can I get some breakfast?" All she received by way of reply was a blank look, so she went over to the table and returned with the menu which she waved at him. He put up his hand and disappeared into one of the shed-like buildings beside him and immediately another young man appeared: "you take breakfast?" He asked.

"Yes please."

"What you want?"

"Porridge, toast, black tea, please." Polly pointed at the items in emphasis.

"Okay. Please sit." Polly did as instructed, feeling pleasure in the warm November morning. Shortly a middle- aged couple came into the garden who quickly rejected the other vacant table, then stood a while looking lost until Polly invited them to join her. As they struck up conversation Polly learned that they were Canadians visiting Nepal for the first time and about to do the trek she had just finished.

"Oh, you'll love it," she assured them. "It was really hard at times, but well worth the effort.'

"That's good to hear. Are you travelling alone?"

Polly hated that question because she always felt she should qualify it, but this time she decided not to. "Yes, I am."

And they were too polite to pursue. "Have you ordered your breakfast?"

"Yes. It took a while to find someone, though. I think they work on Nepali time." Just then the boy who had been sweeping leaves arrived with a shopping bag, the contents of which included bread and eggs, Polly supposed they were part of her breakfast. Before he took them into the kitchen she called him over and showed him the menu again and he went and fetched the kitchen boy. Eventually all three had breakfasted and the Canadian couple took their leave of her. As the table was being cleared Polly asked: "Do you know where Arjun is?"

At first the young man looked puzzled, but then said: "Arjun, where is? – Ah! He has gone to the outside."

They had arranged to meet and make the trip to the bank at ten o'clock so Polly decided to sit on the balcony and read. Her room was on the first floor, but she took her book to the second where there were iron tables and chairs. From here the roof, which housed the water tanks and solar panels, could be accessed via metal steps. The brick work here was painted grey and pink, the concrete balcony ivory, lending the whole floor a more European, less tacky appearance. Before Polly settled to read she took a moment to absorb the view. Immediately in front and to the left of her were hotels of a very similar style, but to her right was a large piece of waste land which bore a notice in English and Nepali saying it was for sale. And next to that was a row of small, one storey, concrete houses with flat tin roofs. A woman dressed in a sari swept the porch with her broom of twigs, a man in European style clothes brushed his teeth beside the outside tap, a bare footed child threw a ball back and forth between himself and the wall. The water buffalo bellowed from time to time from its shelter and a fawn dog lay panting in the sun. In the near distance stood the green heavily forested foothills, in which she had lived and walked for a week, and behind them the Himalayas continued to look one dimensional as they jutted through the cloud.

Polly had hardly started to read when she felt hands on her shoulders "Hi," Arjun said and sat down next to her.

"Good morning, how are you?"

"I fine. So, you require anything?"

"No, I thought I'd read until it was time to go to the bank."

"What time you want go?"

"I thought we were going at ten."

"Okay. I see you in lobby at ten."

And he strolled off, leaving Polly feeling slightly bemused because she had thought a definite arrangement had already been made.

*

A longing that induced restlessness had kept Kabita from falling asleep and the same restlessness woke her before she was ready. She felt it warm and tingling in her solar plexus and breasts, it was strong enough to prohibit concentration on the things she needed to do. When Kabita had felt this before in Ram's absence it had angered her, but now it made her furious. She got up as quietly as she could so as not to disturb the children, took her torch and went to the village tap. Feeling grateful that it was still dark and so she was unlikely to attract anyone's attention, she sent handfuls of water cascading over her body, experiencing the tingle of cold first as punishment, then as relief and finally as cure.

*

At the bank Polly felt like a criminal, as her request for one hundred and sixty six thousand rupees was met with much consternation. The manager was called, the rest of the queue was moved, Polly's passport was requested and a telephone call to her bank in England deemed necessary. The sum sounded large enough in rupees to warrant such a response, Polly had to admit. Arjun put the money, which was in two envelopes, into his small rucksack and carried it next to his chest. Polly imagined walking through her home town with thirty thousand pounds in her possession and so, every time he stopped and shook hands with someone and had a brief conversation it unsettled her. Once the money was deposited in the hotel safe she relaxed and set off to explore some more of Pokhara.

*

CHAPTER FIFTEEN.

The cough was no better. Kabita had only ever travelled once by herself to Kathmandu, this and her distaste for travel had been the cause of her delay, but with only three days until the visit from the English woman she could afford to delay no longer.

The night before they left Kabita could hear her mother in-law wailing into the night, as if she expected to never see her husband again. Her tears disturbed Kabita's sleep, but so too did the anticipation of the journey, not only because of her fear, but also because she associated Kathmandu with visiting Ram. She had always stayed in his one room, concrete apartment, which was chilly and cramped, but it had been good to be with him and it was the only time they shared a bed without children.

The bus left at eight. Kabita wanted to allow at least forty minutes to walk down to the bus stop, feeling her father-in-law couldn't be relied upon to make the descent in twenty minutes in his current state of health, but his wife made that difficult, with her continual weeping and wailing. "We must go now," Kabita finally said, "we don't want to miss the bus." Her mother in-law walked with them so, with the two women as supports, Ram's father was able to walk quite steadily.

They had to stand for most of the two hour journey into town. Kabita clung to the seat and her father in-law to her as the bus bumped and twisted its way. Screaming wheels sent clouds of dust into their eyes and noses, to which Ram's father responded with a fit of coughing so profound that Kabita had to ask the conductor for a plastic bag for him to spit in. Finally a young man offered him a seat, no doubt moved by the violence of the cough and the sight of the frail old man.

The wait for the second bus was just long enough to allow Kabita to eat. She ate hurriedly and scantily mostly from concern for her father-in-law who lay with his head on the table throughout. Then they went directly to the bus to ensure a seat for the two of them. They only just made it for the bus to Kathmandu, they pushed their way through the crowd of people to the back of the bus, where Kabita managed to squeeze her father in-law into a seat that only existed because the two women either side made room by sitting side ways. Despite standing, Kabita started to doze, but was jerked awake by feeling that she was falling forwards and then by another violent coughing fit from Ram's father.

Finally they crawled through the rush hour traffic of Kathmandu and reached the bus station a little before six. From here they took a taxi into Thamel, the tourist district in which Sandeep and Khrisna both worked. Kabita hated Kathmandu, the smell of it, the plastic rubbish on the sides of the street, the layer of dust that hung over everything, but especially the noise, the tooting traffic which seemed to subscribe to no particular rule and made her feel afraid of a fatal accident. And she hated Thamel worst of all, with its souvenir shops and western style hotels that Nepalis couldn't afford to frequent.

They pulled up outside the hotel Khrisna worked in and because he was expecting them he came immediately to greet them, then got into the taxi and directed it to the apartment he and Sandeep shared together with a friend who was currently away. "So how are you?" He asked his father and his reply came in the form of a frenzied coughing fit.

"We'll go to the hospital early tomorrow. Sandeep will go with you, I have to work."

The apartment was very much as Ram's had been. One room with three beds, a cupboard and a gas stove and bottle. The food was already in the process of being prepared by Sandeep, who got up and helped his father to the bed when he saw how ill he appeared to be. After the meal, Sandeep and Khrisna went out without saying where they were going. Kabita helped her father in-law into Sandeep's bed and then laid her straw mat on the floor and tried to settle to sleep herself, but she was kept awake by her father in-laws raspy breathing, the shuffle of a small animal or large insect, she didn't know which, and especially by her memories. Every time she closed her eyes Ram's face was behind them. She recalled the intimacy of the single bed and how they had sex that catered for her needs, not only his, as had been the case ever since the children were born. But it wasn't that she missed, so much as the intimacy of a shared life and the shared purpose of raising their children, and this was closed to her forever now. Even if her culture allowed for the second marriage for women, Kabita knew she would never want that and could never feel about another man as she had about Ram. Faced with a life so empty all she could do was her duty to others in the hope of improving her karma for the next time. And hope that wasn't too long in coming.

She was just falling asleep despite all the hindrances when she was startled awake by the silence. Fearing Ram's father had gone to join his son she got up quickly and crawled over to his bed, putting her ear as close to him as she dared, for she dare not touch him at all, her heart beat so hard it hurt and she could hear the blood pounding in her ears. Finally, after what seemed an eternity she heard a quiet shallow breath and, with a sigh of relief, she returned to her mat. Kabita knew she should have brought him to the hospital before now and that if something terrible happened it would be her fault, she prayed as she lay there, offering any atonement deemed necessary so long as her father in-law got well.

She had no idea how late the hour was when she was woken again by her brothers in-law returning, clearly, from the amount of noise they made and their clumsy actions, having had too much to drink. Whatever the time it sufficiently disturbed Kabita as to spoil the rest of her night, for now she was not only conscious of the rapidly approaching dawn, but subject to stereo snoring.

They arrived at the hospital by eight, while Sandeep went to check them in Kabita settled her father in-law on the wooden bench along with the five other people who were already there. There was only enough space for one other person, Kabita left it for Sandeep. The waiting area was open to the outside; the view from which was out onto a busy street. Directly opposite a house was under construction, its bamboo scaffolding holding it in place while two men laid bricks. Kabita watched a sign writer two doors down from the construction site standing on a narrow plank, as he inscribed the name of the shop keepers, she feared she would be witness to his death if he fell and sure he must if he took so little care. Inside the hospital waiting area there were stairs leading to another floor and on either side of the concrete corridor were rooms, which were curtained off from the sights that took place behind them, but not from the sounds. Currently the doctor, presumably from necessity, was shouting questions of a highly personal nature to the person in her care. Ram's father struggled to stay sitting as he hawked and spat into a plastic bag, the young woman sitting next to him screwed her face up in obvious disgust and slouched away from him, as if fearful of catching a fatal disease. A dog with a prolapse ran panting down the corridor; an elderly woman with a drip descended the stairs supported on either side by two young men. A child of about ten with no obvious ailment wandered in, looked around and then left again. Finally their name was called and they were shown to one of the curtained off areas, behind which were four beds, three of which were already occupied. Sandeep helped his father onto the fourth.

The doctor, a middle aged woman dressed in a blue sari, passed along the row asking questions and issuing appropriate instructions to both the nurse, the patient and their families. Their instructions, which were preceded by a chest examination, included an x-ray and blood test. Kabita took her father in-law and the authorisation paper to wait for the x-ray while Sandeep settled the bill so far. There was only one person in front of them this time, and so in a few minutes they had the x-rays and were waiting with them for the blood test. The full results would take two days they were informed, meantime they were issued with anti-biotics and a dietary supplement and assured that there didn't seem to be too serious a problem and he should be much improved by the time they returned for the blood test results. Kabita was so grateful she almost cried. Sandeep, mistaking her concern to be purely for his father, was moved to touch her on the arm and say: "we're all relieved of course."

Back at the apartment Sandeep first telephoned his mother and then his brother with the good news. To Kabita he said: "Khrisna says he'll stay at the hotel so you can have his bed whilst you're here."

"I was going to leave him in your care and return for him. I need to get the night bus home, the English woman is coming."

"Impossible! I have other things to do. The English woman will have to wait. I'll call Arjun now"

*

The news didn't reach Polly until the late afternoon. The morning had been spent walking Lake Side, first the lake itself and then the main street. At the lower end of the lake she found a small café, with no tourists in it and prices that better suited her budget. She had decided to eat there with a little trepidation because of its scruffy nature. It was constructed of wood that was barely more than sticks, and tin, its pale green walls were dotted black, as if someone had thrown ink at them, and in the wicker chairs were grubby red cushions. The attraction was the price and the lack of customers. She ate pizza, feeling it a safe option and drank black tea. Outside the front door was a sign that read: 'boat on hire.'

At the bottom of the road her hotel was in, was a similar sign advertising the fact that there were bikes for hire and the said bikes were stood in a circle around the large tree to which the sign was attached. Polly thought perhaps she'd hire one someday and explore a little more of Pokhara.

Life was lived on the streets here, Polly decided as she headed for home. The shops displayed their wares outside and the shop keepers sat, squatted or stood outside too, chatting up the customers with offers of 'special prices' and cups of tea. Polly was tempted by every one. For her the main attraction was the colour, but she wasn't buying yet. She had already decided that when she was ready to buy she was purchasing as much as possible from the Women's Skills Project. Not only because it was aimed at empowering women, but also because they sold at a fixed price so she didn't need to barter.

Now she went into one of the many cyber cafes that advertised the fastest internet service and checked her emails. There were messages from both of her children, which were chatty and concerned mainly with the weather and Christmas. There was also one from James, this one in particular made her a little homesick because he responded specifically to all she'd shared about her Nepali experience so far. It was the sharing of her experiences she missed so much without a partner. She wrote replies to all three. Polly carried on up the street feeling a little distracted, noticing for the first time the small homes between the shops, all with clothes hanging from the balcony. In the middle of the road two men squatted painting the black and white lines of a zebra crossing, causing the street traders with their trolleys of fruit and vegetables, doughnuts and samosas, or roasted corn, to have to mount and dismount the pavement. Polly had to leave the pavement herself when she came across a pile of bricks blocking the way. In the gutter next to them lay a small, black and white dog, which she stood staring at for several minutes trying to discern whether or not it was breathing, but she was too afraid to touch it and so walked away without being sure. A school bus tooted loudly and startled her. From it came loud Nepali music, which was in contrast to the way the children were dressed and to the western music that poured out of the pubs and music shops. A book shop advertised a postal service and Polly made an instant decision to write to her mother, suddenly missing her too.

As she walked up her street people put their hands in prayer and offered her a 'namaste' from their shops or outside of their hotels. Not for the first time Polly considered how little it took to constitute a shop. The first had the most logical selection with bread, yogurt and milk in sealed plastic bags and a few tins of something. In the second an assortment of alcohol, toiletries and things with which to amuse children, like coloured pencils, sharpeners, rubbers and some balloons. But the third made the least sense of all, it appeared as if some tourists sometime had made a particular request and the shopkeepers had gone out and purchased one of each in case someone asked in the future. She wondered too, if enough was every sold for a profit to be made.

Arjun wasn't there to give Polly the news in person, but he'd left a message at the reception with the boy who had been left temporarily in charge. Her disappointment was disproportionate to the news. "Did he say why?"

"No, Mam."

"Do you know where he is? Or when he'll be back?"

"He's gone to the outside. I think he'll be back after one hour."

Polly went to her room, lay on her bed and cried.

CHAPTER SIXTEEN.

Polly was sitting in the garden at seven finishing her breakfast in time for the early start when she heard again the retching and vomiting to which she was now accustomed on waking, but now she saw too, the source of the noise. From one of the houses next door the occupant, a man of about her age, could be seen inducing the vomiting by sticking his fingers down his throat. She turned away, partly from disgust and partly trying to protect his dignity. When Arjun came to join her she enquired of him: "why do you think he does that? D'you suppose he feels ill every morning?"

Arjun appeared to ignore her for some time, as he seemed sometimes inclined to do, but just as Polly was becoming irritated and about to repeat her question he said: "No, not ill. Some peoples believe is good thing to clear out stomach every morning."

"Really? How extraordinary!"

And then, as if to emphasise what he'd just said the kitchen boy hawked loudly and spat out of the door, just yards away from where Polly was eating. Arjun said something to him in a harsh tone, which she hoped was a rebuke of his action.

A few minutes later the taxi arrived to take them to the tourist bus station, the first part of their journey would be back towards Kathmandu. The bus station was a pot-holed field with no stands or information to give any clue as to which bus to take. Arjun, however, knew the routine: "is this one." He mounted the bus: "this our seat." And then he was gone, returning just in time for departure like before.

Their stop was just after the breakfast break. With just the two of them leaving the bus together, Polly felt as if she was adventurous and special, not just an average tourist. Here there were shacks selling drinks and snacks, when she saw exactly what was on offer Polly was more than happy that she had already purchased a croissant at the bus station. They boarded a small bus, hardly any bigger than a people carrier, it was so full that two people sat on woven stools in the centre of the aisle, but Arjun had barged his way on and found them both a seat. Polly felt a little guilty that she, a visitor to the country, should be preventing locals from sitting down, but she couldn't have exchanged places with either of the people in the aisle because she was crammed too tightly in her seat. A fact she was soon glad of as the bus bumped its way along the twisty, dusty track, because it was about the only thing that kept her in her seat. Polly knew they were driving into the depths of the foothills and through spectacular scenery, but was prevented from seeing it by her proximity to the other passengers. And being so close to Arjun was more distracting now than it had been on the outward journey; especially since several times he put his arm around her and held onto the back of the seat behind them for support.

They crossed a river as they entered the town of Dhading, from where they would catch another bus. As they alighted Polly had to take a huge step to avoid the stagnant water, whose flow along the gutter was interrupted by a pile of rubbish. In the busy, bustling streets there were no tourist trinket shops, but neither was there a lack of colour. The local women dressed in their brightly coloured saris, haggled with traders of fruit and vegetables, orange and yellow pulses spilled from their sacks, blue, red and green plastic utensils hung in hardware stores. As soon as they left the bus Arjun wandered off and at first she couldn't see him for the crowd, but then spotted the white cap and the familiar stance at the ticket booth.

After the ticket purchase he ushered her onto the bus and into the front seat, ordering her to 'sit there' and then dismounted and wandered to the other side of the street. When Polly lost sight of him for a second time she felt panic rising in her chest, which increased tenfold as other people got on the bus and the driver started the engine, but then he climbed aboard too. "I wish you wouldn't keep getting off," Polly told him, "it makes me very nervous."

"I never miss bus, relax."

Now the bus drove into the bus station, most of the passengers, including Arjun got off again. The driver drove up to one of the two petrol pumps and filled the tank without even turning the engine off, then he reversed out and picked up the passengers who had previously dismounted.

Two women shouted from the back of the bus and the two of them carried on a conversation with the driver at that volume. Now all but those two, Arjun and Polly, left the bus again at exactly the point they had joined it. Then the driver set off out of the town via a fairly steep hill, at the top of which he turned around, with much back and forth movement, drove half-way back down and stopped for the two women to dismount.

"What is going on?" Polly asked Arjun.

He shrugged: "Is local bus."

In a few minutes Polly realised what was happening as the two women returned with the sewing machines they had purchased and, along with the help of the driver, secured them to the top of the bus. The whole process must have taken about twenty minutes. Now the driver drove the rest of the way down the hill and back to the original bus stop. Where, along with all the passengers who were there in the first place, was an elderly man with a goat. An animated conversation between him and the driver took place, during which the other passengers got back on the bus and then most of them including Arjun got off again. Polly didn't think she could be anymore perplexed by the goings on until she realised that the goat was being tethered to the roof.

Finally the bus set out on the full journey with all the passengers aboard. It began with the ascent of the same hill out of the town and continued to climb for most of the journey. The roads now could hardly be described as such, they were single lane dirt tracks which were full of potholes and rocks in several places and took them perilously close to the side of the mountain. Polly tried not to look. She fixed her gaze ahead and was often rewarded with stunning views of both the foothills and the Himalayas. Despite the road conditions drivers tooted and then overtook, or suddenly appeared from the other direction and the two vehicles had to crawl past each other almost touching. The more she travelled the more she understood how Ned's accident had happened and several times she was convinced she would soon join him.

After about two hours they stopped in a small village that was shanty-like, with houses that were no more than shacks and made from wood. Even here there were make-shift shops selling snacks and bottles of water; outside one of which a troupe of ponies were tethered. A group of about six children approached Polly as she alighted from the bus, their hands in prayer saying 'namaste' and she realised they wanted sweets so had to purchase some.

All of the men disappeared behind a rock near to the river. The first time this had happened in Polly's experience had been on the road between Kathmandu and Pokhara. When all of the men dismounted and disappeared a few yards up the road she had been at first confused and then amused as she realised, watching them all stand in a line backs to the roads, hands in front of them, what they were doing. When Arjun returned she asked: "Is that the only toilet there is?"

"Yes. You can go there."

"Okay." Polly had little objection to using the bushes, but she was a bit worried that one of the men might come too, especially as she hadn't thought to wear a dress in case something of this sort occurred. But no one did.

The final part of the journey was so dusty that most of the passengers, including Arjun, wore masks to protect against it, but without prior knowledge or expectation Polly had to suffer the stinging eyes and dry throat. By the time they reached their destination it was six in the evening and the bus that should have taken them the rest of the journey had already gone, so they had to walk. The forty minute journey was such that Polly was very glad she hadn't had to do it by bus in the failing light. Although they didn't pass close to the side of any steep drops there were rocks and holes in the road large enough to require climbing or jumping over. And at one point there was a large stream at the bottom of a dip that Polly was certain a bus would never have been able to negotiate.

They reached the accommodation in pitch darkness. Her room was concrete from top to bottom with a small shuttered window, a table the size of a stool and three beds with very thin, worn mattresses and duvets of the same quality, which were also full of holes. The door was metallic and locked by way of a padlock, the one saving grace was the electric light, but currently it was load shedding time and so the electricity was off and the light was provided from a gas lamp. She put her bag down on one of the beds and then her head in her hands. If Kabita's home was like this she would be more easily able to accept it, but the thought that she was paying to stay in this 'guest house' was not a welcome one. Because of their late arrival Polly was the only diner in the garage-like dining area. She sat at a table, which so closely resembled a school desk it only required the lifting lid and ink well, forcing down dhal baht that was both cold and too spicy and following it with cold sweet tea. From politeness and necessity she ate as much as she could bear and offered assurances that she simply wasn't that hungry.

Arjun was nowhere to be seen. Polly wandered outside and looked up at the sky then lay on her back in the warm night gazing up at the myriad bright stars. Only once before had she ever witnessed so many and so bright, it was on the camping holiday on which she and Ned had celebrated their birthdays in the company of their adult children. She remembered how all four of them had laid looking skywards in admiration and amazement. It had been an unusually warm night for Scotland, so they were able to tolerate the outside temperatures without coats. Now she remembered how, from a genuine and simple happiness, she had tried to make the moment last forever .Perhaps in one respect it had, because she remembered it now with such clarity it hurt. Polly mused on the fact that a whole life time is made up of moments; the moment is soon gone, but without it there would be no now, no future. They, Ned and Ram, were already past as Arjun had pointed out, but the fact that they had once been present was enough to affect the future of those who had shared their lives. And the tiny part they'd played in history was, nonetheless significant. In this sense too, a person was immortal and never truly past. If one individual were taken out of history who knows what might happen to the now. Polly felt sure that this was exactly the reason why Native Americans, whose culture Ned so much admired, practiced ancestor worship.

*

The chicken had already been killed and plucked by the time Kabita and her father in-law returned from Kathmandu, now it hung in the porch waiting for her attention. She had decided chicken was the safest option, assuming goat to be an unfamiliar taste to the western pallet and if it turned out the English woman was vegetarian there were plenty of eggs. She wished she knew what time to expect her guests and how long they would be staying so that she might be better prepared.

When everyone was breakfasted and the two boys had set off for school Kabita began preparation of the meal, she kept the spices to the minimum and she boiled some water and put it aside in a separate jug for drinking.

Ram's father had not yet risen from bed, but Kabita had heard him talking with his wife and knew from the animated tone that he was continuing to improve. Sandeep had made the return journey with them, saying he too wanted to meet the English woman.

Indira went with Bosiram to pick the marigolds from which they would make their guest a garland. So, Kabita was ready to receive her whenever she arrived.

*

A cockerel crowed, a buffalo bellowed, a man called out in response and the light trickled through the slats in the shutters. For a second Polly couldn't remember where she was, but the hard bed and musty smell soon reminded her. She had slept only fitfully and had woken in the night wanting the toilet, but the idea of walking down the concrete stairs and out through the metal gate to the side of the house in the pitch black made her unwilling enough to put up with the discomfort of a full bladder. Now, as she did its bidding she was very glad that she hadn't done so in the dark, as she wouldn't have known about the puddles of urine at her feet.

Polly washed her hands under the cold water tap and dried them on her clothes because she couldn't find anything else available, then she went in search of her hostess and Arjun in the hope of obtaining some clean warm water. They were both sat at the table and the proprietor immediately jumped up when she saw Polly and returned shortly with tea, noodle soup and two boiled eggs. The tea was tepid and sweet, the noodle soup salty in the extreme.

"Arjun, could you get me some warm water for having a wash, please?"

He shouted the instruction and a large bowl was put to heat on the wood stove.

"She say will take about twenty minute."

"I only need it tepid on a warm day like this."

"What means this?"

"It doesn't need to be very hot, just not cold."

Arjun pursed his lips and nodded.

After a few minutes Polly got up and gingerly put her hand in the water. "This is fine Arjun; would you take it to my room for me, please?"

As he did so Polly slipped the two boiled eggs into her pocket in case she wasn't offered any food at Kabita's house.

After her wash she opened the shutters and looking out on the scene transformed her opinion of her accommodation. For as far as she could see, with the exception of the man and buffalo she had heard earlier, there was nothing to be seen. True it wasn't as beautiful as the trekking route, but it was every bit as still and silent and the air had the same clean taste. She stood for a while absorbing the experience and then she tipped the used water out of the window onto the soil below and returned the bowl to her hostess.

Arjun was shaving at the tap; he stood with his back to her. She watched for a moment, admiring the way the veins in his arms protruded and wanting so much to run her fingers along his smooth brown skin. Then she caught his eye in the mirror, he paused without looking around or away and smiled so slightly it could have been intended only for himself, but she was sure it wasn't. When he'd finished he straightened himself turned to her and said: "what do you require?"

Now she smiled to herself, loving the quaintness of his question too much to point out how formal it sounded: "what time are we leaving?"

"What time you want to go?"

"I have no idea. You know how far it is and how steep."

"It take maybe half- an- hour, or maybe little bit more."

And the way he said 'hour,' round, in the back of his throat and resonating through his nose had a musical quality to it.

"Well are there customs or anything I should observe – is it rude to arrive at a meal time for example?"

"No. Is okay anytime and I think she want feed you."

"Shall we leave now, then?

"May be after one hour."

"Okay. And that was exactly as it always was. He refused to make a suggestion until she did and then he changed it. "You have the money safe I hope."

"Of course.

While Polly waited for the hour she knew would be nearer to two she drank tea, which was finally hot and sugarless thanks to Arjun's interpretation. She looked through the photographs she'd brought for Kabita and the small gifts for the children. She had bought a photograph frame in Pokhara with the intention of framing one, but had been unable to decide which and then thought it would be better if it were Kabita's own choice in any case. For the children she'd bought colouring pens and books, a ball and a couple of beaded bracelets for the daughter who was about sixteen, she thought.

An hour-and-forty minutes had passed and Polly was beginning to feel bored and annoyed when Arjun finally said. "Okay, we go."

CHAPTER SEVENTEEN.

In places the route was as steep as the trek had been, but the heat was not so intense. Even so Polly struggled much of the time, and today she didn't receive the assistance she had become used to from Arjun. In fact his whole demeanour was different; it was almost as if he wished she wasn't there. He walked a little ahead as usual, but spoke little and even seemed impatient with the questions she asked, leaving Polly feeling annoyed and mystified.

On the way they passed through several villages where the houses were of the same wood and clay style as those Polly had seen on the trek, but they were simpler and the reaction of the inhabitants made it clear they were nowhere near as familiar with the sight of tourists. Mostly they smiled and said: "namaste", as always. But Polly was sure that one woman, despite Arjun's assurances to the contrary, offered unfriendly jeers in response to Polly tripping and almost falling on the muddy stone path in her efforts to keep up with Arjun. Just as she was wondering how much further they had to go he suddenly stopped and said: "We here." And then he spoke to the woman who was standing in the front porch.

"Is this her? Is this Kabita?"

"Yes." Arjun said and then strolled away and chatted to the several men who were squatting around a water pipe.

Polly and Kabita stood staring at each other, neither of them sure what to do. Kabita didn't look as Polly had expected; her above average height was emphasised by her thin physique, and her long hair, which was pulled and tied back from her chiselled face, punctuated the stern expression she wore: "Arjun," Polly felt as though she shouldn't be calling for his help, even though she had, after all, paid him for exactly that. "Aren't you going to introduce us?"

He strolled over nonchalantly: "I tell to her who you are."

"That's not a proper introduction."

"You can do – go on," he said, with a slight inclination of the head.

"Namaste, mero nam Polly ho," she said as she had practised.

"Mero nam Kabita ho," Kabita said, in her tiny voice. "Tapailai kasto cha?"

"She ask how you are."

"Tell her I am fine and ask how she is."

"She say she happy to meet you."

"Tell her I'm sorry about her husband."

As Arjun spoke, tears welled up in Kabita's eyes and she turned and almost ran into the house. Polly was struck by the contradiction between Kabita's features and her meek manner. Kabita was struck by the fact that Polly appeared younger than she had expected and too light in manner for one who had been so recently bereaved.

"Come, sit:" Arjun ordered and directed Polly to the dry stone wall that was in front of the small concreted yard. He put a straw mat down for her to sit on and then returned to the water pipe and chatting with the men.

Polly sat on the wall feeling bemused and conspicuous. In her small rucksack were the photographs and the money and, as she shifted the bag from her back to her lap she felt their weight as burdensome, and Kabita's behaviour as an abnegation of her reason for being there. Whilst she waited for whatever would happen next she reviewed her surroundings. The two storey house was of the same kind she encountered on her way there, rust red clay, wooden slatted glassless windows and a solid wooden door from which she could see a ladder to the upstairs and several churns, like the ones her grandfather used to use for milking the cows. From what she could see of the upper deck there was at least one room and a wooden balcony from which hung clothing and maize. To the right of the house there was a small shelter of woven twigs, bamboo and straw, from which came shuffling noises, indicative of the presence of animals. To the left there was a vegetable area, where only now Polly noticed a quite elderly lady was laying green leafed vegetables on a straw mat, presumably to dry. When she'd finished she dusted herself down and approached with something near to a smile. However, when she reached Polly she turned her head and mouth down, made her arms into a cradle, rocked them, crossed her arms and emphatically uncrossed them towards the floor, then pointed to her heart and mimed tears from her eyes. So that Polly already understood who she was and that she was telling of her broken heart, when Arjun shouted to her: "she Ram's mother."

"Yes, I know. And these are more family members?" Polly had guessed the relationship of Sandeep and his father, as they approached from the other side of the village, because of the similarity in looks to Ram and to each other.

"Yes. I'm Sandeep, Ram's brother and this my father."

Polly stood up and offered both her hand and her condolences.

"Thank you. Was very big shock for us. And same for you. We also sorry about your husband."

Polly nodded her thanks, suddenly feeling as though she might cry herself. She bit her bottom lip to prevent the tears from flowing.

Now Arjun came over and he and Sandeep shook hands and Arjun patted Sandeep's shoulder, holding on to his arm for some time as they spoke with each other in Nepali. Polly knew they spoke about her as she twice heard her name and once Ned's and guessed by the look Sandeep offered that Arjun was telling him about the money.

Ram's parent's sat either side of her talking a little and signing in order to aid communication, but she still had no idea what they were trying to say. Periodically they turned their attention towards their son and Arjun, so that it was now apparent all the adults except Kabita were aware of the nature of her gift. Polly was a little disturbed by this as, being unsure of the customs, she had no idea how much, if any, control these people had over what would happen to the money or to Kabita. In an attempt to gain some control of the situation Polly asked: "Where are the children. I have gifts for them?"

"Boys at school. Bosiram and his sister back soon," Sandeep replied before turning his attention again to talking with Arjun.

"Should I wait for them all before I give them?"

"Is not necessary, you can give when Indira and Bosiram return."

"And what about the gifts for Kabita?"

"You can give her after we eat," Arjun said, in a tone that suggested it should have been obvious, "and Sandeep can tell to her about it."

"No. I want you to. –Why? – Because you agreed, and I have briefed you on what I want you to say."

"Briefed? What means this?"

"We discussed what to say, you know already."

"You can tell to him. He her husband's brother."

Which was exactly why Polly didn't want him to be interpreter: "Why're you trying to get out of it?"

"No, I not. Okay. I talk her."

"Thank you."

And then a young woman and child appeared and as they approached the girl said: "Hello, how are you?" In very precise English.

"I am well, thank you," Polly stood up to greet her.

Indira held her hands in prayer: "We glad to receive you as guest. This my brother, Bosiram. Our father dead. He only two when father dead."

"I know, I'm very sorry."

Polly wanted to ask how they were all feeling, but she worried about convention and misinterpretation and had little confidence in Arjun today. She called him over again as she presented the gifts to Indira: "Please make sure they understand it's for sharing."

"You can tell, she understand."

"But please make sure."

"Okay, okay." He spoke to Indira in Nepali, who nodded her head in response. Then she took the presents into the house. A few minutes later she emerged wearing the bracelets and started kicking the ball around with Bosiram. Neither of them mentioned the gifts or said anything, but they seemed to be enjoying them. Dressed in loose slacks and a T-shirt and playing ball with Bosiram, Indira looked very young, she could easily have passed for twelve or fourteen with her under developed figure. Her face was long and diamond shaped, her nose straight and flared and her mouth set like her mother's, but her eyes were lighter, so she lacked Kabita's stern expression. She was smaller in stature too, because Kabita, although thin, was large boned, where Indira was petite and slim, without even a hint of future plumpness.

Soon bored by the ball Bosiram came over to Polly and pulled at her bag looking inside. She wondered about showing him the photograph's of his father, but decided Kabita should be the first to see them and then, to distract him in case he should find the envelope, she took her camera from its case. Immediately he posed, screwing his nose up in a false smile. Polly took his photograph and then showed it to him. When he angrily stamped and shouted in response to her refusal to hand the camera over, Ram's mother spoke severely to him. When that made no difference Indira took a book from the rafters and began reading to him. A few minutes later Sandeep summoned them into the house.

They were ushered into the room on their right and offered a seat on the unpolished wooden bench at a table of the same. In front of the window there was a tall cupboard, painted egg shell blue and looking as if it were better suited to a bedroom. High in the corner of the room a wicker basket was home to two doves. In the rafters were stored toys, candles and even toothbrushes and toothpaste. The room was quite dark, as most of the light had been blocked out by the position of the wardrobe, but there was a shaft of dusty sunshine spilling in from the open back door. Arjun and Sandeep sat one side of the table, Polly, Indira and Bosiram the other. Kabita served them food on aluminium plates, dhal baht and a huge portion of sticky white rice. Polly tasted the dhal tentatively and even more so the curry, wondering not only about spice, but the freshness of the meat. Both tasted lovely and she was easily able to eat the second portion she was offered. Now Polly poured some water from the jug into her aluminum cup and tried to surreptitiously add a purifying tablet, but Bosiram at least spotted what she had done and scrambled around her pockets looking for one for himself. Polly took one from the bottle and pretended to put it in his drink. "Why isn't Kabita eating with us?" She asked after the second portion had been served.

"She eat with Ram's parents in kitchen." Arjun assured.

"And then she'll join us so we can talk?"

"Yes."

Arjun and Sandeep continued to speak to each other in Nepali. Polly gathered from the manner in which Indira looked at them that they were probably saying something that concerned her, but no one interpreted.

After the meal Indira collected everyone's plates and put them outside the back door. "You want tea now?" She asked Polly.

"Thank you. That would be nice." Then, becoming impatient with the situation she asked the men: "When is Kabita coming?"

"Now, she come now," Arjun assured.

A few minutes later Kabita came in from the kitchen, but walked straight through and out of the open door. Polly's frustration increased tenfold when she went to the toilet and observed her washing the dishes.

In a wood and straw shelter a doe-eyed water buffalo stood chomping on hay, she bellowed slightly in response to Polly's very close proximity, as she tried to avoid the mud and manure on her way to the toilet. Polly washed her hands in the bucket provided for flushing and shook them dry. On her return journey to the house she observed Kabita, still washing up, and paused for a moment wondering if she should offer to help. Kabita didn't take any notice of Polly at all.

As Kabita passed back through Sandeep called her to join them, his words needed no interpretation, as the tone and sign language were clear to read.

*

When she saw Arjun approaching with the English woman Kabita was almost overwhelmed by emotion. It had been her fear that she would see her own experience reflected in Polly and be unable to contain herself, but nostalgia at the sight of Arjun outweighed it all. He had been a stranger to her for years now, but when she saw him it brought childhood memories to her mind. In one very clear memory she recalled being with Anita, eleven or twelve years old, linked arm in arm, leaning against the wall, watching as Arjun and Ram rolled marbles along the courtyard outside the girls' classroom. He and Ram, like she and Anita, had always been together and looked out for each other. Their deep companionship had made it inevitable that Arjun would not only recommend Ram to his company as trekking guide, but also help him learn enough English. Kabita wondered if he had any regrets now that things had turned out as they had.

Polly's introduction in Nepali, albeit rehearsed, had made a good impression, where her appearance had not. Clothes too bright, eyes dressed in liner, smile a little too relaxed all created the impression in Kabita of frivolity. Yet later, as she cooked the meal and observed her guest through the gaps in the open door, sitting alone on the wall, looking as lost as an abandoned new born, Kabita began to feel an affinity with Polly and to realise she was not as she appeared.

Arjun and Sandeep were only visible in silhouette, but she could see enough to know that they were involved in deep conversation. The bursts of steam from the pressure cooker protected her from the sound of their voices, whose whispered tones would have disempowered her.

In the semi-dark room, her eyes stinging and slightly misty from the wood smoke Kabita felt safe, but serving the food left her vulnerable again and she tried to avoid looking directly at Polly; whose light manner was her protection, her face for the world, Kabita now realised. When there were no more chores to hide behind Kabita was finally forced to sit and confront her guest face to face.

*

Polly addressed Kabita directly. "I'd like to give you these first," she waited for Arjun to interpret and then handed her the photographs and frame, which was wrapped in gift paper. Kabita took them without shifting her gaze from a spot just above floor level. She knew without looking what she'd been given and didn't want to scrutinize them in company; which Polly understood instinctively. After a short pause Polly continued: "but the main reason I came today was to bring you something else. Ned, my husband had very much respect for Ram, not only as a guide, but also as a man – in fact he considered him a friend." Polly waited for Arjun who repeated her words in a very reticent manner. "In England there is a tradition of sending flowers to funerals, but a lot of people these days choose to give money instead to charities. Is it alright to say that Arjun? I don't want to insult her."

"Is okay."

"Ned would have been worried about your family and how you would manage without Ram so I asked people who came to his funeral to donate money for your family." Polly took the envelope on which was written: Rs 166,000 and handed it to Kabita. "This money is from Ned's family and friends; it is for you and your family." Tears now formed in Polly's eyes. Kabita took the envelope in the same manner she had taken the photographs, there was no external sign of how she was feeling.

No one spoke. In the room there was a solemn atmosphere, like the anticipation of the vicar arriving to lead the church service. Polly looked expectantly at Arjun, simply because he was the only person she felt able to expect anything of. She hadn't been sure how Kabita would react, but the total lack of a response unnerved her: "Should we should go outside for a while?" She asked Arjun. He didn't answer, but stood up and moved towards the door, as if it had been an instruction. Polly followed and sat on the wall, feeling deflated and bemused. Ram's parents went inside the moment she emerged.

*

Kabita sat a few seconds longer, conscious from the weight of the envelope that there was a considerable sum inside. To look inside in the company of her guest would have been rude and she didn't want to appear too eager now in the presence of her family, so she waited a moment or two. When she did look and saw the amount written on the envelope she couldn't help but let out a gasp.

"Let me see," Ram's mother requested and responded in the same manner as her daughter-in-law.

Initially Kabita felt elated, never could she have imagined being in possession of such a sum. Then almost immediately she felt ashamed and guilty, in the knowledge of the sacrifice she and Polly, but especially their husbands, had had to make in order for this to be the case.

"You need to think carefully about what you do with it," Sandeep instructed. "And we need to keep it to ourselves, we don't want Hari's family thinking you can afford a dowry."

Kabita acknowledged the flickering thought that crossed her mind concerning how the money could be used for college fees and there being no need for a dowry, but really it was too late for that she knew.

"We shouldn't leave our guest sitting on the wall out there alone." Sandeep said.

Kabita picked up the envelope and strolled outside, still reeling from the shock. "Arjun, tell her thank you. Ask if she would like to stay here tonight," as she said this and Arjun interpreted Kabita approached Polly holding her hands in prayer and the envelope close to her chest.

"I don't know. – Do I Arjun? Do I want to stay?"

"Is up to you."

"Who will interpret for me?"

"Sandeep or Indira. I come back in morning."

"And then we go back to Kathmandu tomorrow?"

"Day after, will be too late."

"Okay. I'll stay."

Kabita seemed pleased with the decision.

A few minutes later Arjun had gone and Polly sat with Ram's parents and the children feeling lost.

Kabita went back into the house meaning to put the money in a safe place and then look at the photographs, but Sandeep was still there and she didn't want him witness to either. Although she knew she would probably have to let him deal with the money, as he was the only person she knew with a bank account.

"You could invest," he said immediately. "I know someone, he'd give a good rate of interest. Shall I speak to him?"

"Okay."

"But we must keep it to ourselves other than him. Probably it's best if we don't even tell the children. Do you have somewhere safe to keep it or shall I take care of it?"

"I have a place."

"I'll go and talk with Santosh then."

As soon as Sandeep had gone Kabita went upstairs and took the shirt from its hiding place. First she sniffed for confirmation that the smell had disappeared completely, before she wrapped the envelope in it and placed them both inside Ram's small rucksack and then buried it inside one of the half full bags of rice. She was aware that it would only be a couple of days before the rice bag was disturbed by someone topping up on the kitchen supplies, but a couple of days should be all that was necessary.

Once this was done she sat down on the bed to review the photographs. In the first there was only Ram, a close up of his profile in which he looked too boyish to have been anyone's husband. She skipped through the rest quickly, not wishing to leave Polly alone for too long. With the exception of those that included the English man, the very same man as in the photograph she'd found in Ram's bag, she now realised; the people and places were all strange to her. During his life it hadn't mattered, but suddenly she wanted to know about this other life. To have been excluded so completely from his work now seemed tantamount to only knowing half the man. Although she had no reason to doubt his sexual fidelity, nevertheless she felt jealous of the women who posed with him and the same on behalf of her children on account of those who took their place in his arms. Far from feeling possessive of the photographs, with the exception of the profile shot, which she now hid in the rice sack along with the money, Kabita felt no reluctance at having to share them with the rest of the family. So she took them with her when she returned outside and passed them to Ram's parents, who sighed wistfully over every image.

Kabita wanted to tell Polly that her husband looked kind and she wanted to ask how Polly had felt when she received the news of his death, but she resisted from fear of strong emotion and lack of confidence in Indira's interpretation abilities. Instead she asked lots of questions about the family construction and Polly's plans for her visit. After this she stayed a while feeling awkward because she didn't know what else to talk about until she was rescued by Indira offering to take Polly for a walk around the village on her way to collect more water.

The village consisted of five or six houses some two storey, like Kabita's, others only one. Under foot the stone path was muddied and manured and Polly was grateful for her walking boots rather than the flip flops Indira wore. Outside one of the houses a very young woman rocked a wooden cradle with her foot and shook a large woven sieve at the same time. At another a woman forked hay into a stack, stopping every now and then to chastise a boy child who was naked from the waist down. They walked to the communal tap, where they waited for a woman to finish washing her waist length hair, and then filled two urns with water. Polly struggled with the weight and against spillage as they headed back to the house. Once there they discovered Ram's father lying in a foetal posture, sleeping on a straw mat in the only sunny spot left on the porch as the mid-afternoon drew in and robbed the sun of its heat.

The two older boys were home from school, Indira introduced them and Polly took their photographs. They were both small for their age, but also sturdy looking. It occurred to Polly that the norm seemed to be looking young for one's age until thirty or so when the opposite became true.

Bored by all the sitting around Polly wandered to the back of the house where she noticed now that what she had previously thought to be a store room above the water buffalo's shelter was in fact, another bedroom. It was reached by virtue of an outside ladder. Through the open door Polly was able to see a figure heaped beneath the many blankets.

Then, as she resumed waiting, she was struck by the idea that life in the mountains might be not only hard, as she had always imagined, but tedious too. Perhaps that was why Ram's father slept now, not because he was old and tired, but because he was bored. From her own point of view Polly felt the lack of distractions would be more of a problem than the lack of amenities. The strong social bonds of Nepali culture, which were often espoused by Westerners, were, Polly felt, necessary for the sake of sanity in a world devoid of art and media. She wondered if Kabita had any desire for those things, or if their very absence were responsible for lack of aspiration, she wondered too if this was a good or bad thing. Certainly the philosophies of the East taught that non attachment to material things and freedom from desires was the way to nirvana, but this was just as likely a means of social control as the promise of heaven.

By the time the meal was ready it was almost dark. Because she hadn't yet been invited back into the house Polly was feeling a little chilly. She had nothing with her except her fleece, in fact the lack of a toothbrush and washing equipment had almost made her refuse the offer of staying, but she thought one night without either would do no harm. She put her fleece on at the first sign of the air turning cold. The boys continued to play with the football until it was dark, demonstrating far less patience with Bosiram than their sister had when he tried to join in, so Indira took him with her to help shut the chickens and goats in their pens. The wicker door to the chicken coop looked a long way from secure to Polly and she wondered how it stood up to the rain in the monsoon. The three goats clambered over each other and ran all over the yard in an apparent attempt to escape returning to a pen that was hardly big enough for one, but made no noise once they were in there. Polly remembered how, as a child, she had felt sorry for the pigs and cows on her Grandfather's farm when they were herded in from an open field and closed in small quarters overnight.

When she sat down to eat her second dhal baht meal of the day Polly was grateful to be inside where it was warmer, but the wood smoke stung her eyes a little and the shadows cast by the candle light played tricks on them making her feel quite homesick.

Hardly was the meal over when the family began preparing for bed. Bosiram had already fallen asleep; in the midst of playing he lay down and was snoring in a matter of minutes. Kabita laid two straw mats on the floor in front of the dying embers of the fire and laid him on one without removing any of his clothes.

Indira acted as hostess to Polly, leading her by torch light up the wooden steps and into the bedroom. Although she could see little in torch light, Polly saw enough to know that all four wooden beds were pushed together and that the two older boys were already asleep in theirs. Indira left the room to undress and so allowed Polly to do the same, but she kept most of her clothes on from fear of being cold. She crawled under the thick duvet feeling her bones dig into the thin straw mattress and her head and neck resist the hardness of the pillow.

The dark was absolute. An active imagination was a curse in a silence that was only broken by the children breathing and fired by crickets ticking and goats shuffling menacingly close. Polly was right in her assumption that she would wake several times during the night, but it was not from being too early to bed or even from being uncomfortable as she had expected, but rather from it being too quiet.

CHAPTER EIGHTEEN.

When Polly finally woke it was eight o'clock. The partial darkness was penetrated by shafts of sunlight, pouring in through the gaps in the shutters and door. And with the light the mood changed, so that now the goats, who were still shuffling in their pen, sounded comforting rather than something to be feared. The cockerel crowing, the buffalo munching and the sound of trickling water produced a deep sense of contentment and nostalgia in Polly; it felt like waking up on her grandfather's farm. She was in the process of getting dressed when Indira came looking for her.

"Oh! You awake. Was good sleep?"

"Yes, thank you. Was your sleep good?

"Yes. Good. My mother want you for breakfast, she cook noodle and tea."

It sounded like an instruction rather than an invitation causing Polly to hurry with dressing and tidying up after herself. She shook the duvet, which smelt a little musty and, as she put it back on the bed, felt amazed that there was no ache in her body with only a thin straw mat to protect her from the hard wooden base of the bed. The row of beds, the cotton and woollen clothes hanging from them and from a line made of string, lent the impression of a Dickensian dormitory. She remembered her own children's school days and how harassed she'd felt by the continual mound of laundry piled on the coffee table waiting either to be ironed or put away. In the corner of the room were sacks of grain and from one, which was half full, there came a sound like rushing water as the rice spilled on the floor. Polly intended to draw attention to this fact, but was soon caught up in the daily routine and forgot.

As she ate breakfast on the porch Bosiram climbed all over her, sucking the snot from his nose, as he did so. She struggled to eat noodles which were too salty and drink sweet tea, but she did enjoy the boiled eggs, which looked and tasted really fresh. A group of children, all of them dressed in school uniform, were busy lighting a fire which they fuelled with dry vegetation and sticks. Polly had no idea if the fire were purposeful or only for entertainment. A group of about ten children were involved in the process, some of them looked as young as five or six, but she assumed they were probably older. Even so she felt afraid for them and moved closer, as if to guard their safety. The flames soared high and the sparks wide and the children were perilously close. Suddenly Bosiram came running from the house towards them and began excitedly ripping vegetation up and throwing it on the fire, the children shouted at him in response and moved him away, but he stamped his feet and stubbornly threw more weeds on the fire. Polly was about to pick him up and take him to the house when Indira arrived, but she didn't take him away, as Polly had expected, instead she helped him build a smaller fire of his own and even offered him a stick with which to take the flame from one to the other.

Around the main fire the older children ran backwards and forwards between the flames with bundles of vegetation, or lit the ends of sticks then beat them out on the ground. Polly was relieved to see Kabita a few minutes later, convinced that she would put a stop to the activities, but instead she said something to Indira who then walked away in the opposite direction so that, when Kabita herself returned to the house, Bosiram was left alone with the fire. Polly resisted her instinct to take him away and instead she moved closer and talked to him hoping to distract him. But, Bosiram was not so easily duped and only left the fire when he noticed that the other children had extinguished the remains of theirs and gone off to school; and then he ran after them.

Polly's relief was short lived, as she then wondered if she should go after him or attempt to alert his mother. But she need not have worried; it was only a matter of minutes before one of the children brought him, kicking and screaming, back to the house. Indira laughed as she took him from the girl who was having difficulty holding on to him; "my brother naughty boy," she said to Polly. And put him down, but immediately he ran off again with Indira in close pursuit.

Polly sat on the wall reflecting on the early morning fights she'd had with her children, insisting there would be no television before school and then how, bored with waiting, they had fought with each other.

The sun had not yet burned through the morning mist and she felt a little chilly again, which closeness to the fire had temporarily taken away, but she was aware that inside the house the temperature was probably the same. The small, dark houses were not intended for living in to the same extent as English homes;

shelter and food were all they offered, not solace and entertainment too.

Kabita emerged from the house, paused, looked in Polly's direction and then opened the door of the goat pen, scattering food on the ground, which they fought over. She was heading towards the chicken coup when Indira arrived with Bosiram hanging from her arm and screaming, but the moment he saw what his mother was doing he quietened down and ran to help. As the chickens hopped out Bosiram crawled in, emerging a few minutes later with an egg in each hand, which he willingly surrendered to his mother. Kabita took them, turned towards the house then towards Polly. She moved a little closer, clearly wanting to say something, although really there was no need as their common experience was there for the reading in her eyes. But then the look became searching, as if she were seeking reassurance from Polly. As they held each other's gaze Polly so wished Arjun was there to aid a verbal conversation.

Bosiram broke the moment running up to Polly and presenting her with an egg: "Oh, thank you, dhanyabahd." She said.

Indira took it from Polly, who looked up hoping to continue her dialogue with Kabita, but she had gone back into the house and Polly wondered now if it was her habit to spend so much time inside when no one else seemed to.

Her sleep had been poor. The cold from the floor penetrated the mat and, presumably for the same reason, Bosiram fidgeted and coughed much more than usual, but not only that, the money troubled Kabita. Her initial excitement was soon replaced by a burdening sense of responsibility as she worried about the best way to use the money. She considered the actions of the English woman as an omen, as another sign from beyond the grave and felt a responsibility both to Polly and Ram. Any doubt in that regard had been wiped out when she looked in Polly's eyes.

*

Kabita had worried that she would be disturbed by the mutual pain, but as it turned out the real problem was the shared responsibility. For now she felt obliged to demonstrate that the money had enhanced her existence, as in some respects it would, but significant improvement became impossible the day Ram died. Furthermore, she would now be required to give up her anger towards this woman's husband and instead be grateful to his wife. Kabita knew too, that despite preferring not to, the English woman would go home and try to think of other ways to help. She wondered how many years they would be bound into a relationship of obligation and gratitude. She wished she could somehow explain how she felt and tell Polly that she had done enough and that they would both be better off if she didn't bother anymore.

When Sandeep arrived with the chicken Kabita had sent Indira to request, he had news too, the local business man would take her money to invest and pay her two per cent interest every month: "he says anytime you need some of the lump sum you will need to give one week's notice."

Kabita nodded, thoughtfully. It seemed a sensible and safe way to use the money, but she felt afraid to entrust it to anyone.

"This is a good deal, Kabita."

"I know."

*

When Polly saw Sandeep approaching carrying the feathered chicken by its feet it sent a little shiver through her, as around the yard the live ones clucked and scratched. With him came his mother and a very short time later, Arjun.

"Hi, how are you?" He asked.

"Okay. And you?"

"I okay too. Did you have nice stay?"

"It's been interesting, but I could have done with you to interpret sometimes."

"You have Indira."

"Some things were too complicated for her."

"Like what? I help now."

Polly almost described the scene between herself and Kabita, but then realised that not only had the moment passed, but Arjun was unlikely to understand in any case. "No, it doesn't matter now. Are we leaving soon?"

"I think she feed us first."

"Again! I've never eaten so much in my life."

Arjun laughed.

Polly just wanted to go now; the responsibility she felt for Kabita was such that just being there was an effort from which she needed some respite.

Staying there had been an intense experience which had tired her, but also left her feeling she would never be quite the same. It wasn't simply that it was humbling to glimpse the basic lifestyle. Nor even the subliminal communication that had taken place between herself and Kabita, but it was also that she knew Ned would have loved the opportunity to do as she had done and she felt there was some consolation in having done so on his behalf. Coming here felt as much an act of loyalty to Ned as one of mercy to Kabita and her family. She mused now on how people often thought that. They ran marathons, composed music, or started charities on behalf of a deceased person, as if this in some way continued their existence. It occurred to Polly now that human awareness of mortality was probably the strongest, if not the single, driving force behind creativity. People sought immortality through deeds because the inescapable fact of death was not only impossible to accept, but also to understand.

They left as soon as the meal was over. Indira presented Polly with a garland of marigolds.

"Thank you for your hospitality," Polly said through Arjun. "I hope that you and your family will soon find some peace."

Kabita thanked Polly again for the money and extended an invitation to visit again if she ever returned to Nepal. To which Polly replied that she probably would and she would love to visit again and, although this was only partly true, she was sure she would come back, even if only for the sake of Ned's memory. Indira and Bosiram walked with them to the edge of the village. Kabita retreated again to the house, looking as relieved as Polly felt.

She and Arjun walked in silence for some time. Then, following a heavy sigh from Polly, Arjun slipped his arm around her shoulder. "Was tiring for you, I think?"

"Yes, very."

"You can take a rest when we get back."

"I wonder what she will do with the money."

"She invest with local business man."

"How do you know that?"

"Sandeep tell to me."

"Was that her decision or his?"

"He suggest, but she agree. Is good deal, good interest, all legal with paperwork."

"Are you sure?"

"Yes. I sure. – You don't need worry, no one want take her money they happy for her."

"Oh I didn't mean . . .," now Polly was worried that she had caused offence. "I wasn't suggesting anyone was acting against her best wishes, but she seemed so – passive."

"What means this – passive?"

"Like she would be easily persuaded, but I didn't mean to suggest that someone would take advantage of that."

"Is not unreasonable worry, some peoples in Nepal would, but Sandeep good man and Ram's family want to take care to her."

"It seems a very sensible thing to do, she'll have a bit of money all of the time that way. It's probably better than buying one thing."

"Yes, but she also going to buy nice wedding gifts for Indira and her husband."

"Indira is getting married? She looks so young."

"She is, but she cost money for family to keep and they have good marriage offer."

It all sounded very clinical. Polly thought of Christine at sixteen, silly and irresponsible and crying over exam pressure and tried to imagine how she would have coped as a wife. And then of her twenty-three year old self who had married feeling very much in love, but terrified of her role. But English 'love marriages' didn't exactly present an encouraging statistic. And in the upper classes arranged marriages based on financial considerations were still practiced. Yet despite this she couldn't help but say: "So, where does love come in?"

"If peoples lucky, come later, if not at least is secure. Please to remember this Nepal, it not like England. Nepal not much concerned with the affairs of women, only the affairs of Gods and men. There not much opportunity for girl unless very well educated. That why I want my daughters have good education, then maybe they have choice, may be job and more choice of husband."

"Will you leave it up to them to choose?"

"They can choose, but if bad choice I say no."

Polly laughed. "In England the girl would probably take no notice and marry him anyway."

"In Nepal too sometimes, but then family disown."

"That seems rather harsh. Would you disown your daughter?"

"How can I give my consent if he bad, if he take drug for example?"

"But if you disowned her she would have no one to turn to if she needed help in the future."

"She my daughter, she can always come home," Arjun's eyes were full of love.

"You love your family very much, I think."

"They are my everything."

They were back at the lodgings by early afternoon. After washing, cleaning her teeth and changing her clothes Polly felt a little lost. She lay on her bed thinking back over the events of the past two days. There was an unreality to it all. Polly pushed her spine into the hard mattress as if confirming her existence. She had swapped her 'real life' for two days and caught a glimpse of Kabita's, and on the face of it they seemed very different, literally worlds apart, but in actual fact, although the details varied, the needs and preoccupations were much the same. Polly had glimpsed several reminders of her earlier parenting role in Kabita's and had even felt envious of her, because at least she had the children to focus on. But, by the time Kabita was the same age as Polly was now her children would have grown and that role be finished and, unlike Polly, her options would be very limited and certainly there would be no room for envy then. For, although Polly currently had no idea how to spend the rest of her life, she did at least have choices.

She slept for a while and woke to the sound of Arjun's voice. He must have been very close because she could hear every word, although because it was in Nepali she couldn't understand. Polly knew he was talking to his wife by the familiar and tender tone and she felt a pang of jealousy because there was no one to speak to her like that anymore. And then it triggered a flood of tears, which she tried to muffle in the pillow, but which must have been audible because a few seconds later there was a knock and then Arjun calling her name.

Now she was annoyed with him for arresting the flow, but called out that she was okay.

He'd opened the door a crack and peered around it: "You sure?" Feeling obliged to Polly sat up and began wiping her tears away She was about to offer explanation when Arjun came into the room, leaving the door slightly ajar and, sitting down on the bed put his arm around her, pulled her close and stroked her hair. The action was so caring she started to cry again. "I'm sorry," she said through the tears. "I'm so sorry."

"You don't need be. Is okay."

Being held by him was comforting, he felt solid and safe, but then she was stirred by longing and looking up into his eyes she saw the same in him. He smiled, looked towards the partly opened door, then back at her, holding her gaze a while before whispering directly into her ear: "I have big desire for you," and squeezing her hard. The words were electrifying. She wanted him, but she wanted him to take control, which he did by pulling gently away, kissing her softly on the forehead and saying: "I go now."

At the door he turned and, speaking at his normal volume said: "You okay now." In a tone that wasn't quite an observation, but neither was it a question.

"Yes."

He left the door open. Polly closed it then slid to the floor leaning her weight against it; again needing the solidity of wood to ground her and make her believe in her own reality. She remained sitting there reliving the moment and thinking through the implications. The way she wanted Arjun was not the way she had wanted Malcolm, she now realised, her desire for him was such that it was capable of replacing Ned. Her conscious mind was full of the rationale for her attraction, not least his role in bringing her closer to Ned, but there was another sub-conscious thought not far behind, telling her Arjun had been sent by Ned to help her recover from the loss of him.

There was no sign of Arjun all evening and Polly's mood changed accordingly, as she worried that it had something to do with what had passed between them. After her meal she went to her room and tried to read, but the light was poor and concentration was ruined as Arjun floated in between the text. So, putting the book face down and open on the page she was reading Polly gave in and allowed herself to dream of a sexual encounter with him, but in the midst of it she was seized by guilt. In her imagination she heard the accusations of their families and friends as if they were certain events, and fuel was added by the memory of Malcolm.

Now, feeling ashamed of herself Polly decided to go to bed, but first she went downstairs to clean her teeth at the tap and use the toilet, hoping, as she did so, to encounter Arjun, but there was still no sign of him.

The dark and the silence were not quite as total here as at Kabita's, from the opposite side of the street there shone a dim electric light and just audible voices accompanied their conversation with periodic laughter.

Polly was drifting towards sleep when she became aware of the rattle of the gate and then teetering footsteps up the stairs and across the landing towards her room. This quiet noise was the loudest so far and it called her to consciousness. Now she was alert and listening, holding her breath for fear of missing a vital clue. Just as she was becoming convinced it was part of a dream after all, she heard the same footsteps recede and a door at the end of the corridor close. It was some time before sleep came to rob her anticipation in case he returned.

*

Reflecting on the visit, or more especially the visitor, Kabita felt guilty. Fear, resentment and preconceived ideas, had led her to judge the English woman too harshly. And, though she had behaved politely, she had shown her no warmth. Any time Kabita had thought about the English woman, prior to expecting her visit, it had been with resentment at her more favourable position. But of course she should have realised that that the English woman, Polly, would swap any amount of material comfort for the emotional security she had lost, just the same as Kabita. For a moment she hated the money because the very fact of it was synonymous to their loss.

CHAPTER NINETEEN.

Another day out with her daughter and this one Kabita enjoyed more than the first, both because she felt more engaged with the idea of the wedding and because the money was their own. Sandeep had advised caution over how much they spent saying he didn't want them to appear ostentatious and as far as Hari's family were concerned they were too poor to afford extravagance. The traditional gift of a bed was not a necessary purchase, Hari's family had informed them, as there was a perfectly good one to be inherited from the sister who had departed to a marriage of her own. So, they bought a gold watch, a few articles of clothing and a gold and topaz ring, which they admired and displayed to onlookers several times during the journey home.

On the outward journey they had Uma for company, who was going to Pokhara to visit her aunt and with whom Kabita had shared the secret of the money, knowing it was safe with her friend of so many years. Now, as they returned home she reflected on how she had cut herself off from Uma since Ram's death, the intimacy of the previous evening being the first they had shared since her widowhood. She looked at her daughter now, wishing to offer some psychic reassurance and also hoping to receive the same for herself. Indira replied with a smile so full of innocence it stirred Kabita's protective instincts and achieved the very opposite instead.

Indira read her mother's look as seeking reassurance that the marriage plans and gifts were to her liking; which they were. When she had learned about the money there had been a fleeting moment in which Indira had once again imagined herself a college student, but she didn't allow it to grow into a full blown fantasy. In order to avert bad karma from her misdemeanour, she had to put all of her energy into being a dutiful wife and daughter in-law and encourage Hari with developing a career. This perhaps, would allow their daughters the chance she wasn't able to have herself. And, now that she had made that commitment Indira couldn't wait for married life to begin.

*

As soon as they returned to Pokhara Arjun had a client with whom to trek. He knocked on Polly's door to say goodbye before she was properly up and about :"Hi - I go now," he took hold of her left hand in both of his and held onto it. "I be back in six day. Take care," then he was gone.

Although she was now quite familiar with the city Polly felt a little vulnerable thinking about being there without him, she was going to miss him and she was coming to rely on him to take care of her. In this new and unfamiliar situation Polly had relinquished control to Arjun and, in so doing, felt safe for the first time in a year. Perhaps that was all it was after all, reliance and attraction, masquerading as something more. She quickly pulled herself together and was soon downstairs eating breakfast.

The air was warm already although it wasn't quite nine o'clock and Polly had to remind herself it was December and would soon be Christmas. A fact about which, she felt a little guilty because she wouldn't be spending it with her family. Yet she was also relieved because it had been such a chore the year before. What Polly really wanted was to forget it was happening at all, but she had seen signs that it would be acknowledged, if not actually celebrated, right there in Pokhara. Perhaps Christmas could better be avoided by going on another trek, but Pokhara was drawing her in and making her wish to stay. The beguiling nature of the place was something to which Ned had eluded and now she was experiencing it first-hand.

A whole day ahead with nothing to do was something to which Polly was totally unused. Even when on holiday she and Ned had had every day mapped out with activities. Now as she wandered Lake Side, enjoying the sun, but feeling aimless, she wondered exactly what she had been thinking of in deciding to stay so long. She had performed her duty as far as Ned was concerned and seen a good deal of the things he had seen, she wasn't at all sure what she wanted to do next. Yet she remembered only too well that last year her isolation had increased with the onset of winter and she had longed to be where she was now. True there were moments of homesickness, but she had them even when there because it wasn't home without Ned. Overall she did feel less lonely here, despite the absence of family and friends. Here she had the sense of Ned being with her, and here she could feel whatever she really felt without being concerned for the emotions of others.

Planning the trip Polly had imagined Ram's family and had a firm picture in her mind of their lifestyle; which had been formed from

Ned's diaries and television documentaries, and which was not so very far from the reality. It was with confidence that the money would somehow make up for their loss and that she would feel absolved and at peace, that she made her plans. She could never have imagined that the real result would be an increased sense of responsibility and being left with the feeling she should do more. It was this, she believed, to be her biggest reason for wishing to remain in Nepal. That there might be another, Arjun, was something she pushed to the back of her mind.

After lunch of yak's cheese salad in a side café, she walked again, following one of the roads out of the immediate tourist area towards the centre of the city. As she did so, she thought back to the previous evening and a conversation between, Arjun, herself and one of the other guides. He was older than Arjun, perhaps even her age, and recalled seeing the first generation of hippies arrive in Kathmandu. With their camper vans and almost naked bodies they had both frightened and fascinated, and his mother had warned him against them, the way some English children were warned against gipsies, she supposed. Now, he had observed, speaking through the haze of English cigarettes and Scotch whisky, their children or grandchildren paid him his wages.

Walking up the side streets littered with non-biodegradable waste, and local people talking on mobile phones Polly reflected on the irony of it all. How common place the middle-class, middle-aged, aid workers or bare armed backpackers seemed; and how the local people had acquiesced so completely they built their lives around them. The thought made her feel both sad and hopeful. Hopeful because with the advent of more secular ideas came also a yearning that would generate striving for greater equality, but sad for what would happen in the process of trying to achieving it.

After walking for about twenty minutes she came across a sign which advertised, in English and Nepali, a residential home for orphaned children, and a few minutes later saw what she assumed was the place in question. Because, within a small courtyard twenty or so children of various ages played football with a young European man. She stood at the gate watching for a while, feeling slightly surprised that no one questioned why she was there, as would surely have been the case in England. And also feeling inclined to enquire if they needed volunteers, but she didn't. A few minutes later she walked away having made the decision to at least obtain some information on volunteering in the near future.

She hadn't walked much further when another sign caught her eye, this time advertising a Women's Empowerment Project. Wondering if it was the same project as the one which sold goods in Lake Side, Polly went in search of it. It wasn't hard to find, only a very short distance off the street she had been following.

Entrance was through a wrought iron gate painted egg shell blue, like everything else in Pokhara it seemed. It led to a well- kept garden with a path all around and three distinct buildings. As Polly strolled around she discovered they were an administration block, the residential quarter and a shop. In addition there was a hut-like building, partially open to the outside world in which women wove on looms. Polly stood and watched for a few minutes, before removing her shoes and putting them under the bench with the four other pairs that were already there and then stepping into the shop. On the shelves the goods included bags, purses and pencil cases, as well as woven garments and footwear, all of various colours and sizes. And all so typical of the hippie generation that Polly found herself wondering whether it was they or the local people who generated the style. She didn't recall seeing one Nepali woman with a bag or a purse and, with a few exceptions who dressed like westerners, had never had seen them wearing anything but saris and sandals or flip flops on their feet.

Whoever the instigators were it was a style Polly liked and she decided to buy her daughter a bag and perhaps Mia too. She picked one up to check the price and discovered not only that, but a little information about the project and the dyes that were used. All of which were plant dyes grown in the adjoining garden, she now discovered. Before making her purchase Polly picked up a tiny pair of woven shoes and felt a surge of maternal emotion in response, which was accompanied both by nostalgia and longing for a future that included grandchildren. With her purchase came a leaflet on the project and it was here she discovered it was possible to sponsor a woman to take part. This perhaps, was something for the future.

It was with some excitement that she now ambled around the garden allowing the fantasy of Kabita sitting amongst the weaving women to germinate into an idea and then into a rough plan. She would return to her village and offer it as a suggestion as soon as the opportunity arose, but first it was necessary to find out the details on funding. With this thought uppermost in her mind she meandered slowly towards the administration block, taking in the sights and sounds of the garden as she did so. For a moment her interest was caught by what she believed was a cotton tree and, as she examined it, wondering if indeed that's what it was she was joined by a Nepali woman who first greeted her with 'namaste' and then: "This is cotton tree."

"I thought it was. I was wondering if all the cotton is grown here."

"No. Most we buy from India."

"Oh! You work here?"

"I manager of project."

The introduction excited Polly further and fuelled her sense of there being significance in the visit. "How would someone get onto the project?"

"They apply to board if we have place they can come."

"Are there usually places?"

"We have only small waiting list."

"And any woman can come?"

"If she have money or sponsor, yes. Sometimes village sponsor because she come here and learn everything, all necessary skills, from growing and harvesting dyes to weaving and selling the goods, then they back home and teach those skills to other women in village. The hope is they become economically independent."

"And how many rupees does it cost?"

"For one woman come is five thousand rupee, for teacher go village with whole programme is fifty thousand rupee."

"So, you have your own teachers too. Is all the funding through sponsorship?"

"No, is Christian charity."

"I see. – Do you have volunteers? – Yes, I would be, but I don't have any of those skills."

"Always we want teacher of English."

"Well, I am a teacher, so that's worth considering. Thank you." Polly raised her hands in prayer and said 'namaste' as they parted. Now her excitement was so great she became restless and no longer able to amble, so she decided to go back to the hotel and formulate a plan to present to Arjun on his return. Then, if he agreed it was a good idea, she could go back and offer it as a suggestion to Kabita. As she passed through the gate she was greeted by two women coming in to the project with a: 'namaste,' so warm and informal it was almost as if they knew her.

There was a bounce in her step now and a smile on her face. She felt full of purpose and, although she didn't believe in such things, convinced of direction from beyond the grave. Now she became acutely aware of the highly visible family life of Nepal. A mother grooming the hair of her tiny children; an older child playing with his younger sibling while his mother squatted cooking the meal over a gas stove; still another mending the tyre on a bicycle any westerner would have condemned as dangerous, whilst his teenage sister squatted washing clothes in a bucket. Most poignant of all, the sight of a young woman, hardly more than a girl, spoon feeding an elderly lady in bed. These sights sobered Polly and brought her back down to earth so that she called into question the advantages and disadvantages of doing things the western way.

Now she wondered not only whether and to what extent she wanted to become involved in the process of westernisation, but more importantly whether Kabita herself wanted it. She considered it now to be vanity to assume that she would be offering Kabita something beneficial, when it might well be the case that she preferred the predictability of traditions that dated back hundreds of years. Indeed sometimes she thought the lack of it in her own life made her grief so much worse. Just as surely as she became convinced of the opposite she now became convinced that the afternoon's events were significant for another reason entirely; that being, to raise her own awareness of the fact that all of her actions thus far were about herself and trying to make sense of the nonsense of death.

Alongside these thoughts came an awareness of how she had neglected her own family; of how, in being so wrapped up in her grief and in trying to find a purpose to her own life, she had failed to include her children. And it was with a growing empathy towards her that Polly realised she rejected her mother's sympathy because she herself was unable to face how, just like her mother, she was not only needy, but desirous of being needed. If that were not the case she wouldn't be expending so much energy on trying to find ways to help Kabita and her family.

In response to these thoughts Polly suddenly felt very homesick and wanted most of all to see her mother.

*

CHAPTER TWENTY.

Uma was talking excitedly: "My Uncle says because he has no daughter, only sons, he will lend me the money for the fees and I pay him back when I can. I think that would be no more than two years. I grow the plant dyes here and spin and weave cotton and then the girls and me will make handicrafts to sell. Maybe once a month I'll go to Pokhara or Kathmandu and sell in the streets. Maybe I even make enough to one day have my own shop."

"And does Nabin agree?"

"Oh, yes. He would like to be shop manager. But I wanted to tell you, because you could do it too. You have that money."

"That's my insurance. I need to save it."

"But you would be able to replace it once you started earning."

"No, is too much risk and Bosiram is too young to leave."

"Is only a few weeks. He will be fine with his grandmother."

"I have too many chores already."

"You're thinking too small, not far enough ahead. A little time spent now will save you time and money in future."

"I'm happy for you Uma, but is not for me. I have enough to get by on and I have no business head."

Kabita could easily have been carried away by Uma's enthusiasm, but what she felt overwhelmingly was fear at the prospect of any deviation from the familiar. In other circumstances perhaps she would have had the impetus to do Uma's bidding. If Ram were alive and encouraging her for example, or if he were ill and needed her to support the family. Perhaps even if she had been abandoned by him, because then she would feel vindicated and fuelled by anger, but as it was currently and with regard to the future she felt safe with the predictability of the known. Besides, she couldn't bear to leave Bosiram, not even for a day.

"You don't need business head, only sense and you have plenty of that, but I can see this is the wrong time to discuss with you. Maybe you think differently when you see how it works for me."

"Perhaps!" But Kabita knew that anything outside of the traditional village life was for other women, not her.

*

Feeling lonely, homesick and suddenly so aware of Ned's absence it was as if she had only just learnt of it, Polly emailed everyone at home. She kept it chatty so as not to worry or upset them. When it was done she headed towards the ayuvedic massage she'd pre booked the day before.

With no idea of what to expect she made her way into the barbers shop front and was taken behind a curtain to a small concrete room where a Nepali woman dressed in tunic and trousers directed her first to a curtained off section of the room, in which she stripped down to only her knickers, and then to a high leather couch where she lay down on her back covered by two large, soft white towels.

The day before Polly had completed a health questionnaire and ticking no to every box as always, had provoked a moment's reflection on how healthy Ned had been and the irony of his death despite that. Now she lay trying to relax beneath the firm pressure of the hands that massaged and the strong aromas that teased not only her nose, but her entire olfactory system.

Relaxing was difficult. The massage was rough and the oils profuse, so that she had the sense that she would slide off the couch any moment and felt as if she was being prepared for roasting over a spit. The music, which Polly assumed the masseuse considered relaxing, was of monks chanting with Nepali music in the background; when she closed her eyes it took her to a place in her soul that felt deep and impenetrable. It scared her a bit so she mostly kept them open with her gaze fixed first on the ceiling and then, as she was turned over, on the floor and she observed the stains and defects in both.

When the massage was over Polly was wrapped in a cotton sheet and taken outside to a concrete bathroom in which she was offered a large bucket of warm water and soap to remove the oil from her body and then she was handed her clothes through the partially opened door. Her clothes resisted as she dressed, hampered by the remaining oil and her hair felt lank, so now Polly wondered why she had bothered with the treatment at all. But the masseuse assured her of unimaginable health benefits and promised her later she experience remarkable results.

The plan for the rest of the morning had been to do some souvenir shopping, but suddenly Polly felt very tired and low in spirits so instead went back to the hotel and slept for two hours.

When she woke she felt better than in a long time. There was nothing profound or extreme about it, but simply as if she had returned to herself. She showered and washed her hair, surprised at first by the both the quality and quantity of hot water, but then realising that of course it would be the case at this end of the day when it was solar powered and the demand on it reduced. There was no electricity, Polly had completely forgotten that it was load sharing time and so she wouldn't be able to dry and style her hair. Whilst she waited for it to dry she washed some clothes in the red plastic bathroom bin and hung them out on the balcony; taking a glance at the mountains that she was already taking for granted and a deep breath of warm air she tried to savour the moment. She imagined Ned on this same balcony, first beside her and then on his own. He would have looked at this same view and thought of her, missed her, wished she were with him and in that sense she would have been. And now that she was here she couldn't understand why she hadn't been before or how she wouldn't want to keep coming back. Again Polly conjured up a memory of Ned and realised that, although they were never as real as the spontaneous, unconscious variety, at least they were always available. She didn't have to feel sad or guilty in response, she not only could, but indeed should, enjoy them it was part of keeping him alive.

With her hair now dry Polly styled it with the straighteners and then went in search of first food and after that, suitable souvenirs. Only the climate and bartering culture belied Polly's sense that she was Christmas shopping. Signs outside restaurants from which the usual seasonal music emanated and which were adorned with coloured lights, advertised traditional Christmas food. One was even dressed with tacky decorations. Polly's negative reaction was unfounded and unfair she decided, as she wondered whether any of the Sikh population felt resentment when the Diwali lights went on in her home town. The Nepali's were after all, just trying to make their visitors feel at home.

Just like Christmas at home, it was the men who were hardest to buy for. James always received a book from her as his yuletide gift, but given the circumstances of the purchase she was only prepared to buy one by a Nepali author. She was busy scanning books of that nature when she looked up and saw Ned on the other side of the store. Such was his similarity in appearance to Ned, not merely in dress but in mannerisms too, that it took Polly a few seconds to decide whether the man was real or an apparition. Once she had concluded that the former was the case, it took a few more to compose herself. Now that she looked properly at the stranger she could see that he wasn't so very much like Ned, but enough for the mistake to be understandable and, as he left the shop, she had to resist her desire to follow him. Instead she turned her attention steadfastly back to the books – almost immediately her attention was caught by the title: 'The Teacher of History' and as she turned it over to read on the back that it was a novel about corruption in the Nepali voting system she realised it was the perfect choice.

That left only Anthony to buy for and Polly had pretty much decided on a khukri for him, as he had always admired the one Ned owned. She was standing outside a souvenir shop contemplating whether it would be better to give him Ned's knife instead and wondering if so what she would buy him instead, when she was accosted by the young man who worked in the shop next door.

"Namaste. How are you?"

"Namaste. I'm fine, how are you?"

"I am better for see you. I think you will make me happy man today."

"I'm sorry I'm not buying shawls."

"No. No. I don't want you buy. I just want you have tea with me. You like masala tea? - I'm pleased because is very very good for you and I make for you now."

"Thank you, but I'm not thirsty and I have shopping to do."

"Why you hurry? You on holiday, you go shopping after tea." He put his hands in prayer, then forwards in a gesturing manner: "Please come."

"I really don't want any shawls."

Now he put his hands on his heart. "I am in pain here, you don't trust me, you don't believe me when I say is for tea not sell."

Now Polly felt totally unable to remain outside the trinket shop and didn't want to go in for fear of being approached and offered purchases before she was ready. "I really do have shopping to do," she said and began edging away.

Then maybe you come tomorrow?"

"Perhaps," she crossed the road and continued walking away, feeling a bit annoyed because she had wanted to look at the Tibetan trinkets and make up her mind about Anthony's present. Deciding that a cup of tea was a good idea after all she headed for a café in a side road, partly because she had been there before, but also because she was well out of sight of the keeper of the shawls shop whom she didn't wish to offend.

She thought she would take the time to consider whether or not to buy the khukri, but had no time to consider anything as very soon a young Nepali man asked if he could sit opposite her and as soon as he did so he struck up a conversation. Asking first of all about where she came from then about her circumstances. Polly always stumbled over mentioning her widowhood for fear of it provoking pity or, in this culture, reproach, but in this instance he seemed almost pleased.

"You have boyfriend?"

"No. No, I don't."

"And you travelling alone?"

"Yes."

"Then maybe I can do something for you?"

"What!"

Her shocked reply was clearly misunderstood as something else. "Maybe you have need of man?"

She took a big swig of tea, stalling for time to think how to respond, but before she had the chance he said: "We can help each other. I have mother and sister to support."

Now she was outraged as well as shocked. "No, I don't think so." And she swallowed the last of her tea and left in such a hurry she almost forgot to pay. The young man followed her.

"I sorry, I didn't mean to insult you."

What Polly wanted to say was that he had very much and that she knew he would never have said such a thing to a Nepali woman so how dare he to her, but she was too polite and too aware of the impression created by the half-clad European women, so she said nothing at all. She quickened her pace. So did he.

"I don't understand," he continued as he walked beside her. "I hear European lady like sex and talk freely."

Polly still didn't respond. Much to her surprise she felt alarmed almost to the point of fear. The feeling was reinforced when the very young man, barely out of his teens by the look of him, continued to tell her in rather too graphic terms about what he believed European women liked and how he was able to supply her with it. She quickly crossed the road and realised too late she was right outside the shop she'd been trying to avoid.

The young man had followed her, but walked away angrily shaking his fist at the shop keeper in response to his chastisement. Now, when offered masala tea for a second time, Polly felt unable to refuse.

"I sorry about him," Anil said, after he'd introduced himself and sent the boy who assisted him in the shop to fetch tea from somewhere. "He make me ashamed of my country, he always try make European woman sleep with him for money. He tell them he have sick mother and crazy sister, is not true."

"Well, it's a world- wide trade." Polly said, laughingly, belying how shocked she really felt. The self-contempt Polly felt at her lack of assertiveness was reinforced by the drinking of tea she didn't even want.

"But I think maybe I should be grateful to him because now you in my shop and I think you wouldn't come if not for him." Anil raised his eyes slightly in a questioning manner, but didn't wait for an answer: "I think this is will of Allah."

Polly had heard all of this before and knew any second the shawls would come out and Anil would tell her how each complimented her eyes or hair. At first she had found the banter and the offers of tea charming and the bartering a challenge, but already it was getting on her nerves and she wanted to just pay the asking price without listening to the sales pitch at all.

"Is tea good? – I'm so pleased. I want only please you. When first I see you I know you are from Allah, He send you be my friend. You want be my friend?"

"I'm only here a short while."

"But you have email, yes? We can be friend by mail, yes?"

"Well, I don't know what would be the point of that."

"No, don't say that." Anil quickly put both hands to his heart as if he had been stabbed. "Maybe you don't like me because I'm Muslim."

"I don't mind at all that you're Muslim."

"Then is okay give me your email address."

The conversation wasn't taking the predicted route and Polly floundered as she sought responses to Anil that were neither encouraging nor insulting. An email address wasn't comparable with a postal one, it lent no clue as to her physical whereabouts and yet to give it seemed also to give the wrong impression. "Why don't you give me yours?"

"I think you never send me mail," he said somewhat sulkily as he wrote it down for her. "And I really like be your friend. Will you come have tea with me again tomorrow?"

"I have plans for tomorrow."

"Then day after?"

"Maybe."

"I think you go other way to shop now so you don't have see me and this make me very unhappy." He put both hands on his heart again and Polly noticed how big they looked because the arms from which they extended were so thin, as was the rest of him. His body was almost skeletal and his eyes looked huge inside the drawn pale face. Suddenly she felt sympathetic rather than suspicious.

"If I come this way I'll call in."

"But you won't make special journey?"

"I have plans I must keep. Anyway, I have no need of a shawl, although they are of course beautiful."

"Still you think I want sell you shawl when I tell to you I want be your friend."

"I'm sure you have plenty of friends without me."

"I like friend in other country. Maybe one day I come visit. I have English girl for friend, but she write me mail and say she marry and her husband don't want her write me." Anil glanced at Polly's left hand as he had several times already. "I think maybe you have husband already?"

Polly didn't answer.

"But if you travel alone maybe you no longer together, or he don't mind you have friend in Nepal?"

"In England it's not unusual for men and women to be friends, but I think in Nepal it's different and may be you mean something else when you say 'friend' – I don't want that kind of friend. Anyway, Anil, you might not like England, it's very wet and not often very sunny."

"But I see pictures and is beautiful and clean and English people I meet are friendly. Is not fair. You come Nepal - you go anywhere and decide like or don't like, stay or go home, but for Nepali people this impossible. That's why I need friend to sponsor me." Polly wanted to object that it wasn't quite true. The English people who could afford to do as he was suggesting were in the minority too, but when the whole of Lakeside was geared to catering for tourists it was unlikely he would believe her. And her guilt at being one of that minority not only kept her silent on that subject, but also led her to say: "I'll write you an email, I promise."

"And you come again for tea?"

"Yes. I won't leave Pokhara without coming back for more masala tea."

One advantage of the encounter was that Polly felt perfectly able to browse the trinket shop now until she had made up her mind to buy Anthony a singing bowl and give him his father's khukri.

With no interest other than an academic one in the healing qualities of the singing bowl Polly had made her choice on size and price alone, but of course the Tibetan shop keeper demonstrated several and informed her on how effective different pitches were in the treatment of particular health problems. And of course, he tried to talk her into buying other trinkets and lamented at length on the plight of the Tibetan people.

Polly returned to the hotel quite exhausted by the complexity of thoughts and emotions with which she'd been bombarded in a single afternoon. As she lay on the bed thinking through the events of the afternoon and wishing there were someone with whom she could share her feelings she was momentarily overcome by self-pity. It was arrested by recalling the conversation with Anil and the Tibetan refugee and replaced by guilt at her comparatively privileged position. Again she thought she might remain in Nepal and taking up some kind of voluntary work. Though this seemed right in many respects it also felt patronising and it was her belief that by living in, and contributing towards, a capitalist society, she was part of the cause and voluntary work only perpetuated the problem. Yet alongside this she felt not only gratitude at being one of the lucky ones, but also a sense of responsibility to make the best of her advantaged position exactly because there were those who were unable to do so.

Polly got up and walked out on to the balcony. This time the light was fading into evening and the sun was setting pink over the Fishtail mountain. Again she imagined Ned beside her and tried to decide what he would have liked her do, but instantly she realised that she would never have been considering what to do with the rest of her life if he were still alive. He was enough to give it meaning, although she hadn't always fully appreciated that at the time. And then she thought of Arjun, imagining him sitting with his guest in one of the tea houses and she tried to remember which one it would be on day four of the trek. Thinking of him she felt lonely and sad, warm at the prospect of his return, and yet more than a little ashamed of her desire for him. Not only because of his family, but also because it was proof that her memory of Ned was becoming less sacrosanct.

The sun descended, removing Machhapuchhare from visibility, but when it rose again in the morning she would see the mountain was still there. Sometimes it was obscured by cloud, others it stood stark in bright blue skies, but always it was there. And so it was with her love for Ned.

*

Uma's words echoed back from time to time in the next few days. Whilst she washed clothes, swept the yard, cooked dhal baht, Kabita drifted into a dream world in which she stood behind a market stall smiling as English speaking costumers, with whom she was able to converse, tried to barter for lower prices. In her imagination she had already learnt the full range of skills, put aside enough of her land for growing the plants for dyes and completed an English course at college. Bosiram was no more than ten and she had earned enough to consider the possibility of moving to the city where he could attend an English school, but come home every day; and where there was a house big enough to have separate rooms for all, her daughters and parents in-law. Sometimes too Bishnu crept into the fantasy. Now, independently wealthy, she had no need of his financial support only of his company.

Kabita thought of her cousin Sawsati, whom she secretly admired for having the courage to abandon both husband and young daughter to move to the city with the man she claimed love for. And how, although there had been the inevitable scandal at the time, in barely more than five years it became an historical event of little importance to anyone. The husband had remarried and the daughter moved to the city to be with her mother. If only Kabita had the same courage she could pursue Bishnu as a husband and expect a scandal of comparatively minor proportions which would soon be forgotten, but she was far too ordinary and orthodox for that. Besides, even as she thought it Kabita felt she tainted Ram's memory and negated his love. Not that she would expect to love or be loved by Bishnu; only that there might be some mutual respite from the all-consuming loneliness and someone worth making her dream future a reality for.

The dusky light played tricks on her eyes and for a second it seemed that Ram was standing in the shadow of the doorway offering a pleading look, the meaning of which it was difficult to interpret, but it startled her back to reality. Kabita knew that if she left this house she would lose the few moments when Ram returned to her and that no one could ever take his place in her life or her bed unless she did so.

*

It was early afternoon when Arjun knocked on the door to announce his return from the trek. "It's good to have you back." Polly said, finding true sentiment in the words.

"Did you miss me?"

"A little. Did you miss me?"

"Yes" - he was standing just inside the door which was open only a fraction, "too much!" The foot distance between them was full of apprehension. "I come speak with you later about what you want do. Okay?" Arjun made a small movement with his head that was tick-like.

"Okay."

After a seconds hesitation he turned, opened the door and left. But the room remained full of him.

CHAPTER TWENTY-ONE.

Christmas day. Polly sat outside in the front garden eating breakfast, feeling the warmth of the sun on her back. On the table opposite two Japanese men talked with Arjun in their native language. He rested his hand on the shoulder of the younger, which he patted as he left them to sit opposite Polly.

"Happy Christmas."

"Thanks. Actually I'm trying to forget about it."

"Why? Why you want forget?" He asked, inclining his head to the right and shrugging his shoulders.

Because she thought Arjun had probably had enough of her grief she minimised the real reason. "Christmas is for children. I haven't enjoyed it so much since mine grew up. And it's not the same without Ned."

"Of course will be different, but still can be good. Everything change."

Polly wondered if, in reality, he accepted change as readily as in his rhetoric. Then she thought back to the previous year and how all she had wanted was for the day to be over. She remembered how it was the very routine aspects of Christmas day that had induced the most extraordinary sense of loss. And how she had longed for one year hence and to be exactly where she was now. Though there was a little sadness and guilt because she wasn't at home now, she knew she hadn't really been there last year either. Her feelings must have shown on her face because Arjun said: "You still want go home when planned?"

A few days earlier she and Arjun had discussed the possibility of extending her ticket for another month, but Polly had decided it would be better to go home, research what voluntary work she'd like to do and then return next year. The decision was made in part, in light of the knowledge that Arjun planned to spend most of February with his family and Polly thought if she stayed longer she'd need his help to find a cheaper way to live. Besides this, in the back of her mind was the acknowledgement that there was less point in staying an extra month if he wasn't there. "Yes. I do."

"When you want go back to Kathmandu?"

"I'm not sure, what do you think?"

"Maybe you want see other things there. Pashupatinath Temple,

Bodhnath, maybe you want go to Bhaktapur, very beautiful place with many temple. Maybe you bored with Pokhara."

"No, I love it here, but I have to go back to Kathmandu to fly home so I guess I may as well spend some time sight-seeing. I'll give myself a week there, I think."

That left her with almost two in Pokhara and no plans, but the ambience was such that just to be there produced a calmness and ability to live in the moment so that she needed none. Ned was right, Pokhara was a very special place and she knew she would return someday. The boy from the kitchen came to take away her breakfast dishes: "Happy Christmas," he said with a big smile and near perfect pronunciation despite his very limited vocabulary.

"Dhanyabahd." As Polly thanked him she realised that here too was a potential friend of the future, as they had been teaching each other bits and pieces of their prospective languages and she had grown rather fond of him.

Arjun said something to him in a jovial tone.

"What did you say to him?"

"I tell him you don't like Christmas."

"Oh! I wish you hadn't, he was so proud of himself."

"Why he proud of two word? He can be proud when fluent."

"He needs praise to encourage him to learn."

Arjun looked hurt. "Was only joke and he know that," he said in a sulky tone.

"I wasn't criticising you Arjun. Please don't be hurt."

He sat sideways on the chair with his arms folded and a pout on his face.

Polly reached her hand across the table to touch his. "I wasn't criticising," she repeated, "really I wasn't."

"Okay!" Now he smiled and inclined his head in a tick-like movement. "When I learn no one praise unless I very good, always they say work harder, try more."

Polly thought in that case no wonder he was so sensitive to criticism. "Well, English teachers think every effort no matter how small should be praised."

Arjun nodded. "Maybe is better way, I don't know. What you going to do today?"

"I have no plans. How about you?"

He shrugged: "Maybe I call to my boss in Kathmandu and see if anyone come for trek and I hang out in Lakeside with my friends."

Polly felt disappointed at the thought of him going trekking again and spending more time without him, even though it only amounted to a couple of conversations a day.

"Maybe you go see your shop keeper friend." Arjun teased.

"Maybe I will."

Polly had told him about Anil and about the young man who'd propositioned her. It was the evening of the day he'd returned from the last trek and they'd been sitting on the balcony outside the rooms, Polly reading, Arjun waiting for the kitchen boy to bring him some cigarettes.

"I was really shocked by the things he said to me."

"This man, he want make money from sex and these people exist in all culture. But also Nepali men think European women good for sex because they freer. Nepali women only do to please men and have baby."

"What all Nepali women?"

"Yes, I think." He nodded vigorously, pursing his lips.

"I find that hard to believe."

"Is true. Nepali man and woman don't talk each other about sex they are too shy. This why Nepali men want European women and always they fascinated by her."

"Really?" Polly said, with incredulity and perhaps a little scorn because Arjun then said: "Yes, really," in a very firm tone.

"I think I'm a bit old for men to be fascinated by me."

"No, I don't think." And his eyes, as he held her gaze a little too long, revealed the utmost sincerity, so that Polly was embarrassed and looked away.

"Anil wants a visa, perhaps that's what other men want." Polly wondered if that was perhaps Arjun's motive for flirting with her, but instinct told her otherwise.

"Maybe some, but other want benefit of your experience. You very sexy lady."

"It's not proper to speak that way to me," she made her tone exaggeratedly playful to ensure he understood she was teasing him.

And Arjun laughed heartily.

Now as Polly considered suggesting they go on another trek, she contemplated the implications of doing so and decided against it, but not firmly enough to keep her from returning to it as a possibility several times during the day. The prospect seemed most attractive when she strolled along the main street to the accompaniment of Paul McCartney, Bob Geldof and Greg Lake, and least attractive as she sat at the far end of the lake in comparative solitude; enjoying the stillness and experiencing every moment fully.

The quietude made Polly consider how it was one thing to savour the moment, but quite another to live only in the present as Buddhist philosophy suggested. It occurred to her to be fully in the now it was necessary to lose both memory and aspiration, but in so doing surely ones humanity was also lost. But perhaps that was the point. There were times, at the height of her grief, when Polly had been so stuck in the moment that, far from memory being lost, it became fixated on a single event.

The minutes ticked away, edging slowly towards the time when it would be convenient to telephone Christine and speak with the whole family who would be there for lunch. Strange to think that Christmas had started five hours earlier for her than for her family. The relative nature of time was most apparent when measured by a particular event. If she thought about the time that had passed since Ned's death it could only be understood in those terms: two Christmases without him, one birthday, one wedding anniversary; but if she were asked how long it felt, it seemed both forever ago and only a few days.

*

There had been tears, in fact almost a full blown tantrum, from Indira when Sandeep had come to take the goat for slaughter. It had been sufficient to create the impression in both her mother and uncle that she was still too much of a child for the marriage in whose honour the goat was being killed. Secretly Kabita shared her daughter's feelings because she too considered the goats to have personalities, which the chickens did not. The remainder of the preparations she put her heart into fully and in the village generally there was a growing sense of excitement as the wedding day drew closer.

The atmosphere in the house was utterly altered by the impending wedding, suspending normal life; although for Kabita at least, it had never restarted after Ram's death. In Indira it induced restlessness causing her to start and abandon tasks before they were complete. Her behaviour reflected the conflicting emotions she experienced. Feeling sometimes every bit the child her family observed her to be she wanted to stamp her feet, cling to her mother, her grandparents and brothers and cry. Yet equally she looked forward to her new role and imagined a future in which she was respected and adored by Hari and his family alike, for reaching far beyond being merely a dutiful wife and daughter in-law. Very secretly, so much so it was almost a secret even to her own heart, she looked forward to developing a proper knowledge of what she had tasted with Kapil.

The same restlessness could be observed in Ram's mother. At least Kabita hoped that it was excitement which produced these symptoms and not a problem related to age. Often she wondered how her in-laws really were, because sometimes she heard one or other crying when they thought they were unobserved. And both, especially Ram's father, had aged since the loss of their son. How would she cope with aged in-laws who needed care? She wondered now, remembering from her childhood days how Sanita's grandmother had several times wandered into their family home and frightened her with her silly talk. Once she had even defecated on the floor; angering Sanita's mother; which seemed a more real response than her own mother's orders to be patient and understanding. How would she cope if one or both of them should end up that way? Without her daughter's assistance, she could only pray that it if it happened she would have a good daughter in-law to help. These thoughts produced not only concern for her daughter at the knowledge Indira's soon to be mother in-law was already in need of considerable help, but also fear for own future. The taken for granted idea that she would be cared for, if necessary, by a daughter in-law she couldn't even imagine the like of, was unnerving. Perhaps she should embark on the project with Uma, because at least if she had some money she could pay for help if it were needed. Things were changing in Nepal, the traditional ways giving way to new ideas and she should have the courage to change with them.

Kabita wished she had the same courage and imagination that Ram had had, which was sufficient to work towards a different kind of future for his family. Now she considered another possibility. That it was no coincidence Uma had tried to persuade her to go to the project, but was in fact another way in which Ram continued to influence things indirectly now that he was no longer able to do so any other way. That Ram had wanted a different future for his children, one with greater choices, couldn't be questioned; perhaps the project was Kabita's opportunity to help both her daughter and herself. Even when Ram was alive to consult with, making a decision had often been hard for fear of divine retribution, but without him she feared not only the wrath of Brahma, but of Ram too.

*

The red banners wished 'Happy New Year' in yellow italic writing, swaying almost imperceptibly above the heads of those at whom it was aimed. On the ground the sun glinted on the aluminium trays of the restaurateurs who had moved their wares outside into the cordoned off roads and dressed themselves and their tables in oranges, golds and reds. The atmosphere was one of expectation and celebration, but Polly stayed home.

Earlier she had taken her daily walk along Lakeside and observed the preparations, but she had no desire to join in with the festivities, not because of any inherent dislike, but because she felt self-conscious being alone at such a time. The departure to Kathmandu had been delayed by Arjun going away on a five day trek from which he would return only just in time for leaving Pokhara.

The occasion of New Year led her again to thinking about her future and how, with all predictability removed it was impossible to imagine how it would be. In all previous scenarios there were common, taken for granted aspects; the most predictable of all being Ned's presence. So, now that he had gone, Polly knew, really knew, there was nothing to be relied upon forever. However now, for the first time since his death, thinking about the future didn't only make her feel insecure, but excited too because of the many and varied potentials. Potentials which she acknowledged, again for the first time since Ned's death, she had some control over. There was even irony in the fact that in many respects her options were greater without the need for considering Ned.

The day before she left for Kathmandu Polly drank masala tea with Anil and he finally showed her the shawls. She bought two, one for Mia and one for herself.

CHAPTER TWENTY TWO

Outside the Pashupatinath Temple tellers sold incense and garlands of marigolds to the devotees, many of whom could be observed practising ritual bathing in the waters of the Bagmati river; along with sadhus, their bodies coloured grey by ash. By the gates of the temple the more traditional holy men, dressed in saffron robes, joined the destitute in begging for money. Polly, like all non- Hindus was forbidden entry to the temple itself, but through the entrance could see the mighty statue of Nandi, Shiva's bull, which dated back to the nineteenth century, her guide informed her. He then led her, without warning, to the commoner's side of the river and invited her to photograph the funeral pyre. From whose embers, which still glowed under the care of the single relative squat beside it, a foot protruded. Polly declined, imaging how she would have felt if someone had photographed Ned's coffin as it the curtains closed on it and feeling more than a little disgust towards the tourists who clicked their cameras readily. If she had been consulted she would have chosen not to come at all.

After the tour she complained to Arjun, who sat on the bank of the river waiting for her because only official temple guides were permitted here and he had no desire to enter the temple for other reasons.

"I'm sorry," he said, "most tourists want see."

"Well, it doesn't seem right to me."

He put his arm around her shoulder and rubbed her left arm, "I think people don't mind, but next tourist I bring, I tell them first." Then he edged her gently forwards. "I take you Bodhnath now."

Arjun sat in the front of the taxi for the short ride between the two places, he wore a down jacket and woollen hat, Polly felt perfectly warm enough in her thick cardigan, although the temperature in Kathmandu was noticeably much cooler than in Pokhara.

Bodhnath Stupa lay at the centre of a Tibetan village, comprised largely of refugees who had fled the Chinese in the late nineteen-fifties. The Stupa itself was a huge white dome crowned by a square head painted pink and culminating in a hay coloured pinnacle, which was reminiscent of an English seventeenth century hair style as it rose into the air. On the square head a face was depicted, oval eyes, slanted brows, between which the dot of a third eye had been painted, and a squiggle for a nose. There was no mouth and Polly wondered if that were deliberate, a place to contemplate, not speak. And this reminded her of one of Ned's favourite Native American quotes: 'Listen or your tongue may make you deaf.' Around the Stupa was a wall, which a man with a bucket of white wash was repainting with a broom and inside the wall people practised Tai Chi.

As Polly and Arjun walked the perimeter Arjun explained that the building of the Stupa had been commissioned by a wealthy woman who had born five children by five different husbands. Polly was most interested in this fact and asked Arjun wasn't that kind of behaviour considered scandalous in Nepal?

He shrugged. "She rich, she do what she like."

They ate lunch and drank tea in a roof top café that overlooked the whole village; which was comprised mainly of three story terracotta coloured buildings, with iron balconies and flat roofs that housed water storage tanks, solar panels and potted plants. On the ground floor from beneath canopies, vendors sold traditional Tibetan wares and throughout the entire village multi-coloured prayer flags flew, creating a sense of celebration. Arjun explained that each of the five colours represented an element and on each flag was a prayer, which would eventually, when left to those elements, be taken off into the cosmos. Polly didn't tell him that she already knew because Ned had been fascinated by the idea.

The sun was out now and Arjun had removed both his hat and jacket and, as he rolled up the sleeves of his sweat shirt Polly looked with admiration on his fore arms and remembered how much she had loved the same in Ned, but his had culminated in large square hands that were so in keeping with his practical nature, whereas Arjun's were long and slender. As if aware of her thoughts Arjun cracked the fingers of his left hand one by one then apologised: "Sorry, I forget you don't like."

They took the same taxi back to Thamel and arranged a pick up for Bhaktapur the following morning. As they walked back towards the hotel they were approached first by a man selling flutes and then another selling beaded jewellery. Polly was becoming good at ignoring their requests for her to purchase. But the beggars were quite a different storey and she always kept some small notes easily accessible. This time they saw three, one of whom was a very elderly looking man to whom Polly gave one hundred rupees. Arjun gave him money too: "I think in England old peoples with no family is look after by Government," he said as if an explanation were required, "in Nepal is not so. There only one Government home, it in Kathmandu, but is no good and not enough room for everyone."

Polly didn't bother to say that it was a similar situation in England as she had done so many times to ill effect. "Aren't there any charities working with older people?"

"I don't know, maybe, but mostly charity work with childrens or with project for village."

Polly had no difficulty imagining why that would be; work with older people was hardly considered valuable in her own country, after all. She thought of the grimy man to whom she had given what amounted to about one pound and how he had smiled and offered a 'namaste' as if it were one hundred. Two brown teeth clung half- heartedly to his upper gums, she didn't think there were any on the bottom. She remembered how abhorrent it had been witnessing the removal of false teeth when she worked, during her student years, at a home for older people and she compared it to how appealing the naked gums of a new born baby appeared. She remembered too, the constant smell of faeces and urine and the feel of thin skin, often bruised purple or breaking down with sores. Then, she imagined washing the Nepali man in a primitive shower or even a bucket and struggling with his wasted limbs as she tried to dress him in clean clothes. There would doubtless be satisfaction in bringing water to a village that previously had none, in being part of an empowerment project for a minority group and certainly any work with children was rewarding. But no, it wasn't hard to imagine that there were few people who would choose to concern themselves with the needs of the elderly Nepalis. Yet such a charity must exist, she felt sure, for there was certainly a need and she began to consider it as an option for her voluntary work.

Back at the hotel there was little to do. About eight o'clock she would go to one of the many restaurants for her meal and then to bed, but in the meantime all she could do was read. Now that it was imminent she just wanted to go home, suddenly feeling the absence of her family and friends acutely.

*

Two evenings before the wedding Kabita and Indira walked together. They held hands as Kabita led the way up the hill and, as they finally sat down, perilously close to the spot Kapil had taken her to, Indira felt an intense sense of portent.

Kabita placed her arm around her daughter and coaxed her head down onto her shoulder so that she could stroke her hair as she used to do when Indira was a child. She wanted to talk to her about what to expect on her wedding night, so that she wouldn't be as frightened as Kabita herself had been and to reassure her that if it was a marriage as good as hers had been with Ram, it would soon become so much more than a chore. But she was too embarrassed and also a little concerned that her daughter might lose some respect for a mother who confessed to enjoying sex, so instead she said: "Everything will be fine for you and Hari. He is a nice boy; he will treat you with respect."

Indira felt ashamed, she was unworthy of such respect and she wanted to confess to her mother what she and Kapil had done, because she feared Hari would know it wasn't he who took her virginity. She wanted Kabita to either confirm or allay her fears, which, in the past few days had grown to almost obsessive proportion and seemed vindicated by the choosing of this very spot. If Hari did realise he might refuse her as his wife and with the secret out there would be even more shame on her family and herself. Yet, if he didn't know she would have confessed to her mother needlessly and risked the loss of her respect unnecessarily; which she feared still more than any other thing. Fleetingly she wished to have never done it, but in her heart knew it to be a lie because a part of her still wanted Kapil, and to have had a little of him was better than none at all.

Kabita brushed her daughter's hair away from her forehead and kissed her and as she enjoyed her last moments of mothering Indira, she thought about change. A chosen change was one thing, though often reason enough for apprehension as was clear from the way Indira was feeling now, but the change from wife to widow had come without warning. Until it happened there was an equal chance that she would be the first to die, but fate deemed otherwise and from that point on dictated a different future. She had been so sure of Ram's love, but it was part of her karma to lose him and she had yet to determine why and what lesson was required of her.

Though she sometimes still felt the effects of his love, it was no longer possible to experience it directly. It had gone up in the smoke of the funeral pyre, dispersed into the universe and was no longer attached to her. It had left her certain of one thing only – that nothing could be relied upon to turn out as expected. And so, because the only reassurance she was really able to offer her daughter was that she loved her, she remained silent, but continued to convey the message through her finger tips as she stroked Indira's hair and face. Maybe the time had come for her to accept Ram as the past and focus on the people who were still alive and whom she had so badly neglected in her grief.

*

It was their last supper together, indeed Polly's last in Nepal. By this time tomorrow she would be flying over Europe, well on her way home.

Yesterday they had visited Bhaktapur. The beautiful medieval town, whose input from European project workers was evident in the cleanliness of the streets and the restoration of the buildings. In the fourteenth century it was the capital of the Kathmandu valley, Arjun informed Polly as he led her around Durbar Square, where two stone lions guarded the entry gate to the school and King Bhupatinrda Malla sat on his column, arms folded, studying the entrance to his palace.

In the art gallery Arjun enhanced the English explanatory scripts with his own knowledge of Hindu Gods; and Polly considered how, although the style was very different to European art, the content was very similar with the basis on religious stories.

In Potter's Square she watched a potter turn his wheel and transform damp clay into a pot in minutes. They went from there to the Thanka school of art, where she purchased a small mandala, having first learnt about the method and materials used in their creation. As they headed towards Taumadhi Tole they stopped for a few minutes to watch an elderly lady as she wove on a manual loom and who demanded fifty rupees in return for the photograph Polly took.

In Taumadhi Tole they viewed the five-story thirty-metre tall Nyatapola Temple, which was built in traditional Newari pagoda style, its steps lined on either side by carved elephants. Polly was overwhelmed by both the quantity and quality of the historic buildings in Bhaktapur. And amidst it all, the colour of every day Nepali life, pulses pouring from sacks, grains and dyed yarns laid out to dry in the sun. From the balcony of Café Nyatapola, they joined the throng of tourists who looked out over the square as they ate lunch and drank tea. Below them a teenage girl washed her hair at the communal tap; children played a game that looked to Polly like hop scotch and two men played backgammon, sitting opposite each other on stools.

When Polly had returned to the hotel she had felt deflated and this underlined the desire she felt to have someone special with whom to share her excitement over what had been a lovely day out.

She was in similar mood now, enjoyment tainted by the knowledge that these were her last few hours with Arjun. She watched him pushing the food around his plate, his head almost on the arm that rested on the table.

"Don't you like it – you can order something else."

"Is fine." He took a mouthful as if in emphasis, quickly followed by another, but hardly raised his head. Then he pushed the plate away: "I'm sorry, I'm not hungry, I pay for this since I waste."

"It doesn't matter!"

He looked up as he called the waiter over. Although she didn't understand the language Polly knew he would have ordered two cigarettes, because that's what he always did at the end of a meal. When the waiter returned, Polly realised he ordered another drink too.

Under the circumstances Polly found it difficult to finish her meal, but she wanted to prolong the time with Arjun. As she ate he watched her intently, taking long draws on his cigarette and twisting his mouth and head to blow the smoke away from the table. He finished it quickly, stubbed it out hard took several large gulps of beer, which emptied his glass half-way. "What I'm going to do tomorrow?"

"What d'you mean?"

"Tomorrow you be gone, what I'm going to do?"

"I'm sure it won't be long before another trekker comes along."

"You know what I mean."

"Yes," Polly lowered her eyes.

Arjun scrambled in his pocket, finally pulling his company's business card from his wallet and writing on it before presenting it to Polly. This my email address and this my cell phone number, you must promise you write me mail."

"I promise."

"You must give me yours. I want you give me now, I don't want take chance you don't mail me, may be you lose then we lose each other." He passed another business card to Polly, on which she obediently wrote both her telephone numbers and her email address.

They each had another drink by which time the restaurant was filling up and the waiters were hovering, obviously wanting them to pay up and leave. The now familiar streets that led back to the hotel were populated with tourists and touts as usual, but now Polly was annoyed by them. She felt like shouting in response to the requests to browse in shops and like pushing the strolling tourists out of her way so that she could run back to the safety of the hotel and vent her true feelings in private.

But at the hotel Arjun said: "I come with you."

The hotelier passed her the key, knowing her well enough to have no need of enquiring which room number, and he and Arjun exchanged a few words, which Polly knew were concerned with her.

Inside her room Arjun said: "I think I say goodbye now, I don't want come airport. I already ask man on desk to order taxi for you, for six am."

"Thank you. – So, this is goodbye then?" Polly swallowed hard and then feigned cheer as she offered her hand to shake and said: "I plan to come back."

Arjun ignored the gesture and pulled her roughly towards him into an embrace. Polly wrapped her arms around him and laid her head on his chest, feeling relief at finally being where she wanted to be. Arjun lifted her face towards him, brushed back her hair and gently kissed her on the mouth, to which she responded in the same manner. They held each other for several minutes. Polly's whole consciousness became filled with him and she felt the bliss of losing herself. They kissed again: "I could stay." Arjun whispered. One word, one small word and they would be united. In Arjun's embrace she felt as lost and safe as she had with Ned and she wanted to fall into him, but a part of her was still not quite ready and Malcolm teased the back of her mind. But this wasn't like with Malcolm. Then she had wanted company and sex, this time she wanted the man; and, if she was really careful she could afford a journey here every year. But what was she thinking of? What about his wife? And to heighten their feelings for each other would be to sharpen loss and then, like the original one, it would pulse through every heart beat and undermine healing: "There's nothing I'd like more but. . . ."

"My wife?"

"Yes. And tomorrow."

Arjun pushed her head back into his chest and stroked her hair. "You will come back?"

"Yes."

Now he eased away slightly and looked at her: "tell me to go."

Stay, hovered on Polly's lips; she said nothing.

"Tell me to stay, then."

Now it teased the end of her tongue, but still she said nothing. The air between them was too thick to breathe.

Then suddenly Arjun said: "Don't forget mail me," and pushed her away quite definitely.

"I won't," Polly grabbed at him as he turned his back towards her and headed for the door: they exchanged a hard and guarded kiss. He held her by the shoulders and looked deep into her as he said: "I go now. Goodbye."

As the door closed behind him Polly flung herself on the bed and let go of the tears that had waited for release all evening.

*

CHAPTER TWENTY THREE.

From inside the house Indira heard the music of the panche baja, which was her only clue that the procession from Hari's village was almost with her. Outside, in the street, the villagers were out in force and there was much celebration and jubilation which would soon be followed by the parsone feast.

Indira's body felt fixed to the spot, but her consciousness soared above the scene; so that she felt she was a spectator, as her mother and grandmother dressed her in the gold necklace and bangles that Hari had presented as a gift and then led her to the door to meet him. As he accepted their presents Indira kept her eyes on her feet, noticing that there was a hole in the embroidery of the slipper on her left foot. As they were led towards the platform on which they would sit together she was forced to raise them in order to avoid tripping; although still she managed not to look at Hari.

Throughout the parsone feast Indira was acutely aware of him, she could feel that he was barely any taller than her and tell that he was boyish still. She sensed his fear was as great as hers. She knew he ate heartily of the khasiko mahsu; whilst she couldn't bear even a mouthful because she had known the goat when alive. And, in fact she had little appetite for anything at all, which clearly delighted the guests who no doubt perceived it as coyness.

Indira sat through the feast like a statue, feeling the same inside. She thought about her father and wished he were there; then realised that none of this would be taking place if he were still alive and felt again regret, because perhaps she and Kapil could really have been together then. Yet she felt relief too because her guilt would have been ten- fold if he were. Then, as she wondered if her encounter with Kapil would have happened at all without her father's death she felt something else, something akin to consolation. And this shamed her deeply. So much so that she was sure it showed in her eyes as she was finally forced to look directly at Hari during the swayambar in which they exchanged their garlands. Now that she did she saw that she had been right in her assessment, he was indeed handsome and in his eyes she was relieved to see both fear and compassion in equal measure.

Yet, as the ceremonial fire sparked into flame Indira couldn't help but think of the flames of the funeral pyre to which she had not been witness, and how, obedience to Gods and men had led, in the not so distant past, to the practice of sati. As they cast the grain into the fire she thought of it, not as an offering to the Gods to ensure prosperity for their futures, but as a sign of her mother's sacrifice. Not only literally in the providing of the grain and the bride, but symbolically too, but as soon as Hari took her hand and led her around the fire she felt reassured again. There was firmness to his touch that was decidedly masculine, yet it was tempered by a fineness that promised a lack of dominance.

Although Kabita's eyes were not always on her daughter, the only time her heart and mind strayed away from her was for the second she mistook Hari's uncle for Bishnu. A mistake probably sparked by wondering the evening before if Sandeep would have invited him, but she knew that really he wasn't close enough in blood or friendship. She was in fact relieved, because his presence would no doubt have distracted her from dutiful thoughts; if not behaviour. It was from such that Kabita now drank the duordai-pathi offered by Hari's family to repay her years of suckling Indira, because she liked neither cardamom nor molasses.

Being so physically close to her daughter whilst watching her being taken ever further away with each ritual was like experiencing a second bereavement, resurrecting many of the feelings from the first. Now she looked across at Sandeep engrossed in raksi and conversation and hated him; for looking so much like Ram, whilst being so unlike him.

*

It seemed a life time ago that Polly had watched the Himalayas come into view, feeling not only an affinity for the emotions Ned had described, but also full of anticipation at where her own journey would lead her. Now, as she watched them recede she felt a great sense of loss and knew that the uncharted places to which she'd been led had changed her forever. And she felt strangely closer to her deceased husband.

As Polly sat in the transfer lounge at Delhi airport, she felt full of misery. There were two hours to wait for the connecting flight to London and she spent them in depressive contemplation. Nepal represented a climax in the accepting of Ned's death, a final thing to do, but now that it was done, far from feeling like a conclusion it seemed only the beginning; and her grief was redoubled because it wasn't only Ned she missed.

She took her mobile telephone from her pocket and wrote a text: 'I'm missing you, can't wait until I return.' Then she hesitated, wondering if he would understand either the English or the intention and whether there would there be any chance that someone else would read it and trouble be caused for him as a result. Neither worry prevented the pressing of the send button. It was only seconds before the message arrived: 'sending failed. Retry?' Polly pressed the yes option, but when she received the same message a few seconds later she deleted the text entirely, feeling disappointed and relieved. Now it seemed an omen, a sign that she must go home and forget she and Arjun had ever met. Because of the many distances between them it should be easy, but even as she thought it she was tempted by the sight of the laptop offering free internet connection. If it became available in time she would test out the email, Polly decided.

She bought tea. For which she had to pay over the odds in pounds as she had no Indian rupees and they no English change. Before she had finished drinking the tea, which was too strong and almost cold, the laptop became available. Logging in was a lengthy process. Her mobile number was required, which she didn't know by heart so she had to rummage in her bag for her pocket diary and then through it until she found the number, and then wait for a text message to say she was registered. Polly started several times, erasing each message after the first few words, but finally she wrote: "Hi Arjun, I'm testing this out to make sure it works. Thank you so much for everything you did for me. I hope it won't be too long until we meet again," then she agonised for several minutes over how to sign it before deciding on, 'love Polly;' which was, after all, how she signed all informal emails. And then, because there was still time remaining before her free half-an-hour was up she emailed her children and Mia and James to say that she was looking forward to seeing them all soon.

When they called her through to security Polly put the single valium pill into her purse, deciding to take it as soon as she was on the aeroplane.

*

Indira tried to mean it and block Kapil from her mind as she repeated with Hari: "May our hearts and minds be united by our vows, full of love for each other. May we remember God has brought our unison with infinite grace. From today onwards your heart is mine, mine yours." The priest had witnessed their words, now she was obliged to mean them, but how could she silence what was already in her heart enough to 'listen attentively and lovingly' as she had promised? And how could she be sure to love Hari when she didn't even know him? The best she could do was to try her hardest and this she promised herself silently as she spoke the mantra aloud.

As Hari rubbed the sindura into her forehead Indira could feel the shaking of his hand and heard a slight change in the rhythm of his breathing. Assuming it to be in anticipation of taking away the virginity it symbolised filled her once more with guilt and fear. She knew how little she deserved the goodwill and affection of the guests that was being offered by the shower of flowers. As Indira received the petals from her mother's hand she remembered that her honour was at stake too, and prayed that her own mistake would not be discovered.

Kabita prayed too. That her daughter might have the happy marriage she had, and that her own karma was not so bad her daughter need suffer the pain and indignity of widowhood.

*

Despite the valium haze Polly felt total empathy for Fanny Brawne, as she watched her portrayed by Abbie Cornish in Bright Star. And, as she collapsed at the news of John Keats death and cried: "I can't breathe, Mama," Polly wept aloud; feeling the grief as if it were her own, empathising with both Fanny's loss and unconsummated love.

*

Ram's mother watched Kabita wandering in and out of the house as if searching for something, feeling again the empty space that had never been quite refilled since Ram's passing. Now, watching Kabita, it was clear that she too was feeling the other loss resurrected.

Indira had clung to her mother and cried almost to the point of indignity and had kept her eyes on Kabita until the very last minute, as she was led away on the back of the donkey. Kabita felt her stomach sink, she felt the hole left by Ram become a pit into which she wished to throw herself, but then Bosiram and duty rescued her. Now, as the sun was setting and the family preparing for bed, she imagined her daughter in her new home, performing the familiarising ceremonies with her new mother and felt jealous and empty and wished Ram was there.

*

Drizzle greeted Polly at Heathrow. Descending onto the tarmac she couldn't help but make a comparison with the landing in Kathmandu. The alienation she had felt then was entirely due to unfamiliar surroundings and customs, and exactly because those had become known to her she now experienced the same in her well-known environment.

Just inside the terminal she spotted Christine and Dan before they saw her, so was well prepared with a smile at the ready by the time her daughter ran towards her, but still tensed a little in response to her embrace.

"Oh, we've missed you," Christine said. "It's good to have you back safe and sound. Is it good to be back, or have you had such a great time you wish you were still there?"

"Well, both I guess."

Dan hugged her too and took the rucksack from her back. She watched as he threw it effortlessly onto one shoulder – the action reminding her of another man.

In the car she was bombarded with questions, which she answered enthusiastically, whilst knowing really the most meaningful parts lay in the spaces between the words and could never be communicated even if she felt inclined to try. The windscreen wipers dashed away the persistent rain leaving a misty view of the darkening motorway that appeared clinically tidy.

As they pulled up outside her house Polly checked her watch, which remained on Nepalese time, noticing that it was a little after one in the morning she pictured Arjun's sleeping face, as clearly as if she'd actually been witness to it. Inside the house there was a strange atmosphere that unnerved her. It felt as if a stranger had just recently left the room and all of her possessions seemed out of time. It was like looking at an old family photograph, in which everyone was familiar, but exactly who they were was impossible to recall.

"Gosh! It feels like a very long time since I was home." She said.

*

The night was still as stone - in perfect keeping with Indira's heart, which she prayed would stop for real. Beside her Hari lay in noiseless sleep, the rigidity having left his body only moments earlier as he finally relaxed. Indira thought in misery of what had gone before and Hari's words prevented sleep from coming: "I can't, I'm sorry - I can't." He must have known from touching her, or perhaps, as she tried to be neither too eager nor unwilling, some clue of previous knowledge had slipped into her behaviour. Then, as now, she tried to keep comparison with Kapil out of her mind from fear of audible thoughts or whispers in her sleep, but maybe her body had let her down. The only thing for which Indira was grateful was the darkness. There was no sense of reprieve as he rolled onto his side, turning his back towards her, because she wanted the accusation to be voiced and in the open. As things were, her future was as uncertain as before the marriage.

Several times during the night Indira sensed Hari's wakefulness and feigned sleep and the more so in the morning as he rose without looking at her and hurried from the room. Manners required her to follow, but she had no idea how quickly she should do so.

As she descended into the kitchen area she was met by the homely smell of wood smoke, but it was the only thing that was familiar. The wood pile was in the corner where the pots should have been stored and the doorway was on the wrong side of the room, so that the light came from the wrong direction, but most significantly, the wrong woman squatted by the fire cooking breakfast. And, although she greeted Indira with a large smile, there was no real sense of warmth from either her or the fire she tended. Indira stood rigidly in front of her mother-in-law awaiting instructions, feeling like a servant.

"Did you have a good sleep?" There was a glint of knowledge, recognition and also jealousy in her mother-in-laws gaze.

"Yes."

"Good. You can go outside to Hari. He is with his father."

Indira did as she was bidden. Hari and his father were engaged in conversation which ceased as soon as she arrived, and she couldn't help but feel the conversation had been about her. Perhaps Hari had even told his father and sought advice on how to deal with her. Confirmation came in the fact that Hari looked away from his bride. Indira's embarrassment was such that she felt naked before their eyes and her consequential shame made her desire to be beaten to death.

*

Polly woke at four in the morning after five hours sleep. For a second she couldn't remember where she was, but when she did felt disappointed. For almost an hour she lay thinking back over her trip, her marriage, her life.

There was no uncertainty as to whether the kitchen light would come on in response to the press of a switch. The boiling water for her cup of tea was almost instantaneous in arriving. A second switch responded instantly to her touch and boosted the heating system. Polly looked at her watch, eleven-fifteen, Friday, the load shedding would be coming to an end and she would be reluctantly leaving the sunny garden to take her shower in time to use the hair dryer before the electricity was cut again. Then she looked at the digital display on the DVD and finally adjusted her watch back to English time, feeling it a final act of arrival.

It was still dark outside, too early to open the heavy floor length curtains. She turned the dimmer switch up full so that her living room was full of bright, artificial light. She removed her crocs and sank her bare feet into the thick pile carpet, remembering the threadbare one in her hotel room and then the bare stone floor in Kabita's house. Polly surveyed the china plates that decorated her Welsh dresser and remembered the metal ones from which she ate her meal at Kabita's house. And, as she perched on the edge of the sofa, thought of the wooden bench on which they'd sat. Now Polly felt alienated by her affluence.

*

Everyone, it seemed, was interested in viewing her. People from the village came with any small excuse to visit, or to their doors as she passed by carrying out some duty. Indira felt like an exhibit and wondered how long it would take before gossip about her failing marriage reached the ears of those who surveyed her now with curiosity, but soon with accusations. Four more nights had passed and on every occasion Hari had climbed into the bed beside her and fallen asleep without so much as speaking to her. During the day his dutiful behaviour was performed with such distance it seemed he was one of those who had come to view the new arrival.

Indira felt utterly lost, knowing there was neither end nor happy solution to her situation. She missed her mother, her brothers and grandparents. And she wished she could be with her father.

*

Sleep had come slowly to Kabita on the wedding night as awareness that her daughter would be having her first sexual encounter made her think of her own. The memory was hazy because she had been full of fear, reserve and even a little guilt, which had kept her slightly remote from the experience, but it wasn't long before Ram's considerate nature and their closeness changed things. And, as her body responded with longing to the memories Kabita felt enraged at herself and her situation and then profoundly lonely.

CHAPTER TWENTY-FOUR

Every time she related any of her experiences Polly felt she was misleading her listeners by failing to convey the way it really was, but also she enjoyed the feeling that she held a secret knowledge. It was a knowledge Ned had understood and had tried to share with her, but until now that had not been possible. It had taken his death to make her hear. Nepal had touched her soul and healed her in a much deeper way than she could ever have imagined before she went there. She was liberated by her rescuer role. And if it seemed that Nepal was possessed by some magical quality, she knew it was because it was Ned's special place and that she had connected with a part of him which remained mysterious to her, despite so many years together. The surprise of it reminded her of how he would always continue to influence her life. She was only the person she was now, because of the relationship they had shared. In this sense there was immortality. He would only disappear completely if she allowed him to.

Of Arjun she thought often with fondness and without regret. She recognised now that he had freed her from the belief that she could never love again and yet, in resisting the temptation of him, she understood she had the choice. No longer did she fear being alone, but neither was she afraid to open her heart to the possibility of loving another man.

Now she opened her mail box and read Arjun's message for the third time: "My dear friend Polly, I fel like fish who have no water now you go to home. Plese to return soon. Your dear friend Arjun."

She had yet to reply; she had after all promised him to return and she did feel inclined towards some voluntary work, but somehow it seemed better to leave her memories sacrosanct.

The morning was cold and crisp and, as Polly peered through the curtains at the white frost glinting on the pavement, she desired to be outside. Wrapping herself up in warm clothes she walked out of the front door towards the town. It was a dawn so cold it numbed her nose. It occurred to her now that the winter was the most honest of seasons; it promised nothing but what it gave. Perhaps the same would be true of the winter years of life when there was nothing left to prove. Although she hardly looked forward to it, the idea of living her older years alone worried her less these days, now it was possible to imagine a future productive enough to dampen the fear of death.

It still made her shudder to think of the method of Ned's death. Once she'd seen the drop off for herself Polly had stopped wondering if he would have been afraid, although really it had already been confirmed by the expression on his dead face. Consolation, if there were any to be had, came from remembering how he had once said that the greater the fear or pain the greater the release from it. Ned was released from everything now and finally she felt she could accept him as past from the world, yet ever present within her heart.

David, the only other man she had loved and on whom her own existence had once seemed to depend, was hardly more than a passing thought to her now, but she never wanted for that to be the case with Ned. Besides, as far as she knew David was alive somewhere thinking, being, doing; accepting Ned as nowhere and not being was the hardest thing she had ever had to do.

Dawn was breaking fully as she reached the town and the streets lights were going out one by one. The temperature was noticeably warmer here because of the shop lights. In Pokhara, with a few exceptions, the closed shops were clad in total darkness.

From the doorway of Boots a human form stirred inside his sleeping bag. Not for the first time, Polly wondered how anyone could survive outside in these temperatures, and she recognised the need for help for these victims of capitalism was as great as any in Nepal.

At the top of the main street she took a left turn to walk home through the park. A jogging couple reminded her that on her way out of Kathmandu on the tourist bus, she had seen people practicing tai chi in the park and soldiers on early morning exercise. Beneath the frost the grass was green and plentiful. In Pokhara it was brown and sparse and the three beer cans, which Polly collected and put into the recycling bin, were the only litter here. Despite the different smells, the air tasted the same there as here and the same sense of anticipation at the dawning of a new day stirred in Polly's stomach.

As she walked through the front door of her home she felt the sense that someone had just left. She sat in Ned's chair and surveyed the room, painted by him in the colours of her choice. On the bookcase she spotted his signed copy of a book by Chris Bonnington acquired at a talk they had both gone to. On the wall hung a painting he'd brought back from his first trip to Nepal and on the coffee table were the diaries, which she had been reading the night before. Everywhere there was evidence of the person Ned had been, but today there was more than this for Polly felt such a strong sense of him that it was as if she had gone on holiday alone, but returned with him.

*

On the wall, her left arm shielding the light from her eyes Ram's mother lay, unaware that she was being surreptitiously watched by Kabita, to whom it seemed her mother-in-law had done little else since the wedding.

Kabita continued sweeping the yard, feeling it was an act of no importance or need and considering it no less a waste of time than what her mother-in-law was doing. It was simply that the space left by family members needed somehow to be filled because the emotions that entered into every inactive moment threatened to overwhelm her.

Death robbed not only the dead of life, but the living too. In the unoccupied moments Kabita's heart and mind were filled by an emptiness that extended farther into the future than she could even imagine. In twenty- years- time when Bosiram was more than grown she would still be younger than Ram's mother was now, but without him she was doomed to fill her empty moments with pointless chores; or worse, to lie on the wall in either remembrance or forgetfulness.

By then she would probably have forgotten more of him than she remembered, because already he was becoming further from her thoughts. She no longer woke with his name in the forefront of her mind, some days it was even necessary to consciously resurrect him. Kabita wanted neither to forget him nor to misrepresent him with her memory, but she didn't know how to avoid either. Bosiram interrupted her musings by grabbing her around the leg and squeezing. His behaviour in the past few days indicated that he missed his sister perhaps more than he'd ever missed his father. Kabita picked him up, hugged him hard and kissed his forehead. When her older sons returned from school she noticed that they underlined Indira's absence.

*

The milk from the water buffalo felt thick, warm and slightly sticky to her hands as it flowed through them into the pail. She had to remember to look down at it from time to time to make sure it hadn't reached overflowing, because most of the time her eyes and attention were on Hari. Indira watched him as he tended the animals and chopped wood, knowing that in a matter of days he would be returning to his hotel job in Kathmandu and that she was genuinely going to miss him.

There was beauty in the way he did everything. She noticed the sinews in his forearms as he clenched the axe tight and raised it over his head; and each individual vertebra in his spine as he lent forward to collect the wood from the ground. She'd run her fingers up that same spine, as he slept with his back to her as usual, on the night he kissed her and held her close and she thought for a moment there would be more, as he stroked her hair and she felt the stirrings of desire against her thigh.

Now she observed his easy relationship with his mother. Envying as much the teasing way she scolded him as she did the laughter that passed between them. Lamenting the fact that they had not yet and might not ever, have that special knowledge of each other, but grateful that he hadn't sent her home and was even kind to her.

Indira's heart leapt as Hari looked back and smiled at her, as he strolled away towards the village on whatever errand his mother had sent him. She had just finished the milking when Hari's mother summoned her. Struggling to straighten her back, as she rose from the stool she was sitting on, she presented her daughter-in-law with a large urn and asked her to please fill it with water.

The urn slipped lightly onto her head but Indira knew that once full, the weight would bear down on her neck and shoulders and condemn her spine, in future years, to the same fate her mother-in-law now endured. And beneath her sandaled feet the cobble stones promised her feet no less.

Indira was becoming familiar with the route now that took her past the house in which Reikha lived with her four brothers and two sisters. Their skinny, black- eyed mother had been widowed like her own, but this time by the war. She was outside now, throwing clothes over the washing line and, as Indira passed, she called out to her that Reikha was engaged on the same errand.

Indira's heart leapt at the sight of Hari as she rounded the corner to the tap, then immediately sank to her stomach with the realisation.

"I was offering to carry the water for her," he said a little guiltily.

Indira acknowledged the other girl then said to Hari: "yes, it's very heavy."

"I'll come back and help you," he placed Reikha's urn on his head with seemingly little effort and no spillage.

Indira watched their backs until they disappeared from view. The synchronised steps, the faces forced forwards and the carefully respected distance between them confirmed what she had observed on arrival - something small enough to doubt, but large enough to cause distress.

Hari returned quickly and put Indira's urn on his head with the same confidence. As they walked he slipped one arm around her waist and Indira's soul rejoiced. Now she understood - she hadn't been his first choice either. But second choice didn't have to mean second best and, in a situation like theirs, where choices were limited, it was fortunate indeed that fate had given them each other.

*

As soon as the door- bell rang Polly knew who it was, James never arrived unannounced and Mia was out for the evening, and actually she'd been expecting him.

"Hi, Polly I thought I'd come and hear all about Nepal."

"Well, you hardly need me to tell you, you've been yourself."

"I'm sure your experience was very different to mine. Anyway, I need someone to help me drink this," Malcolm put one foot over the threshold, as he pushed the bottle towards her.

Polly routed him to the spot with her body and her will: "And where's your wife this time?"

"A girl's night in. I won't be able to stay all night."

"Why don't you take it home and share it with her later?"

"Huh!" It was a cross between a laugh and a sigh: "We had such a nice time before. Didn't we?"

"Last time, was the last time. I'm not going to say I shouldn't have or anything because that's stupid, but . . . "

"Let me in for a minute so we can talk."

"What would be the point?"

"You afraid you can't resist me?"

Polly didn't answer, neither did she move.

"I want to hear what you thought of Nepal."

"Loved it of course. I'll meet all you guys in the pub with some photos sometime."

"That'll be nice," he looked hard at her, with the sincerity she had noticed him capable of before: "So, you're sure?"

"Quite."

"See you around then."

It was a few minutes before Polly could settle back to her book. Although there wasn't even a second in which she considered allowing Malcolm in it nevertheless felt like a triumph, like she was vindicated by the passing of another test.

*

Uma came to say goodbye her face full of hope and enthusiasm, although Kabita knew it was only for a while she felt lonely at the prospect. They walked hand in hand together as far as the river, but the bus was already coming and so they parted in a rush, Uma turning to wave as she stepped on board. Kabita felt sad and bored and as if she was always the one left behind.

She sat by the river for a while feeling sorry for herself. How easy it would be and how desirable it seemed to slip into the water and allow the current to take her wherever it desired; how much easier than trying to shape her own destiny. Now she imagined she heard Ram's voice, speaking in scolding tone and chastising her for lacking courage. Cowardice had not only robbed her of any future happiness, but more than this it threatened the same for her children. She had behaved irresponsibly, looking all the time for Ram to guide her with signs, expecting him to be responsible for his family even after death.

It was no longer possible to experience love and guidance from him. As the flames took his body in the funeral pyre, the smoke carried his love away from her and his responsibility to his family went with it. Yet it was still possible to experience the effects of his love, in fact it was everywhere to be found. None less than in the respect her children showed her, or in the way they had such regard for his memory that they tried to do as they thought he would have wished.

Kabita knew now that this was the way he would stay with them and she was his living representative. There would be no mystical signs, neither would there be a return of Ram in the embodiment of a special child, it was up to her to live out his wishes on his behalf. And she knew exactly where to start.

*

Polly stared at the name and dates on the plaque; for only half of the fifty-eight years between the dates Ned had been part of her life. Before she met him he had never existed for her, now he didn't exist at all. And yet, if she chose it she could make it seem as if he did.

Sometimes the memory was in her head, like a thought, without substance; and sometimes it was a picture. Yet other times, like now, the memory was in her body, solid, and so real she could feel again the safety of being held by him, smell his smell, even hear his heart like she used to when pressed against his chest. It was a heart-beat so solid and strong it sounded as if it would continue forever. She recalled how she thought, just after his death, that if his heart could stop beating then the world could end, but it hadn't. Not even her world had ended.

His heart was always hers she knew, but when it stopped his love stopped too. He would never have chosen to leave her, but now that he had she must accept it. Death was always there in the midst of life. Life and death were like two sides of the same coin, one flip was all it took to change things forever. But it was also true that life was present in the midst of death, and the sapling tree that grew on Ned's grave was there to remind her of exactly that.

As she turned now and whispered a goodbye in her mind, Polly noticed the swallows swooping to the ground in search of food.

*

Indira mounted the bus nervously, she had never travelled alone to Kathmandu but she looked forward to the challenge and knew Hari would see her onto the bus for Pokhara. She couldn't wait to see him and have another taste of the intimacy they had finally enjoyed.

As the bus drew away she turned to wave to her mother, clutching the bag with the money in close, as Kabita had advised, and she noticed now how much more relaxed her mother appeared. And, although Indira wished they could have had more time together she was excited too at the new direction her life was taking and so looking forward to seeing Uma.